THE STONE MAS

A VAMPIRE'S

DOMINION

BOOK III

Vanessa Fewings

First edition 2011.

Printed in the United States of America.

For information or permission contact:

vanessafewings.com

ISBN 978-0-9894784-7-2

Cover Design ©Shutterstock/conrado

For Brad

The Stone Masters Vampire Series

A Vampire's Rise (Book I)

A Vampire's Reckoning (Book II)

A Vampire's Dominion (Book III)

PR⊕L⊕GUE

LIKE ALL NIGHTMARES, I wanted out.

Naked and barefoot, I sprinted along the uneven rain soaked pathway, my mouth dry and thirsting, terror constricting my throat and threatening to choke me. I tasted freedom as though for the first time.

Remembering nothing.

A cold salty sea mist hit my nostrils and I shook my head trying to repel nature's sting. Night wrapped her arms around me as I fled past the grey crumbling wall, bolting left under an ivy-covered archway, descending faster still down slippery stone steps.

Don't look back.

Taking two at a time, I landed on the grassy bank and ran onward, following the sound of crashing waves.

I struggled to recall this place and how I'd gotten here, my memories seemingly just out of reach and my rambling thoughts making no sense and threatening to sabotage my focus.

There was no time to question.

My gut insisted someone was closing in and dread shot up my spine forcing me to run faster. Rustling dead leaves swirled around my feet causing me to stumble. Quickly, I found my footing again. I crunched over a pebbled beach toward the vast ocean crashing six-foot waves onto a dappled-grey shoreline and rolling them into foam. The force with which I hit the icy water shoved my shoulders back and snatched my breath.

This was no dream.

Descending further, spiraling into the darkest depths, the ocean buffered against me and with outstretched arms I thrashed blindly to stay afloat, braving to glance back.

The towering rogue wave broke over my head, dragging me lower and delivering me into the path of a riptide that snatched me further into the blackness, sucking me into the swirling undercurrent and forcing seawater down my throat.

Drowning me . . .

Surrendering to the infinite darkness, I passed out.

Unsure of how much time had passed, my eyes opened to a blanket of white cloud revealing pockets of stars and a glimpse of the thumbnail moon, only for it to soon shy away. The night chilled my bones causing me to shiver and pebbles scratched my back.

Turning awkwardly, there was that same castle rising out of the granite, an intimidating symbol of supremacy conveying the gut wrenching realization.

I'd not made it.

A grinding pain in my right shoulder blade; I cradled my arm with the sudden awareness I'd dislocated it.

With mixed feelings that I failed to understand, I took in that dark silhouetted castle looming large on the horizon, trying to recall why it instilled such trepidation. My mind scrambled to piece together memories of having wandered along its sprawling corridors, losing hours within its age-old library, reading my way through its infinite collection of well-worn books, each one pulled from the antique mahogany shelves. With nothing but quiet for company.

More curious still was a faint recollection of whiling away endless days in there, waiting until sunset so I could return to the highest tower once more and paint my beloved nightscapes.

Daylight, that part of my life I'd long given up, exchanging her burning mortal kiss to become night's lover, surrendering to that endless promise of eternity.

As only a vampire can.

With an unsteady hand I stroked my clean shaven jaw and ran my fingers up and over the rest of my body, relieved to find that other than my arm there were no other injuries. Using my good arm, I staggered to my feet trying to distance myself from the waves spraying foam.

Across the shoreline Penzance lit up the night skyline, the sleepy town still, quiet, and desolate.

I turned and there, standing serenely staring back at me with dark brown eyes, was a tall young priest.

"Jadeon?" The stranger stepped closer.

I went to give an answer but had none to give and considered diving back in to get away from the one whom I assumed had been chasing me. He reflected an easy confidence that went beyond his thirty years. He still hadn't blinked.

Trying to judge if I could trust him, I struggled to hold onto the faintest memories that dissipated like cruel whispers clashing with each other, tightening my throat.

"You've hurt your arm," he said. "Let me help you."

Ignoring the pain, refusing to reveal any weakness I asked, "Who are you?"

"Father Jacob Roch." His fingers worked their way down each button of his long, brown coat and he slipped it off. "Here you are."

Cautiously I accepted his coat from him and pulled the left arm through, wrapping it over the shoulder of the right, unable to lift it.

He made a gesture to help.

"I'm fine." Though clearly I wasn't.

"You're adjusting, even now."

"To what?"

He went to answer but stopped himself as though unsure. Rubbing my forehead I tried to find the answers and not be influenced by the man who I had no reason to trust.

Far off lightening lit up the night sky, and a few seconds later came the crack of thunder.

The sound of footfalls signaled someone fast approaching. Over the ridge a young man appeared and skidded to a stop when he saw us.

"Steady, Alex." Jacob gestured for him not to come any further.

Alex's expression was one of horror and I tried to decipher whether it was disgust or hate. Lost in a fog of thoughts I tried to recall how I knew him.

"Let's go inside," Jacob said.

The rhythm of the ocean sounded like it was now inside my head and my legs weakened. My feet gave way.

My mind blurred, threatening to slide off. *"Who am I?"* My face struck the pebbles.

"That's what we're going to find out." Jacob's voice grew distant.

I

IT WASN'T SO MUCH that I'd woken up inside a coffin that was alarming, it was the fact it was locked shut and I had no idea how long I'd been sealed inside.

I was still wearing Jacob's coat and hoped to find the opportunity to return it. And then suffocate him with it.

At least the fresh scented velvet lining hinted I was the casket's first guest and I knew better than to punch my fist through the walnut lid. With an upward jolt I broke the locks and peered out, relieved I hadn't been buried.

There was a wave of regret for not taking my chance to escape when I'd had it. I climbed out into a prison cell, the gate shut and secured with an oversized padlock.

Well-worn rusty shackles lay discarded on the floor, revealing this chamber dated back centuries. More disturbing was its musty odor omitting a peculiar familiarity. The only relief was seeing my shoulder was back in its socket.

I struggled to get my bearings.

And remember.

Halfway up the brickwork of the far wall someone had scribed in scratchy handwriting *'Find Dominatio.'* And they'd used blood. I backed away from it and peered out through the bars and down a long black corridor.

Jacob stepped out of the darkness, and his iridescent irises locked on me. "How are you feeling?"

My answer was merely to gesture into the cell.

His brow furrowed. "Let me know when you're ready to talk."

"I'm ready now."

He tapped his pockets as though trying to find something, the key perhaps. "Ah."

I reached into his mind but if he was thinking, I couldn't hear it.

"How long have I been in here?" I asked.

"A few hours."

I peered down the passageway wondering if that was the way out.

"We were concerned for your safety," he said. "You were thrashing around quite a bit."

"Well I'm fine now."

He seemed to notice the bloody words '*Find Dominatio,*' and his careful face changed as though judging what I'd made of it.

"Hard to miss." I answered his unspoken question.

My mind reached out beyond these dank walls and I sensed it was midmorning. I cursed the fact I was trapped in here until nightfall.

Jacob stepped back into focus. "You're the proverbial Gordian's Knot, I'm afraid."

I waited for him to continue, hoping for some clue that might lead me back to remembering.

"You consider me an intricate problem?" I asked. "Care to elaborate?"

"Gordian's Knot, the phrase based on the legend of king of Phrygia. He tied a knot meant to be incapable of being untied. Alexander the Great swept in dramatically—"

"Arrogantly, and sliced through the knot with his sword, thus establishing him as sovereign. I know what Gordian's Knot is, I just can't remember—"

"Your name."

I hated this moment, hated him with his never ending psychological torture of vagueness.

"Perhaps this will help?" He stepped closer. "Stonehenge, you were there last night."

"I don't . . ." A wave of frustration.

The only thing preventing me from having a go at the lock was that damned daylight. His lips curled sympathetically and I had a sneaking suspicion he'd read my mind.

"Enlighten me," I said.

"Now more than ever you'll need your friends."

"Any of them here?" It was worth a chance.

"You can trust me."

I went to question his strange idea of hospitality, but knew better.

"Last night everything changed," said Jacob.

"How?" I resisted the urge to yell, *'fucking tell me.'*

He dismissed my last question with a wave of his slender arm and his long fingers brushed through the air.

"What was I doing on the beach?" I asked.

"Minutes after it happened, you ran." He slipped both his hands into the pockets of his cassock. "It's probably better if you remember naturally."

"And how long do you think that might take?"

"You must believe me when I say you're safe here."

I glanced back at the coffin to make a point.

"With the return of your memory," said Jacob, "new challenges will arise. I want you to prepare yourself for that."

I went to ask what he meant but he'd gone and I was left staring at nothing. I slipped my hands through the bars and fiddled with the silver lock.

Alex, the young man from the beach, appeared out of the shadows and leaned against the cell gate opposite. I let go of the lock.

He was holding a blanket. "You really don't know who I am, do you?" he said.

"Alexander?"

He sucked in his breath and then realized. "Bastard."

I ran my fingers through my matted hair. "I need to take a shower."

"I think that's a good idea." He slid the blanket between the bars and let it go.

It fell at my feet. "I'm not planning on staying."

"Won't be for long."

"Did I mess up?" I asked.

"I did."

I wrapped my fingers around the bars. "Then why am I the one in here?"

He flinched, uncomfortable with that question.

"Well you're forgiven." I glanced at the lock. "Now let me out."

"Jadeon?" he asked, searching.

"That's my name?" On his reaction I asked, "That's *not* my name?"

"What do you think your name is?"

"What . . . is . . . my . . . name?" I clenched my teeth.

"William," Alex said flatly.

I hesitated and then said, "You just called me Jadeon?"

"Your father's name was William too."

"How do we know each other again?"

"It'll come back," he said.

"How long have we known each other?"

He didn't answer.

"A while I take it," I pressed.

"Jacob thinks if—"

"I remember naturally?"

He shrugged. "He seems to know how to handle this."

"*This* being . . . ?"

"Complicated."

I wanted to scream. "You were with me last night? When it happened?"

His focus shot back to me.

I feigned remembering and then said, "Stonehenge."

He leaned in closer.

"We weren't the only ones there?" I watched his reaction. "I messed up . . . it wasn't your fault."

"What else do you remember?"

I waited for him to weaken, hoping he'd start talking.

He narrowed his gaze. "You don't remember."

I reached through the bars and grabbed his throat, squeezing. Alex struggled, gurgling for breath, his fingers fighting to remove mine.

Sashaying toward us was a young woman dressed in blue jeans and a man's shirt, her raven hair tumbling over her slender shoulders and down her back; bewitching almond-shaped, turquoise eyes holding mine.

She reached for Alex's head and with a jolt, snapped his neck.

Alex fell from my grip, crumpling into a heap, hissing in an effort to breathe, still alive but paralyzed.

Yet the woman's expression revealed nothing of the terrible act she'd just committed. The softest, longest eyelashes fluttered ever so slightly and her rouged lips pouted innocently.

Speechless, I stepped back, wondering if she was about to use the same move on me. Seeing the unemotional expression of the strikingly attractive vixen, I was now actually relieved there was a locked gate between us. I felt terrible for Alex.

She yanked at the silver lock. The gate was open and she was now inside, moving closer. My back met the wall and she leaned into my chest and nestled there, wrapping her arms around me, my own arms hesitating to embrace her.

"I feel like I've been asleep," she whispered.

I resisted the urge to ease her off and glanced down to see if there was anything familiar about her. By the way she nuzzled into my chest she clearly knew me.

"Who are you?" It came out wrong.

Her expression of indignity quickly fell away. "Sunaria."

"And . . . who am I?"

Her eyes danced with sadness. "Orpheus."

My shoulders dropped a little, relieved that finally someone was answering my questions.

"I know a way out." Her face lit up and she grabbed my hand, pulling me out of the cell.

We both stepped over Alex's body and headed off in silence.

Struggling with whether I should trust her or not I followed her down the longest, darkest corridor, glancing back occasionally to check if we were being followed.

"There's a tunnel beneath the castle," she said. "We can wait in there until sunset."

"How do you know?"

On her face was written a kind of pain, as though remembering something. "It doesn't feel like two hundred years . . ." Her eyes shone with tears. "Since the Stone Masters tortured me here."

"Who?"

She rose up on her toes and kissed my cheek, pressing her soft full lips against me as though time had never wedged its way between us.

"That's what this place is," she said. "Or was?" She looked confused.

Not wanting to be locked up in that cell again or secured back inside that coffin, I picked up my pace. We quickly reached a stone wall and on seeing the dead-end I turned to head back the way we'd come. But Sunaria gripped my arm, insisting, motioning toward the brickwork. Realizing what she was suggesting, my fingers traced the irregularities along each brick, feeling for the one that might give.

"You forgive me?" Her voice was soft, vulnerable even.

"For what?" Something gave beneath my touch and stone scraped along the ground, opening up a gaping tunnel. A burst of cold air.

Peering down the endless blackness, I felt a wave of relief.

"This runs under the sea." Sunaria moved pass me and stepped into the never-ending passageway.

I hesitated. "What should I forgive you for?"

"I didn't know the ashes were joined," she admitted.

Her words stormed into my mind, sending my thoughts into a frenzy as though some part of me had understood her meaning, and that same taunting sensation that had gripped me back on the beach overwhelmed me again.

A black violin case, resting on an oak table.

I doubled over, the twisting, wrenching agony in my gut snatching away my breath. Reaching out for her hand, my vision blurred.

"Orpheus?" Sunaria's voice seemingly distant.

Snow blanketing London's rooftops with a perfect powdery white. I was back in Belshazzar's, my old London mansion, sitting quietly and watching a bloodhound sluggishly pad across the length of a room before settling beside the roaring fireplace.

Crawling along the floor, I tried to make it to Sunaria.

With two clicks, the black violin case sprang open and I revered the walnut violin within.

Gasping for air.

Lifting out the violin and positioning the black chin-rest naturally into place, my fingertips settled on the lower end of the finger board. I brought up the bow upon the strings, caressing the fine cords and bursting forth a chorus of harmonic colors of sound. This violin was an extension of me, conveying more than just the secrets of the soul, its memories too . . .

Spellbound, I tried to grasp ahold of each memory.

That same violin . . . caught up in its maelstrom, swallowed whole and entranced completely by the instrument's curse, an impossible spell to break free from.

I was unraveling.

Sword fighting, the wooden blade slicing through the air, this ten-year-old boy swearing to save this castle with my brother . . .

"Alex!"

Memories were lying, implying I'd lived through two different childhoods, the images gushing in like a torrent, threatening to drown me.

On my knees now, trying to grab the violin hovering just out of reach.

. . . Orpheus plays the violin.

Fighting off the vertigo I rose, resisting the drag of nothingness snapping at my heels, threatening to lose my grip on time and place, clutching my abdomen and clenching my teeth as the twisting agony threatened to ravage my insides.

Sunaria had my right hand in hers and she was dragging me along the tunnel but I broke free and staggered back, leaving her standing there.

With both hands on the stone doorway I gave it a shove, securing it closed.

If Sunaria was screaming at me from the other side, I didn't hear her.

I I

THE SHOWER CASCADED OVER me; it was invigorating.

Within the marble tiled bathroom, I tried to subdue my frantic internal dialogue that threatened to send me over the edge, resisting the urge to smash my forehead against the glass door . . . through which I saw Alex, leaning forward in a corner chair, his elbows resting on his knees.

Realizing I was studying him, he said, "You once told me taking a shower helped you think."

"Ironic that I have to be in the shower to think about that," I said.

Trying to read him I assumed he was far from forgiving me for what had occurred within the hour and pulled a guilty expression, gesturing to his throat.

He rubbed his neck.

"What day is it?" I asked.

"June 24th. What do you remember?"

"Doesn't make any sense."

He seemed to find interest in the hardwood floor.

"Quid pro quo?" I asked.

Alex looked away telling me this game would not be played.

This illusion of normality was impossible to sustain. Even so I did my best to go with it, lathering my body with the rich soap and taking some comfort from the way the pressure from the oversized showerhead pounded my scalp, relieved to be washing off the seawater.

"Who's Orpheus?" I asked, watching him carefully.

Alex's attention focused on the door.

I ran my fingers through my hair, massaging my scalp. "Sunaria called me Orpheus."

"She can't be trusted."

I twisted off the faucet and stepped out, reaching for the large plush towel and wrapping it around my waist. "And you can?"

"Yes." He rose and pointed to several folded garments balanced on the hamper. "Jeans, shirt, jacket." Then he pointed lower to the shoes.

"Tell me about Sunaria?" I pulled on the underpants.

"She's an old girlfriend." He raised an eyebrow. "Kind of."

Great, confusion infused with cryptics.

Alex looked thoughtful. "You're remembering bits and pieces."

"I just need to know why I feel like a stranger in my own home."

His expression tensed.

"So Sunaria?" I pushed.

"You knew to be wary of her. That's a good thing." He shook his head. "Sunaria took advantage of your situation."

I gave Alex a nudge, pressing him to continue.

He shrugged. "She has her own agenda."

"Which is?"

"I dare to think."

With each question there came the distinct realization there were endless answers. Trying to stay focused, I stepped toward him. "So far I've been addressed as Jadeon, Orpheus and William." I pressed my fingertips to my forehead. "Is it any wonder I'm confused?"

"I'll let you get dressed."

"Where's my bedroom?"

Alex hesitated and then said, "Turn left out of here and it's six rooms down. The one with the thick oak door."

"How did I lose my memory?"

"Jacob's in the library," he said, turning to go. "Meet us down there."

"Alex, I'm sorry about . . ."

He lowered his chin, still clutching the doorknob. "You didn't know."

I was still staring at where he'd been standing, wondering if I'd convinced him how terrible I felt.

The clothes fit reasonably well.

My hand squeaked along the mirror, smearing the moisture away and I turned slightly to see the chair in the corner and then back to see it reversed in the mirror, contemplating the room's image, minus the one who stood before it.

Sensing nightfall eased the tension of my circadian rhythm and reassured me it was safe to explore. I paused at the top of the huge sweeping staircase, admiring the low hung chandelier illuminating the vast foyer, hoping to see something familiar. A mortal was here; her perfume lingering like the subtlest reminder of a midsummer's day.

Intrigued, I headed in her direction down the east corridor, taking in my surroundings as though clarity might just find me.

There, asleep on the age-old four poster bed, lay a strikingly beautiful brunette. Gently so as not to awaken her, I sat beside her, considering it remarkable that a mortal was in a vampire's lair.

The long green drapes were drawn closed. The only painting on the wall was of a fierce looking middle-aged gentleman wearing seventieth century clothes.

My attention returned to the woman and I focused in on the small notebook she was clutching. I eased it out of her grasp. On the last page was written yesterday's date and beneath that were lines of scribbled notes.

A hand came from behind me and snatched the book away. I spun round to see Jacob tucking it into his pocket. He gripped my arm and guided me out of the room and along the corridor.

"Who is she?" I glanced at the tip of the notebook.

He nudged it further in. "Ingrid."

Considering returning to her, I wondered why I felt so drawn to the young woman.

"We agreed to meet downstairs," he said firmly.

"Memory's been a little shaky lately."

"You must be thirsty."

"Who's Sunaria?"

"You haven't fed since you woke up."

"I nearly left with her."

"But you didn't."

"Sunaria told me it's too dangerous to stay here." I folded my arms.

"She's misinformed." He glanced back toward the bedroom. "We have to get you fed, before . . ."

"Are you suggesting I might bite her?" I broke away from him and headed off. "I've got a feeling this place will tell me everything I need to know." I ambled away down the sprawling corridor, sensing Jacob was willing to give me the space I needed.

Within a minute I'd found the room Alex had told me was mine; the oak door swung heaving on its hinges.

The décor was simple, understated, with a four poster bed in the center, a writing desk pushed up along the left wall, a large window to the right, black drapes pulled across its arched frame.

My fingers slid along the well-tailored suits hanging neatly in the wardrobe; none of them were my size.

On the writing desk lay a book titled *Voltaire,* a feeling of familiarity as I picked it up and peeked inside. Closing my eyes, trying to grasp the intricate details, I could remember from reading this that I'd derived pleasure from François-Marie Arouet's work. He'd died in 1778, an outspoken writer and philosopher, having changed his name to Voltaire to distance himself from his family. He'd dared to criticize both France's politicians and its religious leaders, which had resulted in his banishment from his homeland. I considered why I'd found his work appealing. Perhaps I was similar to him in nature, a risk taker, a bohemian.

A man whose name didn't fit.

Clutching the book to my chest, grasping it tightly as though this small piece of my past might be a key to the rest of it, I strolled over to the window and pulled back the curtain, peering out at the night, admiring the sprawling well-tended gardens and then gazing out further at the wall I'd passed when I'd tried to escape.

"Are you following me?" I turned.

Alex was sitting on the edge of the bed. "No." He raised an eyebrow. "Maybe."

"You told me this is my room?"

"It is."

I pointed to the cupboard and its row of shirts and suits.

His expression changed.

"Explain," I said.

"Clothes?"

"Where are mine?"

He cringed. Alex joined me by the window and said, "Those are mine. I ran out of space."

"You're a bad liar." I walked away, toward the walnut writing bureau and leaned against it. "What kind of person am I?"

"A deep thinker." He pointed to the book *Voltaire* I was holding. "Well-read."

"Go on."

"Cautious—usually that is. Kind. Thoughtful."

"Then why are you wary of me?"

He shook his head, as though apologetic.

"Nothing adds up." Nearing Alex, I tried to extract more from him with the mere persuasion of my intensity. "Where are *my* clothes?"

He blinked several times as though considering how best to answer.

I shook my head and started for the door.

"You were a good brother," he burst out.

"Still am, hopefully."

"Ingrid's gone."

"And why would I care about that?"

Alex looked away.

Jacob cut me off in the doorway and I tried to nudge past him.

He pressed his hand to my chest. "You had a breakthrough. Share it with us?"

I eased his hand off. "If you're going to access my thoughts at least give me the privilege of reading yours."

"Of course." Jacob opened up to me, yet adroitly controlled each thought. *"I'm here to help you,"* was all he gave me.

I barged past him and into the corridor, hoping this time Alex wouldn't follow. With my mind closed to prevent them tracking me, I flew toward the upper rooms of the castle.

Inside the small dark room I nudged between the numerous painted canvasses, nightscapes laying here and there, a disarray of half-finished artwork seemingly long given up on.

Finding a space on the floor, I sat with my back against the wall, staring at Ingrid's notebook that I'd just pick-pocketed from Jacob.

The quiet closed in.

Leafing through the pages I read Ingrid's scribbled notes, her words unraveling as though in my head, exposing what she'd seen and heard while in the castle last night. I browsed her last entry.

"The Mount's dungeons. Alex is here. A priest. Two young women, one blonde the other has raven hair. I recognize the blonde woman from Stonehenge. They're staring at something moving in the shadows, a naked man is doubled over. Now standing. Jadeon. No . . . Orpheus's features, as though . . ."

With my head resting against the cold brick, I braved the nightmarish memories teeming in, frantically crawling around my brain, insistent on devouring my last bit of sanity. Ghosts raging within, a constant flow of experiences I'd not earned or lived through. Jaw gaping, I tried to fathom what I'd done.

Stonehenge's monumental pillars looming large in their magnificence, this sacred circle where the Stone Masters' rituals had taken place; the bloodiest of ceremonies. The fierce sunrise . . .

A fight to the death.
My death.
Mingling our ashes, our destinies . . .
I flew into a blinding rage.

Canvasses ripped from their frames, others flung and lay smashed where they'd landed. The small chamber where I'd kept my paints now lay decimated and the vast collection of paintings I'd lovingly crafted over two hundred years destroyed.

Staring at my hands like a madman, guilty of having caused the mayhem, I tried to remember the years of my life and find something good in them. So cruel, how a place can be familiar and yet so foreign; this once sacred room had been my sanctuary, but now offered nothing but grief.

Alex's long sigh. "William?"

My vision blurred with tears. "That's not my name."

Jacob caught up with Alex and he scanned the mess.

"Why didn't you tell me?" I slid down the wall, pressing my face into my hands, burying my shame, sobbing uncontrollably.

And they let me, both of them waiting for my cries to dissipate.

Alex sat beside me, wiping away his own tears. Jacob kept his distance taking in the room, and though he didn't glance at Ingrid's notebook lying discarded on the floor I knew he'd seen it.

"I suppose we're doing it your way then?" said Jacob.

I tried to read the truth in their eyes, yet at the same time hoping not too. "Joined as one?" The words tasted foul as I spoke to them.

Jacob's frown deepened. "Yes."

My throat tightened like a vice and I struggled to catch my breath. Alex reached out to comfort me again.

I waved off his gesture and said, "This is worse than being dead."

Jacob motioned to Alex that he wanted to handle this, handle me.

"He doesn't remember everything," Alex murmured.

"But I know who you are." I threw an angry look. "Brother." My glare shot to Jacob. "And you're my son."

"I am Orpheus's son," Jacob acknowledged.

"Everything's muddled up." My sob choked me and I held out my hands turning them around and finding nothing familiar.

"Has this ever happened before?" Alex asked Jacob.

Jacob's slender arms fell to his side. "Once that I know of."

"Is it reversible?" The confusion of what I was actually asking sinking in.

Jacob glanced at Alex.

"Tell me," I whispered through gritted teeth.

Jacob shifted closer. "There is a real possibility, yes."

My hands were still shaking.

"William, we'll talk about this later," Jacob said, "when you're calmer."

"We talk now." My voice wavered with emotion.

"There are ancient scrolls," Jacob said, "Documented evidence of how one might attempt this. If we're able to translate them, maybe . . ."

"What language?" asked Alex.

"Egyptian," Jacob answered, distracted.

"We'll find an Egyptian scholar," Alex said.

Jacob's brows furrowed. "We're talking Coptic."

"Then we'll find someone who understands Coptic," I said. "Where are these scrolls?"

"I'll do everything I can," Jacob offered.

The trembling in my hands was getting worse.

Alex climbed to his feet and walked over to the tipped-over chair in the corner, grasped the backrest and righted it. "Here."

I shook my head, feeling somewhat safer on the floor.

"We're going to find a way back for you." Alex turned to face Jacob. "Aren't we?"

"We'll certainly try," Jacob said.

Alex was staring at Jacob as though searching for truth in his words.

I gestured my frustration. "I'm your Gordian's Knot, as you so eloquently pointed out."

"I'm afraid you're a little unstable still." Jacob gestured to the mess.

I hated the fact he was right. "You're not going to tell me where I can find these scrolls, are you?"

He gave what was probably meant as a sympathetic shrug. "As soon as I know, you will."

Alex was now staring at me, trying to figure out what I was thinking and what I might do if I didn't get the answers I needed to hear.

"Lucas Azir is one of the world's foremost Egyptologists," Jacob said. "I'll find him."

Staring at the ceiling, I tried to control all thoughts that might sabotage my one chance of Jacob helping me, I did after all know who Lucas Azir was.

"What are you thinking?" Jacob asked.

I kept my voice low and suppressed the suspicion in my tone. "You met with Jadeon?"

Jacob stepped forward. "I did, yes."

The bitterness of recollection ate away my trust. "Jacob, you betrayed me."

"You *are* Jadeon," he said, puzzled.

I raised a finger to protest and then realized he was right.

"Did you know this was going to happen?" Alex asked him.

"No." Jacob blinked.

From outside the window came the hoot of an owl, the only noise of the night that dared to interrupt.

"You blame Orpheus for this?" Alex asked Jacob.

Jacob formed his hands into a temple. "Jadeon would never have been there had it not been for Orpheus trying to turn Ingrid. And kill Catherine."

The truth of his words stung deep. "But . . . ." I shook my head, feeling the wrenching guilt building in my gut.

Jacob lowered his chin. "William, my concern is that you'll start finding excuses not to revert."

"You think I'd sabotage my way back?" I said.

"What will undoubtedly occur is a desire to stay like this," Jacob said.

"Why would I want that?" My jaw tightened.

Jacob gave a careful pause, and then said, "Over the next few days you'll continue to evolve."

"Into what?" Alex asked the question that was on my mind.

Jacob appeared thoughtful. "You'll settle into what you are."

I clenched my fists but quickly relaxed them again. "Let's make this happen." I rose to my feet.

"We get the scrolls," Alex said, "and interpret them."

"Only then," Jacob said, "can we attempt to restore Jadeon and Orpheus to their individual components."

I pressed my hand against my chest, expressing my conviction. "What do I need to do?"

Jacob picked up Ingrid's notebook. "Nothing."

"You expect me to just pace these corridors waiting for you to find . . . Lucas?"

"Promise me one thing." Jacob's eyes widened. "You won't leave these walls."

My gaze slid beyond the window pane, settling on the darkening horizon; grey clouds were gliding inland. When I looked back, Jacob was zeroing in on me again.

"Sunaria and I were lovers," I said. "That's how I know her?"

Alex grimaced. "Orpheus's lover."

"How did she know it was me?"

Alex looked away. "She was there when you transformed."

Fragile thoughts drifted back to the dungeons and how I'd mishandled her, shoving Sunaria into the tunnel and sealing the stone door between us.

"She's been asleep for over two hundred years. She can't be allowed to wander around out there," I said, weighed down with guilt from abandoning her.

"Sunaria's capable of taking care of herself." Jacob suppressed a cough. "She's over one thousand years old after all."

"I didn't know that," Alex's voice cracked nervously.

"Catherine was also there when it happened," I said.

"She warned me," Alex said. "I didn't listen to her. I believed the ashes were . . ."

"Jadeon's," I answered for him. "Alex, it was you who resurrected me?"

"Sunaria persuaded me to pour my blood over the ashes," he answered. "And then she did the same."

"He didn't know," Jacob said in Alex's defense.

"Sunaria thought the ashes belonged to Orpheus?" I made it a question, though knew the answer. "I thought she was dead."

"Just as you were resurrected from ash," Jacob said, "so was she."

I focused on Jacob. "You knew where she was all this time?"

"Yes," he replied calmly.

I loosened my collar, needing more air. "Alex, open the window." Memories were flooding in and making my head foggy.

Alex twisted the lock and gave the window a shove to open it. The summer breeze was just as stifling.

"I was revived here in the dungeons," I said, remembering the faces I'd looked upon. "And then I ran."

"You were in shock." Jacob shifted his position as though thinking twice about coming any closer. "You still are."

I ignored Jacob's remark. "Catherine's here?" I felt relief to sense this.

Jacob broke my gaze.

"I've never heard of anything like this, ever," I muttered.

"Jadeon," Alex lowered his voice. "You gave your life to save Ingrid."

"Where's she now?" I ignored the name he'd just called me, remembering the intimacy I shared with Ingrid, the love affair that burned too brightly and should never have happened.

"I took her to the hospital," Alex said. "She wouldn't recognize you now anyway."

"Do I look like a monster?" I feared the answer.

"No." Alex came closer. "When you rose you shifted for the first hour between Orpheus and Jadeon."

The painful transition still lingered in the very marrow of my bones. "And now?" I barely said.

"You have Jadeon's eyes," Alex paused. "Orpheus's dark locks, his jaw . . ."

"More like Orpheus, then?" I glanced over at Jacob for confirmation.

Jacob gave a slow, deliberate nod.

"No wonder you're so wary of me." I sighed. "Why call me William?"

"William Artimas was Jadeon's father," Alex said. "My father."

"You chose it to get back at me?" I asked. "Because Orpheus killed Lord William Artimas?"

"You pushed me for a name," Alex said. "So I gave you one."

"I'm joined with the man who killed my father." My feet felt unsteady. "God help me. I'm joined with . . ."

"Your nemesis," Alex whispered it.

III

"I'M FINE, REALLY," Catherine said, letting Jacob know she was ready to be left alone with me.

"Catherine, I'll wait for you outside." Jacob glared at me. "I'll be listening to *every* word."

I sat down in the pew opposite Catherine. Head down, she rested her hands in her lap as though finding the courage to speak. Her blonde curls cascaded over her shoulders and down her back and I imagined how soft they'd feel should I dare to reach out and run my fingers through them.

This old dusty chapel hadn't seen a religious service conducted in centuries, and despite the layers of time that gave away its neglect, it still maintained its dutiful Protestant presence. Catherine seemed to be trying to gain strength from the tipped-over crucifix resting on the once-used altar. Or perhaps I was just making her nervous.

"Jadeon's father died in this castle." She broke the silence at last. "At your hands, Orpheus."

I broke eye contact with her, wishing I'd insisted that Jacob stay.

"And now you've outdone yourself." Hate welled with her tears.

"I'm Jadeon too."

She pressed her hand to her lips as though the true horror of what I was finally hit her. "Jacob promised he'd do whatever it took to protect Jadeon." She flinched, as though the loss was too much for her. "Was your hate for Jadeon your reason for doing this?"

"What?" I sat back, surprised. "No. You think I planned this?"

"You tortured Jadeon for centuries and this is your ultimate revenge."

"I'm finding a way back from this."

"So now you regret it?"

"I chased you relentlessly trying to save you from . . ." It was coming out wrong. "It's complicated."

"I did everything I could to save Jadeon from you, but in the end those two hundred years of staying with you, loving you, being everything you demanded of me, meant nothing."

"Loved?" I asked.

"I misspoke."

"You loved God."

"And you wanted to kill me for that."

"You never once told me you loved me."

"And that surprises you?" she asked.

"Catherine, I'm not ready for this."

"You always hated the truth."

"We were childhood sweethearts, you and I?"

She searched my face, as though hoping to catch a glimpse of her lost love, though seemingly not seeing Jadeon she said, "Even now you manipulate me. Pretending that Jadeon has a say in any of this."

I stood up, wanting to get closer to her but resisting the desire. "I've always loved you."

"You want me to believe that Jadeon is communicating with me? That's your way of further torturing me."

I raised my hand for her to be silent. "I'm going to find a way to reverse this."

"I'm not that naive girl you kidnapped two hundred years ago. I've been around you long enough to know all your tricks."

"That's not what this is."

"So what have you discovered about yourself?" she asked. "Any new abilities which you failed to possess before? You were a Status Regal, a royal blood vampire, and yet it wasn't enough."

"This was a mistake. You must believe me."

"I don't. We're going to reverse this. Jacob and I are going to London to find Lucas Azir." She waved a pointed fingertip. "You'll not leave here until we have undone this."

"Have you considered you may be addressing Jadeon?"

She hesitated, as though hoping she was. "He would never be a willing participant in any of this."

"That's not what I asked."

She paused and her pale blue eyes regarded me. "If you make one wrong move I'll personally put you back in that coffin."

"We grew up together. We used to swim behind the castle walls."

"You stole that memory from Jadeon."

"I *am* Jadeon!"

She weakened and looked away. "You do what we say, when we say."

"Look at me, Catherine," I snapped. "It's me, Jadeon!"

Slowly, she rose. "No apology?"

"To who? I did this to myself."

"No regret?" She motioned to me.

"This was a mistake. I should never have come in here." I leaned against the back of the pew.

Her lip trembled. "I'll never forgive you."

I held back tears. "I need you."

"Orpheus, you have no soul."

"But Jadeon does?" I shook my head.

"You're trying to draw me in." She strolled over toward the altar and gripped the crucifix's base with both hands and righted it. "It won't work." She faced me again.

"This thing is reversible," I said, hoping it really was.

"And what then?"

"You and I will get a second chance—"

"Never," she sounded distant.

I clutched the back of the pew as though it might stop me from falling.

"Jadeon would never try to entice me away from my faith," she said.

A storm was raging outside, and now inside too, threatening to burst its banks and drown me in a tsunami of sorrow; leaving only regret for what could have been, should have been.

Catherine knew her words were destroying me and she folded her arms to emphasize her point and stand her ground.

"I'm sorry for everything I ever did to you," I said softly, hoping she would hear the truth.

"Go to hell!" She stormed passed me and out.

The shock of her words threw me and my gaze stayed on where she'd been standing, as though I might turn back time and have her say the words I'd wanted—no—needed to hear.

And even if Jacob did find these scrolls and Lucas Azir could interpret them, there was still no promise of a way back for me.

I collapsed onto the pew and lay down along it, pulling my legs into my chest, hoping that daylight might do me a favor and seep in through the stained glass windows and punish me with its inevitability.

And then kill me.

I remained in the chapel like that for hours, waiting for dawn.

Even that was apparently ignoring me. When my spiraling thoughts became too much, pestering my very sanity, I rose up and headed out.

Sleep was a reasonable alternative to consciousness right now.

* * * *

The following evening I found a handwritten note from Alex stuck to the bathroom mirror, letting me know he'd stashed several 500ml units of donated human blood in the fridge.

Making my way toward the kitchen, I resented myself for the way I'd dealt with Catherine last night. I wondered if she'd ever look at me without disdain again.

I had to find a way back from this wreckage that was my life, pull myself back from the brink of hell.

Everything was wrong.

And hunger was gnawing away, making it hard to hold a thought.

Just as Alex had promised, inside the fridge were several thick plastic bags full of packed red blood cells. The labels had been ripped off. Alex's way, I assumed, to help me cope with this cold clinical, nightmare.

My fangs pierced the icy bland plastic and I sucked. The consistency was glutinous and the sharp iron taste was nauseating. Leaning over the kitchen sink, I gagged.

I'd hit an all time low.

Yes, I had to eat, but this was cruel and unusual punishment. I longed to feed properly, and yet the guilt from considering burying my fangs into some unsuspecting mortal was unsettling.

Was I softening?

Then I noticed the note from Alex stuck on the front of the microwave.

"William! Empty blood into soup bowl," he'd scribbled. *"Heat for sixty seconds."*

I cursed myself for missing it.

And gagged again.

Unable to look at the half empty bloody units anymore, I threw them into the bin.

Making my way outside, heading down to the water's edge, I wondered if peace might ever find me again. Although such solitary confinement was understood, the loneliness wasn't.

The rocks were slippery and I chose my footing carefully, edging toward the ocean.

The bitterest taste of salt lingered and I swallowed several times, trying to get rid of it. Small crabs scuttled sideways near my feet and I carefully stepped over them. Turning slightly, I glanced up at the castle to check if anyone was watching, hating this feeling of my every move being tracked.

Reassured I was alone, I knelt low and swept my hand through the water, trying to suppress this suffocating ache. I let go, grateful that my sobs were drowned out by the crashing waves striking the rocks in their perfect relentless rhythm.

I'd swum in these waters as a boy, a reckless game that had almost got Alex and Catherine drowned one late night. But that was two hundred years ago.

Jadeon's memories.

And what were Orpheus's? A daring vampiric excursion to this island, seducing Alex and using him to get an invitation to his father's ball, Lord Artimas the Stone Master. Trapping each and every last Stone Lord in the dungeons and then killing them.

The sweetest revenge for Lord Artimas murdering Sunaria, and yet only now did I know she was still alive. Two centuries of tormenting Jadeon and it had all been for nothing, a selfish endeavor based on lies.

Standing now, taking in the horizon, there was a welcome calmness, a resolution born out of understanding my once misled motives, as though forgiveness may just settle into my soul if I just let it.

I wondered how long it would take me to swim to the other side. Out of the corner of my eye I caught Alex watching me, and gestured to let him know I'd seen him.

"Jacob's back," Alex called out, frowning his disapproval.

A four-foot wave reached over the rocks and splashed onto my shoes, soaking them.

Alex was gone.

Desperate to further this inner numbness, I squelched back the way I'd come and strolled toward the winding castle pathway.

Just as Jacob had predicted, the urgency within me to change back was lessoning and this conflicting internal dialogue was starting to settle.

Just inside the front door I kicked off my shoes and ripped off my socks, throwing them down and trudging barefoot into the foyer, full of disdain for the place that confined me with its infinite number of long-neglected rooms and the timeless secrets they refused to share.

And its bloody cold floors.

Alex was standing halfway down the east corridor. "They're waiting for you."

I took a moment to consider the chandelier above me and then followed Alex down the corridor and onward through a familiar doorway. We descended into the basement.

"Tell me it's good news," I said when I saw Jacob sitting on the large trunk.

Alex gestured for me to come closer.

"What's going on?" I sensed the tension and didn't like the way the others were swapping nervous glances.

Jacob glanced at my feet. "We found Lucas."

"That's good news, right?" I said, trying to inject enthusiasm into what seemed like a dour gathering.

"He's working on getting hold of those scrolls for us," Jacob said.

"Well that's progress." I lifted my right foot and examined my dirty sole.

"Where *are* your shoes?" Catherine asked.

"We have a situation in London." Jacob rose and started pacing. "It's slowing our progress."

Catherine leaned against the wall. "Something's poisoning vampires."

"We're not sure what it is," Jacob said. "Nightwalkers are becoming confused and—"

"Committing suicide," Catherine said, visibly shaken.

"They're becoming disorientated." Jacob shook his head. "Strolling out during the day."

A shiver ran up my spine. "How?"

"Drinking poisoned blood," Jacob said. "We think."

I studied their faces, trying to detect if there was something they weren't telling me.

Jacob paused, his face full of worry.

Catherine flashed her anger. "Bravo. Perfect timing, Orpheus."

I tried to keep the annoyance out of my expression and took in their faces one by one.

Catherine came closer. "Do you know anything about this?"

"No," I said flatly.

Alex watched me carefully. "Hundreds have been affected."

"And Lucas? He's okay?" I braced myself for the answer.

"He's fine," Jacob said. "But if he stays in London he'll be at risk."

Catherine seemed to struggle with her anger. "When were you going to tell us about Lucas Azir? You didn't think we'd find out about you both?"

Jacob moved away. "It doesn't change anything."

Catherine inclined her head toward him. "But why not tell us?"

"I know a lot of vampires." I shrugged. "I own a bar for God sake."

Catherine turned back to me. "Lucas filled us in on what you failed to tell us."

"It changes nothing," Jacob said.

"How do you know Lucas?" Alex asked, looking like he was the last one to know.

I answered with merely a raise of an eyebrow.

"I'm not sure why that surprises me," Alex said.

"Can we please refocus on the issue?" I asked, keeping my tone polite. "My personal life pales in comparison to the fact that vampires are dying." I shook my head, trying to clear my thoughts, searching the darkness as though the answers lingered just beyond and might just emerge from the shadows.

Silence ensued.

Jacob straightened his back. "I'm afraid you're on your own, William. For now anyway."

"I've been waiting here, losing time," I said, suppressing my panic.

"Jacob, you can't just abandon us," Alex pleaded. "We're not even sure how much time we have."

"Who mentioned anything about a time limit?" I saw Jacob's expression and cringed. "You're suggesting I may run out of time to revert?"

He stared off past me.

"Great," I snapped. "How much time are we talking about exactly?"

"Days, weeks, perhaps," Jacob answered.

"Where did this time thing come from?" My hands started shaking again.

"This isn't the first time this has happened," Jacob said, "two vampires joined like you."

I opened my mouth to speak and then closed it quickly again.

"Say it." Jacob stepped into my line of sight.

"I don't trust any of you," I said flatly.

"We have a name," Catherine sounded rehearsed. "A vampire that has direct knowledge of what's happened to you."

"Who?" I muttered.

Catherine's frown deepened. "More like what."

My focus lingered on each of them waiting for someone to continue.

It was Jacob who did, saying, "His name's Paradom."

"How do you know him?" I asked.

"Through Lucas," Jacob said. "His charity serves the homeless. That's where Lucas came across Paradom."

"Paradom's homeless?" I asked, hating the sound of this.

Catherine raised her chin. "Go take a look at him and you'll soon want to reverse this mess."

My gut wrenched as my imagination spiraled.

"Our priority must be to find out what is going on in London," Jacob said, "before it migrates to other cities."

"It's self-limiting," Catherine said. "Vampires can't catch it from each other."

"We've only seen cases in London, so far," Jacob added.

"What can I do?" I offered, though it didn't seem to convince any of them.

Catherine's frown deepened. "*Don't* get in the way."

I responded with a careful silence.

"You have our permission to leave here," Catherine said. "But one of us will be keeping track of you."

I stepped toward Jacob. "Where will I find Paradom?"

"King's Cross, beneath the tube station," Jacob answered. "Paradom's been seen there on more than one occasion. He moves around."

"Once Lucas has the scrolls, you'll let me know?" I asked, scrutinizing Jacob's face for reassurance.

"Of course," Jacob said.

I shook my head in frustration. "So that's it?

"Circumstances have changed," Catherine said coldly.

Jacob wagged his chin. "The needs of the many . . . you know how it goes."

"I don't think he should leave here," Alex said.

Catherine rolled her eyes. "Alex, remember who we're dealing with."

I stretched the tension out of my hands but it didn't help.

"You're trapped in your own personal hell, Orpheus," Catherine said. "Ironic, don't you think?"

IV

WAITING PATIENTLY ON King's Cross's tube station platform, I watched the other passengers disappear out of sight. The ground rumbled as the train pulled away; the air forced out from the tunnel billowed my coat.

It doesn't have to be this way, uttered my conscience, entertaining the same idea I'd ruminated over since yesterday when I'd left The Mount. *Death is a reasonable alternative to being stuck in this body.*

Ah, but the possibilities, came that quiet musing of my ego.

As soon as everyone had deserted the platform, I leaped onto the track and flew along it, listening out for any noise that might hint to a lurking nightwalker.

Something crunched beneath my feet and I cringed at the sight of scattered fine animal bones.

Following the trail of skeletons, the apparent remains of rodents led me to a faded red doorway hanging off its hinges. Easing my way through, I sensed someone watching me, though glancing back I saw no one. Spreading out before me was a long service corridor about five feet in width, running the full length of the track.

A blur of movement shifted just up ahead and then something scrambled away in the opposite direction, scurrying upside down along the arched ceiling.

I bolted after it, whatever it was, trying to keep up with the creature that was picking up speed, its claws scraping the brick work and sending dust flying.

Closing in again I flew through the hole right behind it, landing straight back onto the same track I'd just come from, blinded by a train's headlights speeding right at me.

Barely missing the first carriage, I darted upward and clung to the jagged bricks above, my coat flapping wildly, deafened by the screeches of metal on metal. The train rocketed beneath, down the pitch-black track.

When the last carriage finally passed, I flung myself toward side of the track, hoping to avoid repeating that same mistake.

That dark phantom had seemed more like a large rodent than a vampire.

"You'll soon want to reverse this mess." Catherine's words still rung in my ears.

Nausea came out of nowhere and I wretched against the wall.

Wiping my mouth with my sleeve, I headed back up the track trying to shake the feeling of being watched again from the shadows.

A flash of electricity lit up the tunnel and there, standing just a few feet away, was a familiar green-eyed, titian-haired vampire staring back, a man who could have just stepped out of a painting by Botticelli. His steeliness reflected a timeless intensity, a proud and effortless stature eliciting an array of emotions and stirring memories spanning centuries; enough devilish adventures to spill tears of laughter from both of us.

Having rescued this wayward nightwalker over four hundred years ago, it pained me he didn't recognize me.

"Marcus." It felt good to say his name.

"How do you know who I am?" he asked, his cockney accent as rich as ever.

"Everyone knows who you are, Marcus," I said confidently. "You're vampire sovereignty."

His gaze narrowed. "Who are you?"

"William Rolfe," I said it quickly, hoping he'd believe it.

"What are you doing down here?"

I shut my mind down, making it impenetrable. "Searching for someone."

"Who?"

"Paradom."

"Apparently there is a crazy down here but I don't know his name." Marcus lowered his chin and locked on me trying to extract more.

"What are you doing down here?" I asked.

His gaze narrowed, hinting he didn't like being spoken to like that. "One of my men detected a Status Regal in London," he said. "Thought I'd check it out."

"A Status Regal, down here?"

"I lost him," Marcus admitted.

Actually, he hadn't. I was the Status Regal he'd been tracking, but admitting that would result in more questions.

Marcus's gaze scoured the tunnel. "What do you want with Paradom?"

"Information."

"About what?"

"Lots of questions, Marcus."

"Seems like I'm the one with the answers."

"You're looking for Orpheus?" I watched his reaction.

He hesitated. "And how would you know that?"

"I know him. Intimately," I said it too quickly.

"He's never mentioned you."

"Really?"

"I find that rather odd."

"I work for him," I told him. "Deal mostly with the 'tedious crap,' as Orpheus calls it."

"Like?"

Seeing Marcus again brought some comfort, but I knew well enough to keep my distance. "Investments." I hoped that sounded convincing.

"He has a broker."

"Orpheus hates his broker." I bit my lip, thinking of how much better I could have phrased that. "But he likes his accountant." I gave a crooked smile.

"How come I've never met you?"

"I'm rarely in London."

He scratched his chin, staring off. "Do you know where I can find him?"

"He's taking care of some personal business, I believe."

"How do you know him again?"

"We go way back." I wondered whether now was a good time to explain the truth, though knowing Marcus's unpredictable nature, I reconsidered. The last thing I needed was to provoke an assault.

"Prove it," he said.

I tried to work out how best to handle him. "Orpheus rescued you from Blackfriars."

"That's not exactly a secret."

"It's not exactly common knowledge either."

He folded his arms across his chest to let me know it wasn't good enough.

"You once befriended Orpheus's doppelganger . . ." I said wryly.

"Orpheus was of course flattered."

Marcus shifted his stance.

Realizing I'd brought up an intimate instance meant to be held in confidence, I tried to change the subject. "You found Jacob for him."

"His son," Marcus replied. "That was a long time ago. Orpheus told you that?" Marcus was uneasy. "Why has he never mentioned you?"

A train sped past spraying orange sparks. We both waited for it to head off down the track, allowing us to hear each other again.

"He finds me boring." I gave a shrug, pleased to see the relaxed shift in Marcus's demeanor.

He scratched his head, seeming to lose interest.

"He's done this before," I said. "Pissed off without telling anyone."

Marcus took in a deep breath.

I tried to read him but his mind was elsewhere. "Listen, you don't know anything about something poisoning vampires, do you?" I watched his reaction.

Marcus wore an incredulous expression. "I can see why Orpheus never mentioned you."

He clearly knew nothing.

A dark shadow appeared a little way off behind him.

"Well it's been a pleasure." I kept the phantom in my sight.

"If you happen to see Orpheus again—"

"You'll see him before me, I imagine."

"If you do see him," Marcus massaged his brow, "I need to know what he wants us to do with the girl."

"Who?"

"We have a police inspector sniffing around Belshazzar's," Marcus sighed. "She's threatening to shut us down."

"Not Ingrid Jansen?" I asked, trying to act casual.

"Yes, you know her?"

"She's of no consequence." I turned away, as though not caring. "More of a playful distraction, apparently."

"Ingrid was the lead detective on the Stonehenge case," Marcus said. "You know of it?"

I gave a shrug. "Two girls murdered within days of each other. One corpse positioned at Stonehenge, the other at Avebury. Orpheus placed the dead girls there to mess with Jadeon's state of mind."

"Orpheus told you that?" Marcus asked, surprised that I knew so much.

"Yes," I answered casually. "It was Orpheus's way of drawing

Jadeon and Ingrid together, hoping they'd destroy each other." I caressed my chin thoughtfully. "Masterful." And yet inside me raged a silent war of remorse, a self-loathing for all the suffering I'd caused. A selfish game where I'd ironically become the victim.

"The plan backfired," Marcus said disapprovingly. "Jadeon and Ingrid fell in love."

"Still, she's ever obsessed with Orpheus," I said, trying to appease him.

"The last time I saw Orpheus he was about to turn her." He pursed his lips, evidently troubled she was still mortal. "He must have changed his mind." His face was full of regret for saying too much.

Turning away I hoped he'd not caught my thoughts, though avoiding eye contact was equally risky.

Marcus kicked up some dirt. "Anyway, Ingrid seems to have forgotten much of what she knew about him." He shook his head warily. "Her memory's been wiped."

"How can you tell?"

"She's asking questions about Orpheus like she's never actually met him. And she doesn't remember me." Marcus frowned his suspicion. "You didn't ask me *who* wiped her memory."

"Well?"

He hesitated, mistrust smoldering in his gaze. "Whoever did the deed is an ancient. She seems to have a selective memory." Marcus was scrutinizing me. "Orpheus is so incredibly private. I'm surprised I've never met you before."

"Feel the same way about you, Marcus." I gestured my frustration.

"You seem to know an awful lot."

"So do you."

"I'm Orpheus's best friend," he snapped.

I glanced down the tunnel hoping for another train to pass.

Marcus was perturbed. "You kind of remind me of him, which is . . . strange."

I gave a bored sigh. "What are you going to do with Ingrid?"

Marcus shoved his hands into his pockets. "If I can't find Orpheus, that decision rests with me." He went to walk away and then paused as though he too sensed someone. "I'm going to turn her, probably."

I hoped he missed my reaction.

****

As the elevator descended, I grasped the rail, hating the sensation. Out of nowhere I'd developed an annoying phobia of heights.

Another dread came over me as I recalled how Belshazzar's, Belgravia's most exclusive club, had once been my most frequent haunt and yet now all it brought was angst. The part of me that had once found pleasure here was changed irrecoverably and all the joy this place offered was now gone.

Marcus and I had parted ways within the hour, which was easily enough time for him to turn Ingrid.

The lift jolted to a stop.

Had it not been for Ingrid's stubbornness getting her detained here in London's premier vampire lair, I'd have caught that rat-like creature by now and ruled out he wasn't Paradom.

The doors slid open and I realized I'd been holding my breath.

I stepped out warily and came face to face with our resident American Zachary Harris, who was Marcus's servant. He wore the leather collar of a fledging. Just last week Zachary had been transformed from a *Gothica* into a nightwalker. He was evidently still adjusting to his elevated status.

Zachary held up his hand. "That's far enough," he said with a soft Louisiana lilt.

Voices echoed from down the corridor, coming from one of the farthest chambers.

"I'm here to see Marcus," I said, annoyed that I even had to say it, feeling like a stranger in the place I owned.

Zachary gestured back to the elevator. "Not without my permission."

"Zachary . . ." I shoved him against the wall and held him there. "You disappoint me."

He flinched, forming words but unable to speak them.

"Well hello again," Marcus said calmly. "Now let him go."

Zachary twisted out of my grip.

"You okay?" Marcus asked him.

Zachary straightened his shirt, blushing with embarrassment, clearly shaken.

"What are you doing here?" Marcus asked me, gesturing for Zachary to get out of my way.

"Official business," I said.

He waved off Zachary. "What kind?"

"Financial." I winked at Zachary.

He sped up toward the elevator.

"Orpheus asked me to deal with your *problem*," I said.

"Not sure we need your help," Marcus said coldly.

"If you handle this wrong you'll have Scotland Yard all over

Belshazzar's."

"I find it odd that I met you just hours ago and now you've turned up here."

"Stranger things have happened," I said.

"Like what?" he asked.

"The way your barman makes Bloody Marys. He's adding two shots of Vodka. Now, by my calculation he's wasting your money to make his drinks taste better. And if you do the math over a year— "

"What is that?" He saw the necktie I was holding.

"It belongs to Sergeant Blake, Ingrid's colleague. He's in a Rover outside, waiting for her. I removed it from his neck without him noticing. It's a party trick of mine."

"You're a fucking accountant."

"I have *other* skills." I tucked the tie into my pocket.

"I don't trust you, William. And I don't like you."

"Still." I feigned I had no choice.

"Thanks for the offer." Marcus gestured for me to get back into the lift. "I'm handling this just fine."

"Orpheus gave me just one directive," I said flatly. "If Belshazzar's is ever under threat I'm to carry out his instructions."

"What the hell are you talking about?"

I motioned the obvious. "You told me Ingrid was threatening the club." I strolled confidently passed him, ignoring the cell where I believed Ingrid was being held and headed right to the end of the corridor and straight into Orpheus's office.

Marcus seethed from the doorway. "What the hell?"

I went straight for the 1745 oil painting by Francois Boucher hung behind the large oak office desk. Boucher's masterpiece *Brown Odalisque* elegantly portrayed a young woman reclining forward on a generous blue duvet, her sensuous gaze staring confidently at the onlooker and inviting him into the frame.

I glanced back at Marcus. "Admit you're intrigued?"

"Arrogant fuck," he snapped. "Touch nothing."

"You bought this Francois Boucher for Orpheus." Lifting the portrait off its hook I revealed the safe hidden behind and rested the painting against the wall. "One of his favorites."

He shrugged it off but I could see it bothered him.

"I'm proving . . ." I turned away from him, "that I work for Orpheus." I manipulated the mechanism and breathed a sigh of relief that the combination worked. "Only you and Orpheus have access, correct?"

Marcus squinted my way.

With a click I had it open and peered in. "Accountant privilege."

"You don't seem to realize who I am." His temper rose.

"I know you're reasonable."

"If you so much as—"

"In the early 1600's, both you and Orpheus set up orphanages around the city." I pulled out one of the dusty old ledgers. "You still keep the records of every child saved." I lifted out the external drive. "Thank God for technology, right?"

Marcus's eyes were wide with fury and he was quickly beside me. "How the hell do you know about those?"

I held up the flash drive containing the list of current members of the Stone Masters, which we'd gathered over the years. Marcus snatched it from me and threw it back in, then slammed the safe shut and twisted the combination lock and said, "Obviously you don't know everything."

I lifted the painting and he grabbed it from me and hung it back up.

"What are you planning to do with the policewoman?" I asked.

"What has that got to do with you?"

"Orpheus wants to know."

"If I let you in there, you'll tell me where he is." Marcus hands were balled into fists.

"It's a deal."

Marcus lingered, gauging whether he'd get his way.

I followed him out, ever ready for Marcus to change his mind and take out his frustration of losing all communication with Orpheus on me.

Once inside the dungeon, I lingered near the door, leaning against the back wall. The scent of sandalwood incense lingered . . .

Ingrid was hanging from two metal cuffs, her back pressed against the brick and her arms outstretched on either side of her. Her black rimmed spectacles hung on the bridge of her nose like a school teacher and she wore a white shirt, short skirt and leather boots. Her startling black mascara and bright red lipstick reflected a well-polished Goth, an interesting if not daring effort to mingle in.

God she was beautiful.

She had a tiny puncture mark on her right arm where she'd been administered intravenous fluids in the Emergency Room after Alex had dropped her off there. A discarded leather jacket was lying on the floor to her left, and next to that lay a set of handcuffs. I wondered what they'd done to her already.

But she was still mortal. For now, anyway.

By her worn out expression she'd wasted no time getting straight back to pulling her usual stunt of exploring the underworld in the worst possible way—alone. I wondered what she was doing back in London.

Paradom had answers for me and whatever was going on in here was eating away at time I didn't have. Yet as my eyes met with Ingrid's something passed between us and once again I felt drawn by an intangible force that was impossible to resist.

"Now where were we?" Marcus glanced my way. "Before I was rudely interrupted."

I checked out the other characters in the room, the platinum blonde dominatrix wearing a tight bask emphasizing her tiny waist, and she stood next to a brunette, a vampire turned in her forties. And then there was the shifty looking masked master who was threatening Ingrid with the worn end of a leather whip.

"Where's Orpheus?" Ingrid tried.

Marcus ran his fingertips over her left shoulder and along her arm, lingering for a moment on her wrist and then moving over to the shackle to test it was secure.

"Let me go," Ingrid's voice cracked with emotion.

Marcus folded his arms.

"I know what you are," she whispered.

Marcus reached for the top button of her shirt and played with it. "I assume you're here for our expertise in role play?" He undid her top blouse button but left the rest alone.

Ingrid's cheeks flushed.

My interruption had to be timed right. Intervene too soon and Marcus might become suspicious; take too long and it may well be too late for Ingrid's psyche.

I marveled at the situation. Some part of me had tortured patrons in this very chamber, taken delight from pushing them to the edge and nudging them over, plunging them into agony and bringing them back with ecstasy. The fact that they kept returning for more was the mere proof we were doing something right.

But Ingrid didn't belong here. And part of me felt the same way now. I questioned my change of heart and this unusual desire to save this woman from the inevitable.

Marcus played with strands of her hair. "So you're not just here to mix with our distinguished clientele? Or sup our fine wine?" He wrapped his hand behind her back and yanked her into him.

He was trying to scare her, break her down, but I had a feeling it would take more than this. He pulled out her hair tie, loosening strands that tumbled over her face and down her shoulders.

"When you find your wrists in those," he glanced at the shackles, "it means you're no longer in control. Quite simple really." He removed her spectacles and handed them over to the blonde. "Ingrid, love the outfit by the way."

"Is that what this is?" She raised her chin. "Your need for power?"

"Feisty," he said.

"Let's talk about Gillian Stewart," Ingrid said quickly.

Marcus paused, as though intentionally allowing the silence to pressure her.

"Tell me what you know about her." Ingrid pressed him.

"Does this look like an interview room?" Marcus asked.

Ingrid swallowed hard. "How about Tabitha Web?"

He glanced at each one of us. "Anyone know that name?"

"Two girls were found dead." Ingrid shifted her position. "One at Stonehenge, the other at Avebury. You'd have seen it on the news."

Marcus pressed his hand to his chest. "Ah, yes of course. Terrible."

From Ingrid's confused expression she seemed to be searching the recesses of her mind, failing to remember; the dark side of having her memory wiped by Snowstrom.

And Marcus could see she was struggling too.

I detected much of what she'd ascertained about us came from the detailed notes she'd made in her reports. This was what she was drawing from, not her own memories but facts she'd documented and now used to find her way back to Belshazzar's.

Marcus was right, Ingrid didn't seem to remember ever having met Orpheus. Though stirring within her were fragments of moments, delicate trails of thoughts that even now she was chasing after.

"I'm sure I read somewhere," Marcus began, "that incident at Stonehenge was the work of a cult, or a witch's ceremony."

"Vampires murdered those two girls," Ingrid said.

"Are you suggesting there's really such a thing as vampires?" asked Marcus.

"That's what you are," she said. "And I can prove it."

Marcus shrugged. "We merely just enjoy the . . . Gothic lifestyle."

"I've written evidence from my investigation." Ingrid straightened her back. "Blood results. Photographs."

"I'd like to see those," Marcus answered casually. "I'm assuming they're all fakes."

"Unshackle me!" she snapped. "Marcus, please." The way she spoke his name revealed her need to get through, connect with him.

It wasn't working.

"You invited your way down into the heart of Belshazzar's." Marcus adjusted her bra strap through her shirt. "There's only one reason you'd venture down here."

Ingrid flinched. "Where's Orpheus? I need to speak with him."

"I never took you for a Goth," Marcus said, "but we can certainly satisfy your secret proclivity."

She lowered her chin. "He's the one who calls the shots, after all."

I realized what she was doing, flirting with danger by pushing Marcus.

Flirting with death.

Marcus continued, "We pride ourselves on fulfilling the darkest fantasies."

"You're his sidekick, aren't you?" she said.

I was stunned with how she was riling him as though blindly endangering herself without any thought of the consequences.

Marcus leaned toward her. "Fantasizing about being screwed by the undead?"

Perspiration spotted Ingrid's chest. I wasn't the only one picking up on her frantic pulse racing ever faster. The room crackled with anticipation, the energy surging from one vampire to the other, their rising excitement seemingly bouncing off each other, responding to the challenge that hung helpless before them.

The passing seconds felt more like minutes.

"Marcus, I know you're a vampire," Ingrid said. "I'm going to have a forensic team comb this place."

"Ah." Marcus tuned to face us.

Ingrid raised her chin, full of confidence. "I'm not stopping until I find Orpheus."

Marcus broke his trance and gestured for me to join him. He whispered to me, "Let's get this over with, shall we?"

He was ready to turn her.

I motioned to the blonde to give Ingrid more wine and she responded to my order, pouring Bordeaux into a tall crystal glass. She carried it over to Ingrid.

With more subtlety than I knew I had, I took my entitled place in the center, and with that one confident move I gained the lead position ready to dominate the situation.

The blonde grabbed Ingrid's hair, pulling her head back and shoving the glass rim against Ingrid's lips, forcing the wine.

Marcus grabbed my right arm. "Don't fuck it up." He took my place leaning back against on the wall.

Ingrid spluttered, trying to catch her breath as scarlet droplets of Bordeaux spotted her lips and chin; panic seeped through her pores.

Nearing her, knowing the longer I kept her quiet the more likely I'd keep her alive, I removed the necktie from out of my coat pocket and held it up.

Ingrid looked horrified. "Blake's tie! What have you done with him?"

"Do exactly as you're told and Blake won't be harmed." I held her jaw. "You only speak when I permit, understand?"

"Where is he?" she dared.

"Seems you misunderstood." I pinched her jaw. "This remains closed."

Marcus's quizzical frown revealed his intrigue. If he approved the others would follow his lead.

"Prepare to mark her as property of a Status Regal," I ordered the blonde, and faced Ingrid again. "This is an honor you've yet to earn."

The brunette assisted the blonde, preparing the equipment and heating up the small metal brand. They waited for it to glow orange.

"Your life's hanging by a thread," I whispered. "I need you to do exactly as I say." Pressing my fingertips against her lips, I emphasized the need for her to remain silent.

A thin leather strap was placed in the palm of my hand and I rested it against Ingrid's lips and said, "Bite on this."

Ingrid screamed when she caught the blonde approaching with the red hot poker.

I shoved the leather strap into her mouth, forcing her to bite down and then shot a glance at the blonde. "I'll do it."

The blonde held Ingrid still.

I pressed the glowing brand to the center of Ingrid's left inner forearm and the smell of burning flesh arose; a faint sizzle. The small black circle was forever marked there. Ingrid's keening escaped the edges of the leather gag.

The blonde took the poker from me and stepped away.

The strap fell from Ingrid's mouth and her legs gave way leaving her dangling forward, held solely by the shackles. I lifted her, hugging her into me, waiting for her to regain consciousness.

With a kiss I brought her back to me. "You belong to Orpheus now." Though I doubted she'd heard.

The room fell quiet, the only sound was of Ingrid's short breaths, her anguished sighs filling the chamber. Her tears fell faster than I could wipe them away.

"Everyone out," I said.

"Why mark her if you're going to turn her?" Marcus asked.

"Orpheus's command was clear." I ran my fingers around the circle.

He directed them to leave and then threw me an uneasy glance. "You're not an accountant," he snapped.

Fear caught in Ingrid's throat as she gasped, "Don't you dare turn me."

"You've yet to earn that right." My fingertips pressed against her mouth hoping she'd get the hint.

She moved her head from to the side, her lips trembling. "Let me go."

"Ingrid, stay with me," I whispered. "I need you conscious."

She lost her composure, only this time I let her fear turn in on itself and watched her frenzied struggling with nowhere to go.

"She's not ready for Orpheus," I warned Marcus.

"But she's ready for me," he said.

"Tell Zachary to check on Sergeant Blake," I said.

Marcus gestured for me to join him across the room. "Since when do you give *me* orders?"

"I'm getting results." I glanced toward Ingrid. "She's submitting."

He curled his knuckles and rested them against his lips.

"By the time I'm finished with her," I said, "she'll be begging to be turned." I left Marcus standing there and returned to Ingrid, lifting her chin again. "Good girl."

Her eyes burned with fear and she was breathing rapidly, trying to think her way out of this. The door slammed shut. Marcus had gone.

I flicked open Ingrid's right shackle, easing out her wrist. She held back a sob, bracing herself for another attack.

"Do exactly as I say." I had the other shackle open and her left hand was free.

She rubbed her wrists, not trusting the moment, not trusting me, staring wide-eyed at the branded O on her forearm. I picked up what I assumed was her leather jacket and grabbed her hand, pulling her across the room, checking the outside corridor was clear. We made our way toward the lift. Ingrid tried to pull away forcing me to tighten my grip.

I punched the elevator button. "I'm getting you out of here."

"Where's Blake?" she asked, breathless.

"He's not here."

The doors parted and I pushed her in. "Not another word, understand?"

The lift jolted and began its ascent.

She faced me with her back to the elevator doors. "Where are we going?"

I handed her Blake's tie. "In less than a minute, you can give that back to him."

"What the hell did you do to me?"

I tried to tolerate what seemed like an endless climb upward to the ground level.

"You assaulted a police officer," she snapped.

I wanted to tell her she'd thank me later, but now wasn't the time.

"Who are you?" she asked.

"A friend . . . of a friend."

"Jadeon? Tell me where I can find him."

"Have you any idea of the danger you're in?" I asked.

She seethed. "My job is to hunt criminals."

"What are you even doing in London?"

"What do you know about me?"

I punched the up button several times even though the lift was ascending, as though it would make it go faster.

"Where do I know you from?" Her frown deepened. "How are you acquainted with Orpheus? How did you get that tie off Blake?"

I punched the button again. "Should I be listening?"

"He better not be harmed."

The elevator doors slid open and noises from the bar encroached into our small space.

She pointed a black manicured fingernail at me. "You're going to get a taste of a real cell when I lock you in jail." She turned slightly and there, standing right behind her were six leather-donned nightwalkers waiting for us to exit so they could enter.

Ingrid spun round and froze, looking at me for guidance.

"After you," I gestured.

The crowd of nightwalkers made a pathway for her, bowing in a gesture of respect. Ingrid squeezed through them only faintly aware of their regard of her.

I stepped out and grabbed hold of her hand again, guiding her through the bar. "Ingrid, not one more word."

Belshazzar's Friday night crowd mingled but we ignored them, pushing our way toward the long chandelier lit hallway that would lead us out. Vampires watched us in passing interest.

The bouncer opened the front door for us with a half-bored consideration. We were soon welcomed by the brisk night air.

"Be thankful." I wrapped her leather jacket around her shoulders. "It could have been a lot more interesting." I pointed to Blake's car.

She reached into her jacket. "Where the hell are my handcuffs?"

"Marcus has them. There's probably some unsuspecting punter wearing them right now."

"That's misappropriation of police equipment." She was walking too slowly.

I hurried her up. "This embarrassing charade of yours can be our little secret. How about that?"

"Have you any idea how serious this is?" She raised her left forearm.

"You consented."

"The hell I did," she screeched. "You've branded me? This is permanent!"

"Did you really believe you'd mingle in?" I frowned. "How did you get in there anyway?"

"I walked in with a group." She formed her lips into a pout and blew cold air on her arm.

"Promise you'll never return." I glanced up, scanning the windows for any sign we were being watched.

Ingrid grabbed my sleeve. "You have the right to remain silent . . ."

I slid out of her grasp and continued pulling her along toward Blake.

She tried to wriggle out from my hold. "Anything you say can and will be used as evidence against you in a court of law—"

"What will your colleagues make of your slutty attire when you parade me through Scotland Yard?" I asked. "And just try to explain what you're doing out of your jurisdiction."

She slowed her pace.

Blake had exited the Rover and was closing in on us.

Ingrid ignored him and faced me. "Where's Orpheus, aka Daumia Velde?"

"He's dead," I said flatly.

She studied me with those all-seeing eyes of hers.

Blake caught up. "Ingrid, where have you been? Is that my tie?"

I glanced at the club, wondering if Marcus had realized yet that I'd left with her.

Blake reached for his tie. "Where did you find it? One minute I was wearing the thing, the next moment it'd gone. Talk about freaky."

"Maybe you nodded off?" She threw him a scolding glance.

He looked annoyed. "I didn't."

Ingrid turned her back on Blake and stepped toward me. "How did he die?"

"Who died?" asked Blake.

"Long story." I shrugged it off.

"Ingrid, you told me you were going for a pee," Blake interrupted. "You never once mentioned actually going in there." He gestured toward Belshazzar's. "Didn't you get any of my calls? My texts?"

She patted her jacket. "Shit, my phone."

"Well that explains it," Blake said.

Ingrid studied the inflamed circle on her forearm, her expression returning to panic.

"What the hell happened?" Blake asked, horrified. "Is that a burn?"

I wondered if she'd ever recall how the vampires had respectfully parted for her when they'd caught sight of it.

"It's nothing," she whispered, though she was clearly in pain.

Blake shook his head. "Does it hurt?"

She peered up at me, her frown deepening.

Ingrid, the woman whom Orpheus had tried to turn; Ingrid, the lover whom Jadeon had tried to save, was standing there oblivious that both her nemesis and lover were one.

And back in Belshazzar's was Marcus who was strong enough to do some serious damage to both of us if pushed hard enough.

Tension hung so thick it felt like it could choke me. I'd just saved her life, yet Ingrid's hostile glare stayed on me.

"Let's get you out of here." Blake broke the silence and reached for her.

Ingrid pressed her fingertips to her lips. "I'm going to throw up."

"How much did you drink?" Blake shook his head, annoyed.

"I should go." I strolled away from them.

"I will find you," Ingrid called after me.

Tucking my hands into my coat, I crossed Grosvenor Crescent heading toward Mayfair, carefully dodging the cars. *"Not if I don't want you to."*

V

WITHIN MINUTES OF LEAVING Ingrid with Blake outside Belshazzar's, I was flying toward London's Regency Graveyard, tracking the vampire I believed to be Paradom up and over the cemetery wall and heading fast through trees.

Pausing briefly beside a sunken grave, I could no longer see the blur I was tracking and cursed myself for losing him. Wind chimes carried on the breeze; the weather turning colder and threatening rain.

There was a bulldozer parked to the right of the deserted graveyard and something told me they were going to be using it here, making room for the encroaching city. Judging by the few remaining graves this place was hundreds of years old and anyone who might have disputed the desecration was probably dead. A terrible scent carried, and I wondered if the construction had already disrupted one of the graves.

Something struck my back.

I picked up the coin that had been thrown at me and examined the 1829 shilling crested with King George IV's head on one side and a lion standing atop a crown on the other. Directly ahead was a grassy bank camouflaged by overgrown vines and enshrouded in rotting moss was a rusty old gate.

I yanked it open and eased my way through, cautiously following the dirt pathway that seemed to run beneath the small hill.

Ducking to accommodate the low earth ceiling, I proceeded, pinching my nose, trying to stop the pungent smell from stinging my nostrils, tasting putrid air and trying to find the will to continue.

I'd smelt rotting flesh before but this was something altogether different and it stirred such disgust that I questioned going any further.

Up ahead in the darkness, I tried to make sense of what I was seeing.

Hanging upside down in a bat like pose was a creature that almost resembled a human, but his flesh was leathery and his face that of a wrinkled old man with nothing but tufts of hair on his shiny bald head, his mouth twisted in misery.

I brought up my right hand and covered my face with my sleeve, willing the nausea away.

The myth that vampires turned into bats came to mind and I shuddered, studying this creature and wondering how he'd evolved into this.

"Who are you?" I whispered, making sure my pathway was clear in case I needed to break for the exit.

The creature's crinkled eyelids opened.

I gestured. "I mean you no harm."

He inclined his head as though trying to see me the right way up, but his body remained still. I unraveled my fingers to show him the coin in my palm.

His lips moved sluggishly, his crooked mouth revealing the sharpest teeth as he formed silent words. I held up the coin.

He pointed a long wizened finger, exposing his claw. "Someone did it to you, too."

"Did what?"

"Exactly!" he said.

"Who are you?" I feared the answer.

He grinned. "Paradom," he murmured.

I barely stopped myself from stumbling and checked the ground for anything else that might trip me up or trap me in.

"They sent you to kill me?" he mumbled.

"No." I motioned my sincerity.

"Pity," he muttered to himself. "Can you pass me that?"

Before me stood my worst nightmare and Catherine's threat that I'd become him was too much.

The cruelest revenge.

"That." He pointed to the wall.

All I saw was a scurrying rat searching for a way out, seemingly with a lot more sense than me. And then I realized.

His mouth twitched. "Quickly."

Trying to hide my repulsion, I grabbed the vermin by the scruff of its neck and held up the squirming rat. "I'll get rid of it."

The bat-like creature became flustered and he did for a moment show a flicker of excitement in an otherwise frozen face. He gestured for it, revealing a glimpse of crinkled flesh dangling from his upper back. This creature had wings.

Holding the rat out in front of me, I stepped forward and Paradom snatched the rodent out of my hand. He bit into the creature's throat, sucking furiously as it squealed and writhed against his mouth.

I took in his den, trying to find clues to who this being was from the things surrounding him, working hard at keeping my composure and my own expression polite.

There was a stack of old dirty clothes in the corner, and resting beside them, several moldy looking books. Almost hidden behind was an empty collection of bottles stacked in a heap.

"Are you really Paradom?" I asked, hoping there was another.

He continued sucking, closing his eyes to further appreciate the now dead creature, its eyes bulging.

Nausea welled and I warned myself this was a bad time to throw up. "What happened to you?" I tried to say it gently.

"Mustn't say his name. Don't say his name. Don't even dare to think his name."

"Who's name?"

He gawped and dropped the rat. "Nothing bad happened, right?" He hesitated. "I'm still here." He licked the sticky blood off his fingertips. "Listen, do you hear that?"

I wondered whose name mustn't be mentioned.

He cocked his head. "The one I'm joined with."

My head felt light and I leaned against the wall to support myself.

"You're a pretty one." He somersaulted off the ceiling, his black wings expanding wide and then raveling again. He was now standing upright before me. "Such a shame it won't last."

I tried to rally my courage and fight this urge to bolt. "Clearly you're a vampire and yet . . ."

"We're the same, you and I."

"Yes, Paradom, I too am a vampire."

He shook his head in frustration. "No, of course that, but you and I are the same."

"Oh God." It came out.

"They did it to you too." He shrugged. "Two of you, now one, yes?"

"How do you know?"

He stepped closer. "In your eyes. And in your head." He pointed. "See."

"You read my mind?" A strange gift, considering I thought I'd locked down my thoughts. "You say someone did this to you on purpose?"

"His purpose."

"Who?"

He waved a long wrinkled finger at me. "I disgust you."

"No."

"William?"

"How do you know my name?"

"You told me."

I squeezed my eyes shut and gave closing my thoughts down another go.

"Must shut down my thoughts," he mirrored.

"How do you do that?"

"Because I'm twice the vampire I once was!" He let out a maniacal laugh.

Stale blood rose in my throat. "How long have you been joined?"

"A century. Centurion. Center."

I held back, not wanting to ask the question that was screaming so loud in my head. I was sure Paradom would hear it.

He shot up a finger. "You want to go back."

"Separate, yes."

He pointed upward. "Stay here with me."

I could have sworn the rat jerked.

"When you were joined . . ." I braved to say. "Did you look like me, like a man at first?"

"I was beautiful just like you are now." He raised a sparse eyebrow. "I could have anyone I wanted," he said triumphantly. "And did."

"If I may ask . . ."

His jaw clenched and then relaxed like a toothless old man. "He seduced me in with poetic words. He told me he loved me."

"Who?"

Paradom shrunk low. "I was everything he wanted to be." He scurried toward me, closing the gap between us, reaching for and grabbing a lock of my hair. "He wanted to be me so much that he . . . dug out a bit of my brain and ate it right there in front of me."

I tried to close my gaping mouth, ready to duck away, threatening to break his trust.

Paradom tugged on my hair. "No, wait, I think I dreamed that."

I wanted to tell him that was more like a nightmare, but he appeared too unstable to push.

"I am too unstable to push." He stared off.

It was disconcerting that despite having locked down my mind he could still penetrate my thoughts. "Are you saying a vampire tricked you into joining with them?"

Paradom was biting his yellow claws. "We got up to so much. Our power together . . . we are so much better for being two. He was right about that." Paradom seemed to be looking around for another rat. "Can you move things with merely a thought?"

"Haven't tried." I offered the shilling he'd thrown at me back to him.

He took it from me, clutching the coin in his palm. "The world will fall at your feet. It once bowed so low at mine that I felt like a god."

"Paradom, the name of the vampire who you're joined with—"

"Listen!"

I tried to pick up on what he was hearing.

"Can I stay with you?" he asked.

My expression answered before I could. His shoulders slumped.

"How did you become one?" I asked.

"You have to die first." He raised a pointed claw and pointed it my way. "Snowstrom knows how to reverse it."

It suddenly dawned on me that Paradom was probably mad and I wanted to kick myself for taking him seriously.

I studied him carefully. "How long before you . . . became this?"

He held up his withered hand before his face.

"How long do I have?" I pushed.

Paradom seemed to be counting on his fingers. "I think about . . ." More counting.

My legs weakened. "What were the first signs?" I barely got the words out.

He leaned forward, his expression riddled with confusion as though remembering.

"I will find a way back," I mumbled.

His nose twitched. "You'll need the scrolls."

"Yes, the scrolls?" I cringed, realizing he'd just read my mind again.

"Aren't you hungry?" he asked.

I shook my head.

"The Stone Masters have them," he muttered.

"The Stone Masters have the scrolls?" Frowning, I tried to relax my facial muscles, but with the dank smell mixed in with the rotting aroma, it was hard.

"When you find the scrolls will you help me to reverse?" he asked.

"Yes. Now are you sure they're with the Stone Masters? This is very important."

"They have it all. All the books. All the letters. All the scrolls."

I drew closer.

"They have the finest library," he said, as though remembering. "I'm not allowed in there anymore." He let out a sob.

"I'll find the scrolls." I took a step back. "And then I'll come back for you. I promise, Paradom."

The longest primal howl escaped his curled lips.

I gestured my goodwill, trying to calm him.

"He visits me once in a while and lets me drink from him." He pointed to the collection of oddities behind him. "He brings me those."

"Who does?"

"He's a Stone Lord." Paradom shook his head. "Very important."

"What's his name?"

"Jacob."

"Not Jacob Roch?" I regretted giving him the last name so quickly.

"Yes."

"You're sure?"

"The priest."

I shook my head. "He used to be a Stone Lord a long time ago. He isn't any more."

"He was wearing their signet ring last time he visited."

"When was that?"

"Last night."

I studied him trying to work out who was madder, him or me for believing him. Jacob had told me to find Paradom but hadn't mentioned he'd actually met with him.

"Jacob gave me that." Paradom pointed to several tins of cat food stacked up behind him.

"You shouldn't be eating that."

"I promised I'd be good." He gave a grin, but it was out of place.

My jaw fell open though I quickly closed it, hoping to act casual and not derail Paradom's trail of thoughts, wondering again if he'd read my mind and extracted information and was now confusing both me and him with it.

"What did Jacob say?" I asked.

Paradom waved his claw. "They're on our side you know. The Stone Masters."

"Not exactly." My voice was low, unthreatening.

"Why do you say that?"

"Jacob was once aligned with the Stone Masters, but that was in order to spy on them." I said it softly. "Now though, we avoid them

"You messed up royally this time."

I shook my head. "Wait . . . I'm wondering how you're coping, Marcus. Does that sound like me?"

"You're home now, where I can take care of you." He stepped forward and embraced me.

I waited for his hug to end.

Marcus broke away. He had smudges of blood on his shirt, rubbed off from me, but he didn't seem to care.

"That flash drive in the safe?" I said at last.

"What about it?"

"I need to check out the names on it."

"Sure," he said. "Why?"

"Apparently the Stone Masters have something that might help me reverse."

"Now you're really scaring me."

"Just get it for me," I said.

"I'm so relieved to have you back."

"It's good to be here." I suppressed a frown, not sure if those words rung true.

Marcus didn't catch it. "You have to talk to her."

"Sunaria's here?"

"I've never seen her so lost."

I studied the door suddenly aware of why Marcus had led me here.

He reached for the handle. "She's very fragile right now."

Hands trembling, realizing the very reason for every action I'd taken, the catalyst for centuries of yearning was on the other side . . .

. . . *And yet something within me resisted.*

Sunaria was laying upon the King bed surrounded by numerous newspapers and magazines spread over the covers. Her bewitching presence soaked through my flesh like the darkest dreaming, inducing a painful rush of memories.

Although she seemed hesitant, I sensed she was pleased to see me, as though our exchange back in Cornwall was merely a lover's quarrel.

I stepped toward her. "I'm sorry about . . . back at the Mount."

She peered at my scarlet stained shirt and then her steely turquoise gaze settled on me. "You've even got blood in your hair."

"Had a run in with some thugs." I gave a shrug. "They had knives."

"It's your blood?"

"As soon as I knew you were here, I came in."

Her expression reflected disgust. "Apparently they have modern appliances now. Like showers."

Filled with panic that our first real reunion was already going awry, I broke her glare, stung by her tortuous silence, my chest tightening with tension.

Self-conscious, I undid my shirt, ripping the last few buttons off and then removing it, throwing it into the corner.

I glanced over at the TV. "Quite something isn't it?"

"Planes in the sky too," she said.

"Man has walked on the moon." I sighed. "Quite something from our day."

"I recognize nothing." She swung her legs over. "Not even you."

"You've been asleep awhile." I took a step closer.

"Orpheus?" she whispered.

The name sounded like a lie.

She looked fierce. "Jadeon, when this is over, I will kill you for this."

"We were fighting over Stonehenge," I began. "The sun arose and—"

"I know how it happened. I just don't understand why?"

"I was taking revenge for your death," I said.

She seemed suddenly overwhelmed.

I struggled to find the strength to deal with her pain, still reeling with mine. "Jacob . . . saved you." I tried to grasp what those words really meant. "He bribed the Stone Lords for your ashes."

"Fabian only agreed to resurrect me because Jadeon Artimas begged him." She shifted closer to the edge.

I gave a careful gesture of acknowledgment.

"This sudden awakening," she continued, "finding the world has nothing in common with the one I left behind is too much."

"You've been jolted through time," I said, offering my understanding of what she was going through.

Only now did I take in the simple decor of Marcus's suite, the neatness. The comforting intimacy of an old friend's place; cool white walls and furniture with simple lines, a classic, crisp, clean design emanating sophistication.

Sunaria followed my gaze around the room. "Does Marcus believe me now, about you?"

"He seems to." I sat beside her and reached for her hand. "You and I were inseparable."

She pulled her hand away.

I gave her a nudge. "Since when did you become so sensitive?"

"Since Jadeon murdered my lover." She stared into my eyes as though throwing a warning.

"I'm not dead, just . . ." I gently took hold of her chin and lifted her head to look at me. "Sunaria, I have you back." And yet my thoughts betrayed me, devouring each other, as though some part of her terrified me.

She sensed my reticence. "This can be undone?"

"Jacob believes so."

"Can we trust him?"

"What choice do I have?" I stared at nothing.

Sunaria rested her hand on my knee and then quickly withdrew it. "You're . . . not yourself."

Panic washed over me and I tried to save myself from sabotaging this moment. "You're not planning on staying, are you?"

"There's nothing for me here." She stood up though remained close. Close enough to take her hand and kiss it, beg her to love me as she once did.

"You're upset with me because I failed to save you, is that it?" I asked. "On that beach in Spain, I begged you not to go. You should have listened."

"You never forgave me," she said.

"I never got over your death." I clenched my jaw, angry with myself that it had come out wrong. "Look, I'm so far down the rabbit hole I'm beginning to doubt there's a way back."

"Rabbit hole?"

"It's a reference to . . . Alice in Wonderland—" I felt ridiculous. "Which you'd have absolutely no idea about." My shoulders slumped with the realization of what Sunaria was facing. "You can't leave here until one of us has updated you on all the dangers out there."

"You don't get to dictate what I can or cannot do."

"You're not capable of making any decisions."

"I could say the same about you."

Trying to shake off my frustration, I said, "This moment, I never believed it would ever happen."

"You gave up on me."

Her words stung deep and I was stunned with her lack of sympathy.

Marcus was standing in the doorway. "Orpheus plans to reverse this, Sunaria," he said.

"Thought we were calling him William now?" Her tone sliced through the air.

Marcus gestured for me to rejoin him.

"Change your mind," I pleaded with her. "Stay."

"Anyone who attempts to imprison me here . . ." though her inflection was passive, the intimation was clear.

Marcus lowered his gaze. "Sunaria, no one will stop you. You've made it quite clear you're not staying."

"What are your plans for him?" Her mouth twisted with suspicion.

Marcus stood straight, confident. "It's my job to pick up the pieces when you break his heart."

"You left him alone at Stonehenge," she said. "This is your fault for abandoning Orpheus when Jadeon attacked."

"Orpheus ordered me to go," said Marcus. "Don't you think I regret leaving him there now?"

"The only person I trust is me," she said. "Snowstrom will put this right."

Marcus looked harried. "That's where you're going, to find Snowstrom?"

Sunaria was defiant. "You get him all to yourself after all, Marcus."

"I'm right here," I said.

"Not my Orpheus," Sunaria snapped.

Her words struck hard and I grasped the door to steady myself. "Sunaria, my love for you goes so deep inside of me that even I can't reach it anymore."

Yet she stood there expressionless as though she'd not heard my confession.

When those tortuous seconds became too much, I closed my eyes and rested my forehead against the doorframe. *Lord, forgive me for all that I've ever done that may have offended thee . . .*

"He's not listening," she said.

Don't abandon me in my hour of need . . .

"It's a little late for that don't you think?" Her incredulous expression forced me out.

VII

THE FEMALE, TWENTY-TWO year old Gothica Anaïs, stood barefoot on the floor's ornate hexagon. Long, black hair and heavy make-up emphasized her delicate features bestowed by her Japanese heritage. She wore the classic attire of a servant of Belshazzar's, and her body was kissed here and there with tattoos.

Twenty or so other elders stood a little way behind her, all eager to watch the proceedings of the Gothica's initiation on her day of decision.

Zachary approached Anaïs, sharing words of reassurance with her.

Marcus was seated in the center of one of three high-backed chairs upon a high platform. I sat to his right.

His ironclad grip brought my attention back on him. "Sunaria's hurting," he said quietly. "She'll come round."

"I've lost her again," I whispered, not believing it possible.

Marcus looked away, unsure how to placate me.

This was one of Belshazzar's largest subterranean chambers, reserved only for the elite, all mortals forbidden unless expressly authorized by the elders for occasions such as this, tonight's ruling in our vampire court.

But right now my mind was far from this place.

Marcus admired my fresh clothes that Zachary had bought for me. "They fit you well," he said.

I tugged on the pinstripe shirt. "You do realize Jadeon dressed like this."

Marcus looked stunned. "I don't pretend to understand any of this but I know it's you, Orpheus, and this is your home."

"My sanctuary."

He seemed to take comfort in that.

My gaze found the room again. "Not really in the mood."

"What goes on in here is never about us," he said. "You always insisted on presiding."

"Not today."

Penthea, the tall slender nightwalker who managed the bar, took the seat on Marcus's left. Zachary stood nearby, waiting on his master's next order.

"You know why you're here?" Marcus addressed Anaïs, gesturing for her to speak.

Anaïs looked to Penthea for guidance, though Penthea ignored her, hinting the girl was to look at Marcus.

"It's five years to the day," Anaïs began, "that I swore allegiance to Belshazzar's."

Marcus leaned forward. "And what were you promised?"

"If I served loyally, I'd be rewarded."

"And in your opinion have you fulfilled your part?" he asked.

Anaïs froze.

"Answer the question," Penthea commanded.

"I believe so. Yes, mistress," said Anaïs.

Marcus leaned over to Penthea. "Covent Garden?"

"We found Anaïs begging," said Penthea.

"She was only sixteen," Marcus said, remembering. "So, today we decide."

Anaïs's seemed fascinated with me and her attention was making me uncomfortable.

"She's your Gothica?" Marcus asked Penthea. "Anything you'd like to add?"

Penthea gave a bored sigh. "Anaïs has served me well."

Anaïs reacted to her name being spoken as though only now understanding what today was, realizing the door was closing on her once unremarkable life where days, weeks and years had passed ordinarily. As much as it can for a Gothica.

Marcus reached into Anaïs's thoughts. "Come here."

She stepped forward, warily.

"You were good friends with Gill?" Marcus asked flatly.

Anaïs shrugged. "Sort of."

"Shall I ask the question again?" he asked.

Anaïs's pupils dilated. "We were friends."

"And you think your fate could end up like hers?" Marcus glanced at me.

VIII

THE TOWERING FOUR FACED clock kept perfect time.

I slipped passed the lone security guard and headed through the low doorway, ascending the winding staircase toward the tower, trying to think of anything but how high I'd be going.

Or how I was going to achieve anything when I got up there.

Counting at least one hundred steps of the three hundred and thirty-four to the belfry so far, I peered down the way I'd come at the wrought iron staircase, marveling at how Big Ben was still boasted as one of the largest clock's in the world, recalling its construction in 1859 when Queen Victoria had ruled; this darling of landmarks having since survived two world wars as well as the Blitz.

Vertigo hit me and I stepped back.

Again that issue with heights and I questioned if it was a passing phase, a symptom of more recent events. I tried to shake it off and forced myself to look over the banister and face this new fear.

I rallied the courage to continue.

There it was, the other side of the huge clock face made up of stunning cast iron circle sections with twelve or so white pieces of glass perfectly designed within and it was well over twenty feet across, the faint shadow of the small hand inching its way every two seconds closer to the fourth Roman numeral.

The minute hand was carved expertly in solid bronze and beyond the glowing clock face was a spectacular view of the grey city skyline, the grand metropolis below showing signs of life stirring.

Attached to the wall was a brass stairwell that I assumed led to the rooftop and I reached for the first rung and began the short climb upward.

With a nudge the skylight lifted and I rose onto the roof; my long coat flapping.

There, leaning precariously over the edge with his back to me, was the man I'd followed up here.

The handsome, dark complexioned young man, pulled his tatty jacket tight around him, trying to shield himself from the cold. His jeans were dirty and ripped. He peered over, seeming hypnotized by the drop.

I'd found his name amongst fifty or more Stone Lords stored on the flash drive stashed in Belshazzar's safe. I'd been tracking him for just over an hour and was initially annoyed with his choice of locale until I realized his intentions.

The first hammer struck one of the smaller bells and I pressed my hands against my ears, knowing that any second the largest of the three bells would strike.

He stared back wildly, squeezing his hands against his ears.

Despite being in his mid-twenties the lines around his eyes aged him, and his fragility hinted at misery.

There was a mutual sigh of relief when Big Ben finished announcing it was quarter past the hour, though the ringing in my ears was still terrible, and from the stranger's expression he too was suffering the after effects.

His attention fell once more onto the city below. "To die . . ." he whispered with a Welsh lilt, shifting closer to the edge. "To sleep."

I took a step toward him. "Perchance to dream."

He tipped back, frowning. "Don't come any closer."

I peered to my left and a wave of vertigo struck again. I turned back to face the man who was now squinting at me. He pulled his grey worn coat around him.

I glanced at my wristwatch.

"You don't need that." He pointed downward. "You're standing on one of the world's finest time pieces."

"Can't see the clock face from here." A wave of vertigo hit and I coughed it off. "Nice view."

"Yeah right." He gestured. "You first."

I pressed my fingertips against my forehead, trying to decide whether to go back inside the bell tower.

"What's your reason?" he asked.

I ignored him.

"Not so easy, is it?" he said, interrupting my thoughts. "What if we jump together?"

"I came up here to think."

"Sure."

"The vista's something else." I found myself drawn to him, as though his dark irises might just answer all my questions.

He raised his hand. "If you take one more step . . ."

"I thought that's what you wanted?"

"In my own time."

Lost amidst his rambling thoughts, gauging where to go from here; I noticed his worn shoes.

"This is not who I am." He tugged his tatty shirt and his eyes glistened as though dwelling on what had led him here.

"Not that it matters now," I said.

"Does to me." He adjusted his footing, revealing an unsteady gait as he favored his right leg.

"Trust me, whatever I'm thinking right now will be surpassed by those who stroll past your mangled corpse." I pointed. "Down there."

"Grief counselor are you?"

"Is that why you're here? You're grieving?"

"And you?"

"I have a problem with timing, apparently." I marveled how I'd almost forgotten why I was here, becoming so engrossed in this man's life and impending death.

"You remind me of one of my old professors," he said.

"You studied at Cambridge?"

"Law." His frown deepened. "That was a good guess."

"Your accent."

"I'm Welsh."

"With a hint of Cambridge."

"Really?"

"Family tradition?"

He studied me. "My father met my mother there. What do you do?"

"What does it matter now?"

He peered down the side of the tower. "I tried to explain to my father that I found no passion in law."

"He wanted the best for you."

"Much to my father's embarrassment, I left." He pulled his lips into a frown. "We were never that close." He raised his chin. "Instead of following his dream, I followed mine."

"Good for you." Though the irony of that statement now sounded ridiculous. Trying to save the moment and somewhat intrigued, I asked, "What did you do?"

"Why?"

I gave a shrug. "Talking is helping me right now."

He hesitated and then said, "I joined The National Ballet."

"As a dancer?"

"*Yes*, as a dancer." His head snapped my way. "What about you? What do you do?"

"Art," I said it softly.

"You're an artist?"

I thought about how best to answer; the question forcing the deception out like lava, erupting a scolding truth that yes, some part of me had once been hopelessly in love with art. I kept silent, hoping the attention would fall back on him.

He was still waiting for an answer.

"Life's complicated," I said eventually.

"Where did you study?"

"It's not necessarily where, but from whom."

Renoir leaning over my shoulder, holding a paintbrush and smudging the paint delicately on the canvas, masterfully merging the grey to reveal a cloud moving over the horizon as though he'd revealed it and not painted it before my eyes.

The stranger's feet were dangerously close to the edge.

"What happened to your leg?" I asked.

"Why?"

"You mentioned you're a dancer?"

"Was." He glanced over his shoulder. "Got hit by a car." He'd spoken the words so matter-of-factly they sounded rehearsed, used up and almost comfortable. "Leaving a late night rehearsal," he continued, "Taking my usual route home through London."

My thoughts encroached into his and I was seeing his journey through his eyes, his bicycle whipping past houses and shops, navigating the busy roads down twisting lanes, slowing only to take the tight turns.

"It was raining," I whispered, seeing the blur of the road.

"The car came out of nowhere." Dazed, he was reliving the moment all over again. "The driver swerved, but . . ." He reached for his trouser leg and lifted it, revealing a gnarly looking deformity to his lower right calf. "The only time I ever felt alive was when I was dancing." He gave a small gesture as though emphasizing that was why he was here now.

"What's your name?" I asked.

"As you've already suggested, what's the point?"

I already knew it was *Sebastian*.

"Why are you doing it?" he asked.

I came back to the moment, realizing he was still waiting for an answer. "I don't even know if I have a soul." The words tumbled out as though coming from a place deep within.

"Of course you do. I can see it in your eyes." He glanced at the edge.

"What's the worst that can happen?" My ill-timed grin quickly faded.

"I figured the drone of the bell would drown out my scream."

I took a step toward him. "I don't think you're ready."

"What's that meant to mean?"

"I believe you'll regret it."

"Well by the time I reach the ground, it'll be too late." He sneezed.

"Careful," I said.

The clock struck and I covered my ears as the bell rang out, chiming it was half passed the hour.

Sebastian pressed his hands against his ears too, trying to block out the deafening clang. He lost his footing, tipping dangerously, his face twisted in terror, his arms flapping widely as he tumbled backward off the ledge.

Falling . . . flying . . .

Sebastian scooted backward on the pavement, moaning his terror as though still falling.

He froze.

Standing a few feet away, I was astonished that I'd actually caught him and I squinted back up at Big Ben, having swallowed my fear.

Sebastian became reanimated, caressing the ground, trying to make sense of what had just happened. He staggered to his feet, his eyes riddled with confusion, his mouth gaping.

"That was close." I shoved my hands into my pockets.

His face froze and then tension rippled across his brow.

"Second chances are quite something, aren't they?" I headed eastward.

"What are you?" Sebastian shouted after me.

Ignoring him, I picked up speed.

"Can you see him?" Sebastian's voice was strained.

Two scruffy young men were walking our way with their hoods pulled over their faces, protecting them from the morning chill.

The taller of one of the two pointed at Sebastian. "Look."

"Can you see him?" Sebastian asked them again, gesticulating wildly in my direction.

The taller man gave a snide grin. "No mate, don't see no one."

Sebastian mumbled something, clearly on the verge of panicking.

I headed back toward them. "Keep walking," I said to the boys and hailed the oncoming taxi. It slowed, but as soon as the driver caught sight of the two hooded men he sped up and sped off.

I drew closer to the eldest. "Your brother here has carnal knowledge of your girlfriend."

The thug's eyelids flickered. "Knowledge?"

"*Extensive.*" I closed in on him. "David, while you're working hard in your father's garage, breaking your back and shouldering the family business, Ray here is in the office *doing* your girlfriend Becka."

David teetered in a dream-like state and focused on his brother.

Check his phone, I sent the message silently, pointing toward Ray's pocket.

David reached out his hand. "Give me your cell."

Ray removed it from his pocket. "What's wrong with yours?"

I gestured to Sebastian he was to follow me.

David had Ray's phone and was fixed on the small screen. "That's Becka's number!"

I breathed in the freshness of the rain striking the pavement, clearing the dawn air, and returned to the curb. I raised my hand toward yet another taxi that had just turned the corner.

Sebastian was still lingering, fascinated with the entranced brothers.

The black hackney carriage parked in front of me. I opened the rear passenger door and ducked low to climb in.

And then I waited for Sebastian to join me.

IX

SEBASTIAN SAT BESIDE the walnut table, crossing one long leg over the other, taking in the luxurious suite. One of the Savoy's finest.

Though this room was a little too plush for my taste, I still appreciated the unusual collection of objet d'art that were placed here and there, providing an eclectic mood. From the crystal decanter resting on the far side table, I poured Sebastian a large glass of sherry into a tumbler and carried it over to him.

"Thank you, William." He pressed the glass to his lips but didn't sip. "I fell . . ." he said. "You caught me." He went to speak again but instead slumped as though the moment defeated him.

"How is it?"

He downed the sherry, barely tasting it.

Strolling over to the closed curtain, I caressed the thick velvet drapes. "This suite has a wonderful view of the Thames."

He rested the empty glass down. "Isn't the National Gallery about a ten minute walk from here?"

"The gallery houses one of the world's finest collections of European paintings," I said, yearning for the past, regret by another other name.

Unable to push away this longing, a reminder that everything I once held dear was at risk, I faced him again. "These curtains remain closed."

He offered his understanding. I marveled at how easily his thoughts opened up to me.

"Bath first or food?" I asked.

He scanned the room. "I'd love some crisps."

"Room service will be here soon. Shower?"

"You can fly."

I sauntered toward the bathroom and opened the door. "You'll feel better once you've freshened up."

He rose from his chair. "Are you going to tell me what really happened back there?"

"In what respect?"

"You saved me."

"I believe it's the other way around."

He squeezed my forearm as though checking I was real. "Why?"

"It's just a shower."

"I love the Tate. Used to, anyway." His voice softened. "What kind of art do you like?"

"Old masters." I pointed. "There's some spare clothes in there that should fit you."

He headed on in and I shut the door behind him.

Taking a seat in the velvet armchair I allowed my mind to wander and find solace in my imagination, recalling the Gallery's glorious yellow-lit corridors presenting their finest treasures, brave expressions of art including paintings from Botticelli, Leonardo Da Vinci, Cezanne, Turner, Renoir, and Van Gogh; glorious echoes of their souls channeled onto each canvas, sharing their genius.

There came the sound of the shower.

Inevitably my thoughts were drawn to the 1507 portrait by Raphael of St. Catherine of Alexandria, which I'd loaned to the National and was on display there still.

Back in Cornwall, remembering Catherine's haunting glare; the bluest irises portraying fear when she'd seen me for the first time; and something else too—hate.

Not far from where Raphael's St. Catherine was exhibited hung another painting of mine, Rembrandt's Belshazzar's Feast. A grand depiction of a biblical tale where God had sent a message to Prince Belshazzar that his days were numbered.

Were both lost to me now? I wasn't ready to believe that.

Sebastian stood in the bathroom doorway wearing the hotel's luxury robe.

"That was quick," I said.

"Wasn't sure what your plans are," he said. "Don't want to hold you up."

I waved off his concern.

"Can I use your razor?" he asked.

"There should be a complimentary one in there."

A knock signaled room service had arrived.

Within minutes dinner for one was set on the walnut table and the hotel waiter was tilting the 1976 vintage Brevier de Jane for my approval. With a steady hand he uncorked the wine and poured a sample into a crystal glass. I picked up the leather wallet and signed the bill, adding a generous tip. The waiter made a discreet exit.

Although Sebastian and I were alone again, my inner ghosts left me feeling crowded and my thoughts divided as I struggled with my decision to loan St. Catherine to the National, tortured by the way it reminded me of my own Catherine, remembering how she loved to sit and admire it when we were children.

In a daze I froze, still holding the bottle mid-tipped and ready to pour.

"You alright?" Sebastian was dressed in jeans and a blue shirt, and where he'd shaved he was left with a fresh-faced boyish appearance.

"Miles away." I poured the Bordeaux into the tall stemmed glass. "I've already eaten." I answered his question before he asked it.

He reached for the glass.

"Let it breathe," I whispered.

Sebastian lifted the silver lid. "Pasta!" He let out a laugh. "For breakfast!"

"I can order something else."

His face lit up. "No, I haven't eaten like this in . . ."

I pulled out the high-backed dining chair for him and he sat in it, scooting forward, reaching for the silver cutlery placed on either side of the fettuccini-laden porcelain plate. He ate elegant mouthfuls of the yellow creamy dish, pausing briefly to dab his mouth with the napkin. He tried to say, "Thank you so much," with his mouth full.

I strolled back over to my chair, briefly catching the flicker of emotion in his eyes, reflecting the comfort a good meal provides.

A familiar turmoil raged within, reminding me that time was of the essence, though Sebastian didn't catch it. He was far too engrossed in the taste of the Bordeaux. He studied the wine label and caught the age of the vintage. He became fixated on the waiting pot of crème brulee.

"How's the wine?" I asked.

He took a sip. "Delicious."

"Do you trust me?" I asked.

"You saved my life." He smiled and yet it seemed out of place.

"Stay here tonight. You're quite safe."

"Where are you going to stay?" he sounded suspicious.

"I'm going home."

"This place is costly." He dabbed his mouth with the napkin. "I shouldn't stay."

"I insist."

"Where's home?"

"Cornwall."

"Nice. Bit of a drive."

"I live on an island." I rose and reached for the bottle and topped up his drink. "Very private."

He raised his glass. "You're not having one?"

"I don't drink."

"Huh," he said, surprised. "And yet you choose the finest wine. It's my father's favorite vintage." He scratched his chin and said, "You don't know him, do you?"

"No."

I'd hoped such a familiar red might stir his nostalgia, perhaps even nudge him in the direction of home.

Sebastian's fingertips caressed his lips thoughtfully. "You're scared of heights?"

Remarkable. Despite his own problems he'd caught my moment of vertigo back on Big Ben.

He straightened in his chair. "Strange that a man who can fly is scared of heights."

"When was the last time you slept in a bed?" I asked.

He glanced at the one here and gave a deep sigh.

"That's a long time," I whispered.

"I can't trust what I saw. Or what I think I saw." He put down his empty glass. "Why are you being kind to me?"

"You don't think you deserve it?"

"Most people who look at my tatty clothes think I'm a homeless bum."

"Pain has led you to the place where you must come to terms with it. Only then will you find your way out of it." I realized those words were also meant for me.

"You sure my father didn't send you?" He rested back.

"I'm afraid not."

"Are you like a guardian angel?"

I chuckled.

"Did you drug my wine?" he slurred.

Now wasn't the best time to admit to Sebastian that a few drops of vampire blood mixed with, say, a 1976 glass of Brevier de Jane, or any wine for that matter, would eventually make a mortal sleepy.

"You're the best thing that's ever happened to me," he whispered.

"I thought that was dancing."

"I've given up on all that foolishness." His eyelids fluttered, threatening to shut.

Caught off guard, my tears blurred my vision.

GAZING UP AT THE FOYER'S low hanging chandelier, I was distracted by the way the crystal droplets refracted candlelight, throwing off shadows that danced around me like small, taunting demons hauntingly conveying the truth—

I'd have gone for something more gothic.

I broke away and ascended the staircase with a sluggish step, trying to shake off the guilt of leaving Alex alone here.

There was something comforting about his bedroom, the familiarity of being surrounded by some of his things, and I wandered over to his wardrobe to check his clothes were still here. I scrunched up one of his shirts and buried my face in it.

There was a pinewood table that Alex had obviously dragged in here at some point, but I couldn't remember when. I took a closer look at what he was working on, admiring the handmade wooden ship and next to that a finely carved mast yet to be attached; as well as an assortment of miniature paint pots awaiting their application.

The intricate design would have taken him weeks to complete or longer. I read the name on the side of the vessel. *The Blue Rose.*

I jolted up, grabbed the boat and flung it against the wall, shattering it into pieces.

Alex's replica of the very ship Orpheus had sailed upon over from Spain in 1805 was now unrecognizable.

There was a blur of movement in the corridor.

"Alex?" I called out, seeing no one there.

Strange how a place can be familiar and yet foreign at the same time, this once sanctum of mine was now stifling. The only thing offering consolation was Alex, and I needed to see him.

I scoured the castle.

At last I found him balancing upon one of the turrets facing the ocean, staring out at the nightscape, deep in thought.

I braved to shake him from his daydreaming and said, "I owe you an apology."

"I didn't think you were coming back," he said.

Neither did I.

Alex turned round. "Ingrid's still looking for us isn't she?"

"I can handle her."

His expression was full of confusion.

"I'm sorry about your boat," I said. "It's just that . . ."

Several seagulls swooped low, flying across the horizon and I envied their ability to take flight with no explanation required.

"I promise we'll find our way through this." I took a step closer. "A way back."

Alex shrugged. "You really believe that?"

"Come down, please."

His coat flapped against his legs. "All this is my fault."

"Hardly." I sidestepped toward the wall and peered over at the sheer drop.

Alex caught my reaction.

Again I gestured for him to come down.

He hinged on snapping. "We can't be friends."

"You don't see Jadeon in me, is that it?"

He threw me a look.

"I'm determined to put this right," I said.

"I was watching you walk around the castle. Caught you staring at the chandelier." He raised his eyebrows to make his point. "You'd have gone for something more gothic." Alex quoted my thoughts exactly. "That's Orpheus right there."

"Look deeper."

"How could you have done this to me?"

His words stunned me. "Why did you make Orpheus that boat?"

Alex's face changed and he seemed unable to answer.

Pressing my hand against my chest, I gestured sincerely. "I'm your brother."

"My brother's dead."

I felt like I was failing him for not finding the words, or maybe just not saying them right. "I'm here." I was sure if I stepped any closer he'd jump. "We almost drowned in that water, remember?"

"I know what you're doing."

"I'm trying to—"

"Manipulate me."

"No, Alex, no."

"Prove to me that Jadeon's here." He turned back to face me.

"I need you to help me find the scrolls."

"So you can destroy them."

"No. *No.*"

He smiled in a way that hinted he was fast becoming overwhelmed.

"I need you," I whispered.

Time slowed and my vision blurred as I reached the wall that he no longer stood upon, and I collapsed beneath it, knowing I'd let him down for having not seen the agony in his eyes soon enough. My fingers groped at my shirt collar to loosen it.

Though I still couldn't breathe.

Gathering the courage to stand again, my throat constricting, I peered over at the crashing waves battering the rocky shoreline. I spun round and glared at nothing, unable to confront the sheer drop.

My fear of heights was getting worse.

* * * *

No matter how much I shifted my position upon the chapel altar, I couldn't get comfortable, though the view of the frescoed ceiling was quite something.

Despite the fact that Alex still refused to talk to me, it felt good to be back at the Mount. I almost believed my own delusion that it was here I'd find clarity, the faint promise of calmness within the storm.

Having not seen Alex since last night, I decided it was best he came to me when he was ready.

Moonlight backlit the stained-glass windows, softly illuminating an otherwise dark chamber, almost subduing the layers of dust dulling every surface. Copious cobwebs were tangled here and there, testifying to the neglect and willfully reflecting a certain state of mind.

A tickling on the back of my right hand alerted me to the small black spider crawling there, heading fast toward my wrist. I brushed it off, giving the creature a second chance.

The darkest lies were clinging to me, threatening there was no way back.

I turned my head toward the center isle of the long line of pews.

Sebastian was standing there. "There's a young man dragging a coffin across the foyer," he said, his expression incredulous. "Friend of yours, is he?"

I sat upright and slid off the altar.

"Has someone died?" he asked.

I was about to throw in *not yet* but stopped myself.

"This place is huge." Sebastian came closer. "You're probably wondering how I found you?"

"Yes."

"You told me, remember?"

"Wasn't that specific," I said.

"Process of elimination."

"Sebastian, what do you want?"

"To thank you." He gave a weak smile. "For saving my life." He took in the chapel. "I fell asleep and didn't get to—"

"You didn't need to come here."

He ran a fingertip over the edge of the nearest pew and examined the dust. "Why didn't you say goodbye?"

"Don't take it personally."

"Was it something I did?"

"No," I said with a convincing shake of my head.

"Can I ask you about that night?"

"What about it, Seb?"

He grinned but it was the uneasy kind.

I went to say something, anything that would deflect his question and felt relief when Alex appeared in the doorway.

"Sebastian, meet Alex, my brother," I said.

"Half brother," said Alex.

Sebastian stepped forward to shake Alex's hand, but Alex ignored him.

"Same father?" Sebastian dropped his arm to his side.

"Not that kind of half," Alex redirected.

"That coffin?" Sebastian began to ask.

"Halloween," I said.

Sebastian's brow furrowed. "Bit early."

"It's a gift." Alex turned back to me. "For William."

Sebastian started laughing though soon stopped, realizing no one else was. "Right then, it's been great meeting you . . . both." His expression became strained as though wanting to continue, but the awkwardness threw him.

"You can't leave," Alex said.

"What my brother's trying to say . . ." I glared at Alex. "Would you like to stay the night?"

"I should go." Sebastian quick-footed it through the foyer toward the front door.

"The tide's in." I followed him. "Use the rowboat."

Alex caught up. "We don't have a boat." He smiled but it fell away quickly. "Anymore."

I reached for the doorknob.

"I chopped it up for firewood," Alex added, "with an axe."

I opened the door and stepped out, scrutinizing the harbor. "Seriously, where's the boat?"

"Wouldn't recommend swimming at this time of night," Alex offered. "Tide's deadly."

Sebastian suddenly saw the funny side and started chuckling. Alex scratched his head and eventually broke into a laugh.

"Is this your way of making me not feel guilty about staying?" Sebastian asked.

"Absolutely." Alex raised an eyebrow.

I guided Sebastian off toward the kitchen.

As soon as we were out of his sight, Sebastian said, "That brother of yours has quite the sense of humor."

I wondered how Sebastian would react when he realized there was no food in the house.

He opened yet another kitchen cupboard and peered inside, then reached for the small teacup. I filled the kettle with tap water and then rested it on the counter top, studying the plug.

Sebastian took it from me and plugged it into the power socket and flicked it on. "You're not here to serve me," he said.

I sat down on one of the six bar stools that encircled the central marble counter top.

"Do you like to cook?" Sebastian asked, looking around.

Having spent no time in here, I too found myself fascinated with the red stove, the dark green pots and pans hanging from the brass crook above the central isle and the other modern appliances installed to represent normality.

"You probably have a chef," Sebastian said, though it wasn't a question. "Cornwall has, what, twenty castles?"

"Nineteen."

"Has your family always lived here?"

"Yes." I went to answer that I'd been born here, but that truth was now skewered.

He opened the tin filled with teabags, removed two and dropped them into the teacup. "No mug?"

"Um, no."

His attention fell on Renoir's self-portrait hanging on the far wall and then his gaze slid over to the silver wine goblet resting on the corner oak table.

"A gift to Anne Boleyn." I gestured to it. "On her wedding night, from her mother."

"No doubt her mum knew Anne would need a drink before bedding Henry the Eighth." He rolled his eyes. "That marriage didn't end well." Sebastian took a seat on one of the stools opposite. "What's that?" Sebastian pointed to the book on the kitchen counter.

I slid the leather bound hardback across the marble toward him.

"A Tale of Two Cities." He opened the first page. "How old is this?" He glanced up, excited. "This is probably worth something."

"I imagine it is."

Sebastian peeled back the next page. "There's an envelope."

"Open it."

He reached in and flicked through the hundred pound notes.

"Your train ride home." I sat up straight. "And more than enough money to get you back on your feet."

He froze realizing the book had been here all the time. "You knew I'd come?"

The kettle whistled, shrilling through the quiet.

I approached the countertop and yanked out the power cord then poured boiling water into the teacup.

His fingertips tapped the book. "Your idea of goodbye?"

I brought the teacup over and handed it to him. "I had no right to interfere with your life."

"You saved it." He carefully placed down the delicate cup. "I need to know how you did it." He pointed at me. "How you leaped off Big Ben and survived?"

"Messed up didn't I?

"How do you mean?"

"I left the teabags in." I gestured. "I'll take care of it."

"I like it strong." He waved me off. "We were talking about Big Ben."

"*You* were."

He held up the book. "You knew I'd try to find you. You even gave me clues back at the Savoy of where I could find you."

"Sugar?"

"Please, William."

I sighed. "A man sees an island just off in the distance. He wonders what goes on there."

Sebastian was riveted.

"Then one day," I continued, "he decides to investigate that mysterious island. Once there, he looks back at the old island he's just come from and realizes he can never go back."

"Because he sees everything from a different perspective."

"He's standing on the island from where all truth can be seen and once that knowledge is known, it cannot be unknown."

"I'm that man?" He shuffled on his seat. "This place holds secrets you don't want me to know?"

"You could teach dance?" Seeing his expression made me regret saying it. "What you love is worth fighting for."

He pushed the book back toward me.

"Walk away," I said

"It's not me walking away."

"All those whom I've been close to have been irrevocably damaged."

"I don't believe that."

"You don't want to."

"So you're shutting everyone out?"

I nudged the book back toward him. "Chapman and Hall published this in 1859. It's a well-loved copy."

"It's flawless." Sebastian's rested his fingers on the illustrated cover. "A first edition, and with it you're bribing me to go away?" He tucked the envelope back inside the book. "This you can keep. As soon as the tides out, I'll go." He reached into his back pocket and held up a Centurion credit card. "I found this in the jeans you gave me." He slid it across the countertop. "This belongs to Daumia Velde. Do you know him?"

"I'll make sure it gets back to him." My thumb caressed the name on the titanium charge card. "Finish your tea and I'll show you the guest room."

"Does it have a lock?" He offered a smile, seemingly not wanting to offend.

"I believe so."

"This place is like a haunted mansion."

I marveled at his perspective and how close he was to suspecting that it was indeed haunted.

But not by ghosts.

XI

THE FOLLOWING EVENING, I detected Sebastian was still here.

He wasn't alone.

Watching from the balcony with a good view of the foyer, just left of the central staircase, I listened in on his conversation with Ingrid Jansen and Sergeant Blake. The awkward silence of initial introductions still lingering.

Trailing my left hand down the banister, I descended the flight of stairs, and despite the tension rising in my gut, I forced a smile.

Sebastian caught sight of me. "You have visitors."

Ingrid's expression changed and she quickly turned away as though gathering her thoughts before facing me again, reflecting nothing but a stony-faced demeanor. She was dressed elegantly in classic black trousers, a white ruffled shirt and a simple leather jacket. A far cry from the sultry attire I'd last seen her in.

She turned and my breath caught.

"What are you doing here?" Her tone sounded controlled.

I hesitated. "I see you've had the pleasure of meeting Sebastian."

"We met you at Belshazzar's?" Blake asked, and he wasn't looking well.

After a few more seconds of awkwardness, Ingrid shook off whatever thoughts were impeding her and turned to face Sebastian. "We were talking about Alexander?" she asked.

Sebastian inclined his head toward me as though hoping for guidance. "Haven't seen him."

Ingrid caught it and said, "How about Jadeon Artimas?"

"Who?" Sebastian asked.

Ingrid stepped toward me. "Where is he?"

"Jadeon's in Italy." It was a good enough lie.

There was something about Blake's pallor, the newer lines etched around his eyes reflecting an added tension that was only beginning to show.

"Gothica?" The mind message meant solely for Blake hit its mark—

Blake coughed and spun away from me. He locked his attention onto Sebastian. "Do you work here?"

"No," Sebastian answered. "Just visiting."

"Do you need to sit down?" I asked Blake.

"Touch of food poisoning." Blake glanced over at Ingrid. "I'm fine, really."

"How about some water?" I asked him.

"No, thank you," Blake insisted.

Ingrid shared with him an unspoken moment and turned to face me again. "This castle belongs to Lord Artimas and his brother," she said. "And yet neither of you can tell me where Alex is?"

My focus shifted to Blake's necktie.

"Bit of a trek to get here." Blake looked away nervously. "Do you ever get used to living on an island?" He ambled toward the suit of armor to the left of the stairway, one of the two guarding knights. "Those add a nice touch," he said. "How old are they?"

"Medieval." Sebastian peered my way for confirmation and then strolled over toward Blake and added, "The average height of men back then was five foot four." On Ingrid's reaction he said, "Bit of a history buff."

"So we can see," she said.

Blake examined the helmet's jaw. It fell slack and stuck, leaving the knight gaping.

I knew just how the knight felt.

Realizing he couldn't fix it, Blake offered an apologetic grimace and continued to fumble.

Ingrid's attention fell back on me. "How are you acquainted with Jadeon Artimas?"

I watched Sebastian take over where Blake had failed, easing closed the knight's jaw, restoring it to his original dignified pose.

"I'm an acquaintance," I answered.

"Mind if we have a look around?" she said.

"Actually," I said, "this is a bad time."

"Really?" Ingrid called over to Sebastian. "How are you acquainted with the Artimas family?"

Sebastian turned to me for guidance. "Just popped in for a cup of tea."

"What was your last name again?" Blake asked him.

"Price," Sebastian said.

Blake made a notation in his notepad. "And sir, your surname?" He peered up at me, pen poised.

"Rolfe," I told him.

"Do you know Daumia Velde?" Blake asked us. "He also goes by the name Orpheus?"

Sebastian went to answer and then hesitated, seemingly remembering the credit card he'd returned to me. He gave a questionable shake of his head.

"How about you?" Blake asked me.

"I know of him," I said. "As I previously explained to Detective Jansen. Shall I go into detail about what we discussed at the club?"

She waved it off. "Not necessary."

A squawk came from the doorway and we all turned to see the black raven hopping around on the top step, threatening to fly in.

"Well look at that," Sebastian said. "A guardian of the dead."

"Celtic belief," I explained to Ingrid.

"One for sorrow," Blake said, half distracted. "The crow. You know, two for joy."

Sebastian's top lip curled into a smile. "That's the Magpie."

Blake frowned. "What's the difference?"

Sebastian glanced at me, amused. "The crow has black feathers and the magpie has black and white feathers."

Ingrid shook her head. "We appreciate anything you can tell us."

"Those two men you mentioned," Sebastian asked, "you're looking for them?"

"We need to speak with them," Ingrid explained. "Urgently."

"What have they done?" asked Sebastian.

I almost cringed with the thought of Alex dragging that coffin through the foyer.

Blake removed a folded piece of paper from his pocket and unraveled it. "We have a warrant."

"May I?" Sebastian held out his hand.

"Just part of our investigation," Ingrid said.

My thoughts raced with the idea of what they'd find if let loose. "May I speak with you alone?" I asked Ingrid and headed toward the other side of the foyer.

Ingrid caught up and glanced back to make sure Blake could still see her from where he was standing.

"You never told Blake what really happened at Belshazzar's?" I asked.

"Of course not," she said.

I leaned back against the wall. "What are you looking for exactly?"

"Alex, my prime suspect," she said. "What's Jadeon doing in Italy?"

"Touring Florence, I believe."

She bit her bottom lip and peeled back her sleeve revealing her brand. "If Orpheus is dead," she ran a fingertip over it, "why give me this?"

I nudged her out of Blake's line of sight. "Very few people know he's dead."

Her hand lingered near mine and then she withdrew it. "Back in the club you mentioned something about branding me for Orpheus."

"It was important to get you out of there by any means," I replied.

"So you lied to them?"

"Is this a moral discussion?" I asked.

"I detect avoidance."

"More like boredom."

She knitted her eyebrows together. "What's to stop me from arresting you right now?"

"For what?"

"Obstructing justice."

"Merely smoke and mirrors." I grinned off my remark.

She blinked several times, amazed by my daring attitude.

"Illusion is the first of all pleasures." I turned slightly to face the painting of *Voltaire*. "His real name was François-Marie Arouet. He was an advocate for civil liberties as well as a writer and philosopher. He was known as Voltaire."

"His name's an anagram?" she asked.

"Very good. Arouet is the Latinized spelling of his surname."

Ingrid snapped back into the moment. "So, how long have you been staying here?"

I gave silence a try.

"Perhaps you can show me around?" she asked.

Quiet ensued and I let it, trying to savor these last few seconds that I had left with her.

Ingrid's long lashes flickered, her natural pout giving away her boldness. "Was Orpheus buried?"

"Yes," I answered too quickly. "Apparently."

"Where?"

"I'll find out."

"William, you're one of them aren't you?"

I neared the portrait. "In 1726 Voltaire insulted Chevalier De Rohan, an influential nobleman." I took hold of her hand and swept her fingertips up and over the canvas. "Voltaire was given two options, imprisonment or exile."

Her hand trembled beneath mine.

"Ingrid," I whispered, "which one would you choose?"

The artist had captured Voltaire's intelligent eyes, a reflection of hope, his desire for freedom. I wondered if she'd caught it too; that and his wise presence revealing a lifetime contemplating reason.

I left Ingrid standing there and headed back toward Blake and Sebastian. The knight's jaw had slipped again only this time without any help. I paused briefly to ram it shut.

"We have a problem." Sebastian greeted me. "Exhibit A." He squinted at the warrant. "This stipulates a search of the grounds only. No entry into the castle has been granted." He handed it back to Blake.

Blake folded up the warrant and swapped an uneasy glance with Ingrid, who'd rejoined us.

"A misunderstanding?" she asked. "Still, it wouldn't hurt to take a peek here and there." Perhaps it was something in her expression or the way she shifted her position when I slowly approached her that revealed her intrigue.

She flashed the sweetest smile. "Let's start in the dungeons."

I gave a look of frustration. "Haven't had time to clear out all the cadavers."

Sebastian let out a nervous laugh. Ingrid pouted, trying to disguise the fact that she was taking mental notes and threatening to draw on them later.

I gestured to the door, much relieved that Blake took the hint and headed for it. Ingrid hesitated for a moment and then turned and followed him. My hand reached for the lower curve of her back, lingering there though not actually touching.

Sensing my gesture, her brown eyes found mine and unwittingly she let me in. A thrill shot up my spine as I realized I'd just glimpsed her psyche, exposing her secret obsession with the underworld and its intoxicating promise of forbidden pleasures yet to be discovered.

I lingered on the top step waiting just outside the front door, watching her stroll away down the pathway, daring to recall the vision of her shackled to the wall, helpless, fear oozing from her pores twinned with her innate need to be cherished.

To be saved.

Squeezing my right hand into a fist and then relaxing it again, I regretted not being able to tell her who I really was. The door to

Ingrid's world had to close and I was the only one preventing it.

Having watched Ingrid and Blake set off toward the mainland and satisfied they were really leaving, I went back inside and found Sebastian sitting halfway up the staircase.

"Never a dull moment here," he said.

I made a discreet scan of the foyer wondering if Alex had caught any of Ingrid's visit. I headed up the staircase taking two steps at a time, soon passing him.

Sebastian stood up. "How about a thank you?"

I paused, my grip tightening on the banister.

"I did after all prevent them from looking around," he said.

I turned to face him. "Brilliantly executed."

"Why were they here?"

I gave a shrug. "They have nothing better to do?"

"What's Alex done?"

"Nothing."

"Miss police detective believes he has."

"Ingrid's obsessed with this place."

"Ingrid?" He raised an eyebrow.

"Inspector Jansen—"

"Is obsessed with you." He ran his hand over the curve of the banister. "She'll come back."

"Perhaps."

"I can help you." He took a step closer. "I'm dying to know more about you." He cringed. "Dying in a metaphorical sense, not in becoming one of your cadavers sense."

"Seb, there are no dead bodies here."

"So what's up with that coffin?"

I caressed my forehead.

"I want to repay you," he said. "You saved my life."

Peace seemed so far out of reach, and there came that familiar dread that the castle's safety was threatened; our once private domain was slipping from our grasp.

"Come on." I headed down.

"Where are we going?"

"Thought you might like to check out the dungeons. It's a good place to start."

"Start what?"

I waited for him to catch up. "The tour."

"Why the sudden change of heart?" Sebastian sped up, following me down the east corridor.

"I like you, Sebastian, and I trust you."

Moonlight flooded in through the dusty windows illuminating the way ahead with a grayish tinge, weaving along the mutated white hallway.

"This place is over a thousand years old. It has a rich history." I glanced at him. "It's worth saving."

"It's under threat from the Inspector?" he asked.

"There may be some inheritance issues that need straightening out." Which wasn't so far from the truth.

We soon came upon an ordinary looking door and I twisted its well-worn handle.

Sebastian peered into the blackness. "Am I going to regret this?"

"Regret anything so far?" From inside the doorway, I lifted the halogen lamp and with a flick of a switch readied it to light our way.

Sebastian took his first step toward the belly of the castle and said, "My stay at law school only lasted a year but it might prove invaluable."

"Have a feeling it might." I guided him downward. "That's why I'm going to show you everything."

"And tell me everything, too?"

I continued eastward. "Thought you might like to see where they once entertained unwanted guests." Lifting the lamp, I swung it around us. "See, no bodies."

He scratched the back of his head. "You share a crazy sense of humor with your brother."

"That's not all we share."

"What's that?" He followed me into the dim chamber and took in the antique sconces, their candles burned to the wick, rusty chains hanging here and there, and that time-tested torture table artfully rounding out the sinister decor.

"Well, what do you think?" I watched him.

"Is that what I think it is?" His wide-eyed stare was locked on the torture table, rusty shackles hanging from its sides.

"It's no longer in use."

"Why the hell keep it then?" Sebastian shot me a wary look. "Just a suggestion, perhaps next time you should start off your *tour* in the garden?"

"A gentler introduction?"

He emphasized his point, raising his eyebrows.

"Pity, this being my favorite." I suppressed a smile.

XII

THE FRONT DOOR OPENED and the man standing just inside the Knightsbridge flat oozed privilege and he regarded me with annoyance.

"James Lemont," he introduced himself and slipped his hand into mine, his grip matching his icy-stare. He glanced at the gift I'd tucked under my arm.

Though he wouldn't recognize me now, I'd first met James when Ingrid had invited me here to his London flat. He was hosting a party for his well-connected friends, and I remembered thinking then that Ingrid's bohemianism seemed contrary to the upper-class crowd.

"Who is it?" Ingrid froze with a brightness in her eyes. "William?" Her casual T-shirt and yoga pants extenuated her curves.

James moved aside allowing me to enter.

"What a nice surprise." Her eyes widened and she glanced over at James. "This is William."

James didn't notice her reaction. "That a present?" He took the wooden box. "To what pleasure do we owe this visit?"

"We were just about to eat," Ingrid said.

"Like to join us?" James's insincerity was glaring.

An annoying ringtone broke the uncomfortable silence and James shoved the box back into my hands and reached into his pocket. "Have to get this." With his Blackberry pressed to his ear, he ambled into the living room.

Ingrid came closer, her gaze narrowing when she saw the box. "What is it?"

I handed it to her.

"How did you know I'm staying here?" she asked.

"You must have mentioned it."

She frowned. "No I didn't."

"Perhaps Blake did." I rubbed my chin thoughtfully, feigning trying to recall. "Anyway, consider this a peace offering." I glanced at the box she'd just taken from me.

"What are you doing here?" she whispered.

"You asked me to find out where Orpheus is buried."

She pursed her lips and hugged the box, gesturing for me to enter.

I headed on in toward the sitting room. James sat on the arm of a chair, chatting away on his cell.

Ingrid ambled into the kitchen. "I'll check on dinner."

Just as I remembered it, James's flat exuded all the elements of a bachelor pad with its mismatched leather and beige furniture wickedly clashing with the green carpet, a sight hardly saved by the modern light fixtures. African masks screamed from where they hung on stark white washed walls. I was left with the distinct impression James was not only eccentric but also colorblind. Eager to escape the nerve grinding still life, I headed into the kitchen.

Ingrid slammed down the receiver onto the cradle of a wall phone.

I motioned to it. "Don't let me interrupt."

"It can wait." She reached for her glass of Chardonnay and took a sip.

The rich aroma of tomato sauce filled the kitchen and something else too, garlic. I suppressed a frown, baffled by the myth that nightwalkers were fended off with an herb.

I leaned against the counter. "Aren't you going to open your present?"

She shrugged. "You had no right to come here."

"You're right of course. I'll go."

"Wait, where's Orpheus's grave—"

"So, James?" I raised an eyebrow.

"We're just friends," she said. "I'm looking for my own place."

"Kind of him to let you stay," I said, wondering if she'd finally caught on that James was quietly in love with her.

Ingrid seemed to pick up on my ruminations. "What's in the box?" She put down her glass. "Something else to place into evidence?"

"That would be a shame. It's a rare 1945 Monte Saint Claire vintage."

Ingrid's intense brown irises grew larger and that delicate reflex spoke volumes.

A wave of conflicting memories caused my focus to waver and a nagging guilt lingered. I reached for the box and flicked open its two catches, lifting the lid to reveal the red bottle of wine, admiring the label that had stood the test of time.

"Have you seen Alex since we last spoke?" she asked.

"I've been in London."

"Why are you really here?"

I closed the lid.

"Do you really have information for me?" She took another sip.

I wanted to open a window and allow the cool night air in to clear the stifling temperature yet resisted the urge to move in any direction and risk startling her.

"I doubt he's dead." Ingrid came closer, close enough for her Chanel to reach me and stir a desire that was ill-timed. "Want one?" She raised her glass. "That's right, you only drink blood."

"Perhaps you've had too much."

"Perhaps I haven't had enough." She took another sip to make her point. "How come you're friends with *both* Jadeon and Orpheus?"

I caressed my forehead, trying to ease the building tension.

"Looks like I've hit a nerve," she said.

"More like a dead-end."

She rested her drink on the countertop, spilling the liquid over the rim. "What do you do?"

"I'm an art dealer." I made it sound convincing.

"That's how you know Jadeon?"

"Pretty much."

"Where did you meet him?"

"We move in the same circles." I gave a shrug.

"Is William Rolfe your real name?"

"Of course, why?"

"Shakespeare's editor was called William Rolfe."

"It's actually quite common." I shifted my stance. "Ingrid, am I under investigation now?"

"No one gets ruled out," she said, "until proven innocent."

"There are those of us who abhor any wrongdoing."

"You're referring to the murder of the innocent?"

"I'm trying to convince you that the threat is over," I said simply.

"You admit to having knowledge of these murdered girls?"

"All I can say is . . . you're safe."

"Not good enough."

I didn't react.

"Two nights ago an entire gang went missing," she said. "Last seen hanging out around Tottenham Court Road." She folded her arms. "Know anything about that?"

"Maybe they moved to the country. City life can be stifling."

She continued, unfazed. "Witnesses heard screams coming from where the gang was last observed."

I glanced toward the living room. "Where was James? Did you check out his whereabouts?"

"William," she chastised.

"Seriously." I grinned. "He has Jack the Ripper written all over him."

Ingrid almost smiled. "More like one of your crowd took a dislike to them."

"Are you calling *my crowd* a band of crime fighters now?"

This was the moment I wanted to remember, seeing in Ingrid's eyes not hatred, not fear, but a sense of wonder, fondness even.

Her lips came close to mine. "Don't ever come here again."

The spell was shattered.

"I'm not going to let this go." Her gaze fell to my lips. "No matter what bribes you offer me."

"How can I convince you that the continued pursuit of your obsession is futile?"

"You can't."

"Then you'll waste the rest of your life chasing shadows." Realizing I'd been staring at her, I tried to break the intensity. "I should go."

"I never thanked you properly for what you did to me at Belshazzar's," her tone was sarcastic.

"You should never have gone there."

"If I keep digging, what other skeletons am I going to find?"

"It's important for . . . Jadeon to know you're safe. You're happy." I shook my head, trying to shake off this welling grief brought on by seeing her. "It's time for you to move on."

"Jadeon told you that?"

"Yes." I tried to make it sound convincing. "Jadeon's not coming back." These lies tasted foul. "I'll see myself out." I passed James who was still chattering away on his mobile.

I almost made it to the front door but Ingrid was right behind me and she clutched the back of my coat.

I eased off her fingers. "This is your life we're talking about."

She glanced over her shoulder to check James couldn't hear.

I opened the door. "Have you ever questioned just what it is about the underworld that draws you to it?"

"What are you insinuating?"

I stepped out and turned to face her. "Highgate cemetery."

"Orpheus is buried there?"

I backed away. "Enjoy your gift. That vintage survived a Nazi invasion."

I left her standing there.

XIII

NIGHT RETURNED ONCE MORE to Highgate Cemetery, bringing with it the bitterest chill to a fast fading evening and throwing an eerie luminescence from the few flickering light bulbs, failing miserably to scare off the murkiest of shadows.

Wearing a long woolen coat and flat heeled boots, Ingrid strolled through the high-fronted brass gates and crisscrossed along the pathway, pausing now and again to view the names of the departed engraved on the well-tended tombstones.

Undetected and shaded by dusk, I moved amongst the low hung sycamore trees, looming close enough to encroach on her thoughts that trailed quickly away like the falling leaves around me.

The modest mausoleum was the final resting place of one Daumia Velde. Ingrid took the three short steps to the door and found it locked. She rummaged through her handbag and pulled out an L shaped tension wrench, a rake pick, and half-diamond pick. Checking to see no one was watching, she picked the lock.

Ingrid stepped inside, leaving the door ajar.

With a flash of thought, I entered right behind her and settled into a dusky corner.

She rested her flashlight on her handbag and pointed it in the direction of the sarcophagus. She ran her fingers along the marble lid.

I stepped forward. "Never knew you were into burial desecration."

She jumped backwards and bashed into a stone stand upon which rested a porcelain vase filled with wild orchids. It slid toward the wall and cracked.

"You scared me half to death!" she gasped.

"I know how that feels." I examined the vase, running my fingers along the fissure, feigning concern. "Qing dynasty."

She coughed, clearing dust from her throat.

I tutted. "I should press charges. Let me see, breaking and entering, desecrating a tomb."

"I haven't touched anything."

I glanced at the vase.

She hesitated and then said, "I'm here to pay my respects, and you?"

"Careful."

"Jadeon and Orpheus were enemies, so how come I've seen you both at the castle and the club?"

"I'm a peacemaker." I held her gaze, hoping to convince her.

"Are you in touch with either Orpheus or Jadeon?"

My focus turned toward the sarcophagus. "What part of deceased don't you get?"

"The answers I need are in Belshazzar's, I just know it."

"Ingrid, please close this case. It's too dangerous."

"That some kind of threat?"

"From me, no." I sighed. "Next time I might not be around to save your life."

Ingrid reluctantly acknowledged what I'd done for her back at the club. "This case won't be closed until it's solved."

I moved closer. "One day you'll rally the courage to ask for that which you desire. The very reason that has you searching for an underworld."

"The truth?"

"And you and I both know where it really lies, don't we?"

"I'm dedicated to seeing this through."

Realizing I wasn't getting through to her, I closed my eyes, considering how far to take this . . . take her . . .

I ran my fingers over the lid of the sarcophagus admiring the limestone. "Ever been in one of these?"

"What kind of question is that?" She glanced at her handbag.

I walked over to it, reaching for the flashlight balancing precariously on top of it and switching it off, sending the chamber into darkness. I peeked inside her bag. "Pepper spray?"

Ingrid blinked furiously. "That was rude."

"I'm not the one carrying round an arsenal of weapons." I rose. "You're not frightened, are you?"

She wrapped her arms around herself. "It's freezing."

I glanced at the sarcophagus. "You'd soon warm up in there."

She backed toward the door. "Don't even joke about that."

"Where do you think you're going?" I gestured. "I'm not done. I'm still trying to decide whether or not to forgive you."

"What for?"

I motioned for her to come closer. "Your lapse of judgment."

"Trying to get to the truth is a crime now?" She took a careful step toward me.

"Your job is to uphold the law, not break it."

"It's not working, this attempt to intimidate."

"You misunderstand," I said. "I'm merely considering which punishment is best suited to the situation. Something that will leave an indelible reminder that you can't tamper with things that don't concern you." I considered the vase. "After all, that came from the last ruling dynasty of China."

She lowered her lashes.

"It's priceless," I added.

Outside dead leaves whirled against the door.

Her face darkened. "I'm going to get this body exhumed." She pointed to the sarcophagus. "Dissect the corpse."

"Perhaps you should go. I can't be held responsible if you stay."

"I'm not going anywhere."

I moved closer, lingering over her. "Go home."

"What if I don't?" Her eyes burned with determination.

Gently I caressed her cheek with the back of my fingers. "Am I not getting through?"

"Don't . . . touch me like that." She was breathless.

"That's not what your thoughts suggest." I reached for her coat, easing it off her shoulders. It slipped to the floor.

"If you can read my thoughts . . ." Ingrid's lips parted in anticipation. "You're a vampire."

"Exactly."

She reflected defiance; perfectly silhouetted by the balmy moonlight, yet her apparent strength was unwavering and, despite shaking slightly, she reflected dignity.

"You're perfect in every way," I said. "You know that don't you?"

Puffs of cold air left her lips and her breathing became unsteady as her delicate expressions revealed she wasn't ready to let go just yet.

"It was the Marquis de Sade that once said, 'It is always by way of pain that one arrives at pleasure.'" I ran my thumb over her lips. "The term sadism, that is to experience pleasure while inflicting pain, was first presented by the Marquis de Sade."

"I know what it means," her words fell away like a frightened whisper.

"I was once locked up in a Parisian cell with him." I recalled the date. "1810, if you can believe that."

A low mist seeped in beneath the door gathering at our feet, seemingly trying to encroach without being noticed and hoping to share in the dark drama unfolding.

Ingrid's eyelids fluttered but other than that she didn't move.

I flicked a few brunette strands from out of her eyes. "I taught him everything he knew."

She raised her chin higher, hinting I had no effect.

"In the end he went quite mad." I nodded, remembering how far I'd pushed him and then slid my fingers around her neck. "Do you understand why I'm telling you this?"

She stood there quite still, hoping to understand her dangerous fixation, lulled by the numerous frissons I was causing her to feel.

I loosened my grip. "That little voice inside your head that's screaming, 'you're daring too close to the flame,' you should listen to it."

"So you admit I'm close?" She shivered against my touch.

"I'm not sure whether you want me to protect you from it, or deliver it unto you?"

The sound of rain striking the roof filled the tomb, disallowing any chance of tranquility and yet it seemed to calm her.

Delicate blue veins teased along Ingrid's neck and I tilted her head to better expose them. "It takes less than a minute to drain a mortal."

She inclined her neck further, revealing her fearlessness.

"My sweet moth," I said and held her gaze.

Silence wrapped around us as time itself held its breath, quietly coaxing us to that secret place of sighs and whispers where we might just lose ourselves completely and truly find each other.

I let her go. "I think I've made my point."

Disappointment danced in her eyes and she blushed softly.

"You're truly exquisite," I said.

Her lips trembled and her thoughts carried. *I have to hold on.*

"I'm not sure that's the answer." I straightened the vase upon the stand and slid my fingertip over the chink. "Evidence of a moment frozen in time." I caressed the porcelain. "What passed between us is captured here."

"Is Orpheus really in there?" she asked.

"He is." Though I hated lying to her and considered whether I'd started believing Orpheus was indeed entombed here.

That part of me that had once reveled in cruelty, savoring the seductive quality of torture, was now more drawn to exploring the sublime, that which promised to hold my attention and I wondered if such a desire could ever be quenched.

Orpheus seemingly reigned within me and yet, despite my dormant presence it was I, Jadeon who ruled each moment with an uncommon fierceness. And I could only surmise it was the result of having remained centered in death, honoring Snowstrom's counsel.

I met Ingrid's eyes and felt her enrapturing vulnerability and reasoned she might just be the only one to understand me.

Drawing from Ingrid's strength, I was finding mine.

And yet this moment had not been meant for me.

"Orpheus can't hurt you now." I kissed her forehead. "Let's get out of here. This place is starting to creep me out."

"Really?"

I shook my head, assisting her into her coat.

She reached for my hand. "I can't help but think you're using your supernatural ability to seduce me."

"I think it's the other way round." I picked up her bag and handed it to her, guiding her toward the door.

Once outside I refastened the padlock, securing the tomb closed. I used my coat to shield us from the rain, guiding her back down the winding pathway.

A black limousine's headlights flashed on and the chauffeur stepped out from the front seat. He opened the rear passenger door. Ingrid climbed in first and then I joined her, sitting beside her. Within seconds we were navigating our way out through the cemetery gate, the windshield wipers working furiously to clear our view.

"I'm taking you to James's flat," I said.

Classical music struck up, lulling me back into the leather.

"Johann Sebastian Bach." I raised my forefinger. "Ingrid, listen between the notes. Bach became the pain . . . for us."

The music consumed me, igniting my imagination and I searched the faces that seemed to come out of nowhere in my mind's eye, appearing like grim phantasms, their mouths forming frantic words of anguish that I didn't catch.

Past ghosts ever haunting.

Ingrid rested her head back, taking in Highgate.

Notes tumbled out of the speakers.

Savoring these last few minutes with her, I tried to rally the courage to say goodbye and actually mean it this time.

Ingrid was staring at me.

"I've seen inside your bag," I said wryly. "If Orpheus were alive

I'd be more worried about him."

She glanced at the driver to ensure he wasn't eavesdropping and then shifted her position to face me, her thoughts taking her back inside the tomb.

I gestured to her heart. "Don't be afraid to look deeper."

The car pulled alongside the curb.

She glanced up at James's flat. "I can't shake this feeling I've met you before."

"I'll wait till you're safely inside."

She flashed another glance at the chauffer.

"Ingrid, promise me you'll never go back to Belshazzar's."

She waited until the driver had exited the car and then said, "You know I can't promise that."

"Vampires don't play by human rules," I said. "They will kill you if you go back."

"This is what I do."

"Do you want to be one of us, is that it?" I asked flatly.

She shot me a look of horror.

The driver opened her door and she ducked low to climb out.

Just a few feet away from the limousine, Ingrid rummaged through her handbag and already I missed her, regretting our last words shared.

The chauffer was back in the driver's seat, waiting for my next order.

"Turn it up," I said to him.

He touched the volume, filling the car entirely with Bach's Little Fugue in G minor.

Ingrid's scent lingered, interweaving chaos with clarity and I filled my lungs entirely with her.

Despite the cold, I was burning up from the inside, trying to suppress my desire to ravish her and I let out the longest sigh as though it would help, wanting nothing more than to take her back into my arms.

With her now gone, I allowed myself to finally imagine the taste of her blood and dared even further, envisioning the way she'd respond to me after drinking mine.

XIV

THE MOUNT OFFERED UP its quiet familiarity.

Leaving London at one in the morning, I'd reached Marazion within the hour, marveling at my ability to let Ingrid go. Though as I now strolled through the foyer, replaying those moments we'd shared, doubt crept in that I could ever forget her.

From the doorway I watched Sebastian and Alex, who were sitting opposite each other, both of them focused on the checkered inlaid table between them, and by the way Alex's hand hovered over Sebastian's knight, it was his move.

Alex smiled and I couldn't remember the last time I'd seen him so happy. It was good to see him emanating a peace he'd long been without.

"Good choice." I winked at him and then moved my attention to the chess piece he was holding, that just seconds ago had belonged to Sebastian.

"Had a good teacher," Alex said.

Sebastian maneuvered his bishop. "How did your meeting go?"

"Fairly well." I headed toward them. "Ingrid's staying in London."

"Permanently?" Alex asked.

I gave a shrug and sat on his chair's armrest. "I believe we've resolved all our issues."

Alex perked up and pinned Sebastian's bishop.

"Who taught you to play?" Sebastian asked him.

Alex looked my way.

"So that's where he gets his killer moves from." Sebastian said. "His brother."

Alex's expression changed and I searched for the words that might lighten the moment, and then turned to see what Alex was looking at.

"Hello, William," Marcus said, having entered unheard.

My first thought was for Sebastian's safety and I quickly headed toward Marcus, gesturing toward the doorway.

Marcus locked his gaze on Sebastian.

I reached for his arm. "Let's get some fresh air."

Marcus allowed me to guide him into the foyer. "Why didn't you tell me you were leaving Belshazzar's?" he asked.

"I had to deal with Ingrid," I answered. "She's out of the picture now." I led him through the foyer. "So you can forget about her."

"That sounds like an order." Marcus said. "Seems to me you're trying to protect her. Let's not forget Orpheus's plan was to turn her. Weren't you in the middle of doing that when this whole thing blew up?"

I went to answer but the guilt caught in my throat.

We stepped outside and headed toward the garden.

"You'll be happy to hear that Anaïs is thriving," Marcus continued, "thanks to you saving her. Thank God you were there. She keeps asking where you are."

"A normal fledgling reaction," I said. "Make sure Zachary keeps an eye on her."

"Of course," said Marcus. "Who's that man playing chess with Alex?"

"I need Sebastian alive. Please don't kill him."

"Now you've really got me intrigued." Marcus jolted to a stop. "He's a Stone Lord, isn't he?"

I shut my thoughts down.

"Too late for that I'm afraid," said Marcus. "What the hell is a member of the Stone Masters doing here?"

"I'm gaining his trust in order for him to reveal the location of the Stone Masters' headquarters."

"You've lost your mind," he snapped.

"Sebastian has no idea I'm a vampire."

"Five minutes with Alex and most people catch on that something's amiss."

"Did you do it?" I asked, trying to stay calm.

"Close the club?" asked Marcus. "No."

"Leaving it open is a liability."

"You really believe someone's poisoning vampires?" he asked.

"Yes." My frustration rose. "Closing Belshazzar's is temporary, just until we can isolate the cause."

Marcus stepped onto the pathway. "We've weathered storms like this before."

"That's true." Still, my desire to protect Marcus from the harsh reality of what was really going on would be no good to him in the long run.

With each new century another challenge had arisen, bringing an ever advancing threat to our survival. As such we'd evolved, adapting to societal changes by flawlessly integrating with each generation. But this present danger of poisonings was altogether different and though my thoughts had focused primarily on finding my way back, I also had to face the evidence—our extinction was underway.

Marcus nudged up closer. "William, your rightful place is with me."

I navigated the rocks, wanting to harness the serenity of the blue ocean lapping at the shoreline. Marcus hung back. He was sulking.

"What?" I asked.

"You didn't answer me."

"Once I have what I need from Sebastian, I'll return to London."

"Well get back in there," Marcus pointed to the castle, "and take care of it. I'll wait here."

"I get one chance," I reasoned. "I'm not rushing him."

Marcus looked at me sharply. "Drink the knowledge out of him."

"I'm not that vampire anymore."

He glared at me, hating my reticence.

"Look," I said. "Imagine what it's like having memories of being in two places at the same time." The idea of it sounded impossible.

Marcus fixed his stare on me.

"Have you ever woken up from a dream," I asked, "and believed that's where you should be, still in the dream and not the place where you just woke up? That's what I'm going through."

Marcus's expression softened. "I'm sorry. I miss you, that's all."

Jacob appeared just over the ridge, making his way toward us. His long black cassock buffered by the breeze and there was something in his expression, fragility perhaps as he considered us with trepidation.

Marcus squinted. "Jacob?" He snapped his head back to me. "I feel like I'm being mind fucked."

Jacob quickly joined us.

"When was the last time I saw you?" Marcus's voice strained with disbelief.

"Four hundred years," Jacob said, flatly. "Wasn't it?"

"First Sunaria, and now you!" Marcus studied Jacob. "Everyone's crawled out of the woodwork." He frowned his way. "What's with the outfit?"

"Had the pleasure of meeting Paradom," I said, not wasting any time.

"William, I did warn you," said Jacob.

"Seriously?" Marcus said. "What are you, a vicar?"

Jacob looked annoyed. "Yes."

"Since when?" Marcus asked.

"Since I was ordained," Jacob said.

I motioned for us to get back on track. "Jacob, you failed to tell me you know Paradom. And what's with the cat food?"

"Didn't you notice Paradom's confused?" Jacob asked, then realizing this tact wouldn't work, he said, "I didn't actually think you'd find him."

I peered at Jacob's hands to see if he was wearing a signet ring. His fingers were bare.

"Paradom told me you're a Stone Lord," I said. "He really believes you're still one of them. He mentioned something about a ring you were wearing?"

"Don't go back there," Marcus said. "This thing, whatever it is, sounds crazy."

Jacob stared at me as though judging my reaction to that.

Marcus grabbed Jacob's arm and yanked him round. "You knew all this time where Sunaria was and not once did you tell us."

"It wasn't my decision," Jacob said, easing Marcus's hand off. "Snowstrom thought it best—"

"And how does Orpheus feel about his son betraying him?" Marcus asked me.

"Am I really going to end up looking like Paradom?" I asked, almost choking on fear.

"Who told you that?" Marcus asked. "That unbalanced creature?"

"You're not helping," I snapped at Marcus.

Jacob turned his back on Marcus and faced me. "We're doing everything we can to prevent the same thing from happening to you."

"Tell me you're not serious," Marcus said.

"I don't know what to believe." I ran my fingers through my hair, fighting the panic rising in my gut. "Paradom mentioned there was a plan?"

Jacob cleared his throat. "Yes, the plan is to separate you."

I paused, trying to read Jacob. "Apparently Paradom believes the Stone Masters have the scrolls."

Jacob opened his hands. "Paradom's unreliable."

"Then why did you want me to see him?" I asked.

Jacob's careful face changed. "William, you know why."

My throat tightened. "So that I'd want to revert. Want to separate."

"Exactly," Jacob said.

"Do you have *any* idea how frustrating it is talking with you?" I asked.

"Lucas is working hard on your issue," Jacob said. "I understand your frustration, William."

"Jacob," Marcus interrupted, his face flushed with anger. "I was the one who reunited you with your father, four hundred years ago. You owe me."

"What's your point, Marcus?" Jacob seethed.

Marcus pointed to me. "He's standing right in front of us resembling nothing of Orpheus. Why is everyone so slow to help him when time is a major issue?"

Jacob steepled his fingers, clearly trying to remain composed. "Catherine and I are striving to save the lives of vampires everywhere," he said. "We're investigating vampire deaths, trying to find the cause before it wipes us all out."

Marcus snapped back to me. "Is this true?"

I faced Jacob again. "This reunion is all very cozy, but why did you even come here?"

Jacob raised his eyebrows thoughtfully. "I thought Marcus might like to see his sister again."

Marcus sucked in his breath. "Rachel?"

"I believe I owe you that much," Jacob said.

"Where is she?" Marcus's voice broke with emotion. "I haven't seen her in over fifty years."

"We found her wandering outside Belshazzar's," Jacob said. "She was looking for you."

"Where's she been all this time?" Marcus's voice was strained.

Jacob lowered his gaze. "I'm afraid the news isn't good."

"She's been poisoned," I said, realizing.

Marcus flinched.

Jacob bowed his head. "We're keeping her safe."

"Will she live?" Marcus asked.

"As long as we manage to keep her out of the sun," Jacob said. "Confusion seems to be the only side effect."

"I have to see her," Marcus said.

"We're hoping she can answer our questions, and possibly help find the cause," Jacob said. "Though she doesn't seem to remember much. We're watching over her at Salisbury Cathedral."

I gave Marcus's arm a squeeze. "I'll meet you there."

"What keeps you here?" Jacob's tone reeked with suspicion.

More answers than you're prepared to give me, I wanted to say, *but didn't.*

Still reeling with the idea that Rachel was suffering, I headed back toward the castle, now more than ever ready to question Sebastian. I left Jacob and Marcus standing there on the shoreline. These poisonings were fast becoming the worst threat since the Stone Masters and I was eager to vanquish the cause.

Dashing down the endless corridors, I followed Ludwig Van Beethoven's Fur Elise and quickly found its source. Inside the ballroom, Alex was pounding the keys, speeding up the notes into an insane rhythm.

"Where's Sebastian?" I asked him, not wanting to waste anymore time.

Alex slammed his fingers onto the keyboard. "Why?"

I was taken back with his aggression. "I have to talk with him."

Alex grabbed the keyboard cover and slammed it shut. The piano chimed its disapproval. "What happened with Marcus?" he asked. "What did you two talk about?" Alex rummaged around my thoughts.

"Please don't do that," I said.

"Then don't evade me."

"This is difficult for everyone." I studied him. "You spent some time with Jacob recently. Anything you might want to share?'

"I like him."

It was now my turn to penetrate Alex's thoughts.

"I can feel that." He sat forward. "Jadeon would do everything in his power to make this right."

"I am."

"What are you scheming?"

"I'm here right now, with you."

A stack of books rested on top of the piano and I picked one of them up and read the title. *Necromancing the Stones.* I held it up. "Fabian Snowstrom wrote this." Glancing at the other titles, I realized they were all about vampires. "Don't let Sebastian see these." Then I saw Alex's blood stained cuff.

He stretched out his long legs. "You're not going to stay, are you?"

"What did you do?" I feared to see in his eyes or read from his thoughts what he'd done. "I have every intention of taking you with me."

"You didn't last time," Alex snapped.

"Tell me you didn't harm him."

"Even now you don't know me." Alex righted his chair and stood up. "Sebastian was a ballet dancer."

"*Was?*"

"Not just any dancer," Alex blurted, "one of the finest."

I turned toward the doorway, terrified of what I'd find. "Stay here."

"You've never been alone," Alex shouted after me.

I flew back toward him and grabbed his shirt, shoving him against the wall. "What did you do?"

"Why did you bring him here?"

I shook my head. "He wasn't meant to stay."

Alex grasped my forearms. "Tell me you're not going to leave me."

"I would rather lose this place a million times over then lose you."

"I don't believe you!" Alex yelled.

"Promise you'll talk to me before doing anything like this again." My hands were shaking. "I need you."

"You'll help me get Jadeon back?" he begged.

"Yes." I turned away, flashing back to those terrible minutes spent with Paradom, his yellow stained fangs buried deep in that dead rat's carcass, his black orbs like a child's, freakish, and full of pain. "I want it more than you," I murmured.

Alex buried his head into my chest.

I wrapped my arms around him, trying not to choke on my words and asked Alex again, only this time in a whisper, "Where's Sebastian?"

XV

WITHIN THE DUNGEONS, Sebastian was huddled up with his back against the wall, clutching his legs, his stained shirt collar the only evidence of Alex's attack.

I swung open the gate, the rusty hinges squeaking.

"Interestingly place to hide," I said.

"Three cells down there's a coffin." He raised a finger. "No one's in it, yet."

"May I come in?"

"Tell me it's not mine."

"It's not, Seb."

His lips trembled when he saw the three books I carried. "William, how long do you intend to keep me here?"

"You're not staying." I shook my head.

He gulped, hard.

I raised my hand to clarify. "Nothing's going to happen to you. You have my word." On nearing him, I breathed a sigh of relief he hadn't been turned. "Remember when I told you about the island?"

"Yes."

"You've crossed over to it."

Sebastian climbed to his feet and took a step toward me with a steady gait, his limp now gone. "Your brother thinks he's a vampire," he said. "Where is he?"

"In the study."

"With Miss Scarlett, with the candlestick." He let out a nervous high-pitched laugh.

"Sit down."

He did as I asked, leaning back against the wall again.

I knelt close. "You're in shock."

His attention lingered on the books.

I got comfortable and reached for the first one, showing him the cover. "Arthur R. Raker. *Ancient Aztecs.*"

"I'm not going to like this, am I?"

"Perhaps I shouldn't have started with this one." I gave his shoulder an affectionate squeeze.

"Please don't tell me I'm some kind of sacrifice." Sebastian folded his arms around his legs. "Don't kill me, William."

"I saved you, remember?" I took a deep breath. "The Aztecs believed that an ongoing human sacrifice was essential to appease the Gods and drank blood to ensure their debts were paid." I put the book down. "Franciscan monks documented how the Aztecs offered their blood for the sake of humanity. Notice the common denominator."

Sebastian shifted uncomfortably. "Not sure I like where this is going."

"Keep up." I reached for the second book. "The Hindu God Shiva, meaning Auspicious One. The earliest accounts of her life first recorded around 1700 BC, mentioning her ability to have victory over death. Worshipped by millions, this once living being had a third eye and was able to read minds." I placed it back on top of the other and held up the last one. "Great Britain. Archeologists discover evidence that blood rites were conducted at Stonehenge."

"You're trying to convince me it's not your brother's fault?" Sebastian stood up and made his way toward the open gate.

"These are all a gentle introduction," I said.

"Into what?" asked Sebastian.

I stood up. "Alex was trying to heal your leg."

His frown lines deepened. "Makes sense."

"Sebastian, Alex has healed you."

"Thank him for me, won't you." Sebastian's right foot stepped out of the cell, his hand reaching behind him.

"Unfortunately, the side effect is sensitivity to light. Alex gave you just enough blood to heal your leg, but you'll need sunglasses or you'll feel like your orbs are being burned out of your skull."

"Thanks for that little nugget of info."

"Sebastian." I remained still, wary of keeping my distance. "Your limp's gone."

He bolted.

Waiting for a few seconds, I felt my empathy soar and what had seemed like a simple enough endeavor now took on a different meaning. With mindful ease, I headed after him.

Back up at ground level, outside the door to the dungeons I waited, having swiftly slid passed Sebastian unnoticed.

I leaned against the wall with my arms folded, Sebastian's footfalls signaling his imminent appearance at the top of the stairwell. He shot through the doorway, skidding to a halt when he saw me.

"When was the last time you ran like that?" I asked, impressed.

Sebastian turned awkwardly and sprinted down the corridor toward the foyer, almost tripping over himself when he nearly bumped into me.

I bowed slightly. "We could do this all night but it's bound to get tedious."

Fright was etched on his face. "Are you going to kill me?"

I stepped toward him and knelt at his feet, reaching for his right trouser leg, easing up the material to reveal his calf.

"Looks healed to me." I rose and stepped back, giving him the room he needed.

Sebastian was shaking. "That's . . . impossible."

Alex was sitting halfway up the central staircase, watching us.

Sebastian's hand shot to his mouth, suppressing a scream, seemingly not really taking anything in and struggling to grasp what was happening.

"Sebastian, this means you can dance again," Alex called from the stairs.

"I don't want to." Sebastian shook his head, disallowing any chance of accepting the idea.

"Consider it a going away gift," I said.

He grimaced. "Am I a . . . vampire?"

"No," I said flatly.

Alex stood up. "Just gave you enough to cure you."

"He gets it, Alex." I shot up my hand to silence him, wanting to give Sebastian the quiet he needed to process.

I could hear his heart thundering away and his breathing was way too fast.

"You're leaving now," I said. "No one will stop you."

Alex removed a pair of sunglasses from his trouser pocket. "You'll need these tomorrow." He threw them into the air.

Sebastian reached up and caught them, examining the lenses suspiciously.

"Come on." I headed toward the front door.

Keeping some distance from me, Sebastian followed me out into the night. "Are you really a . . . ." He panted behind me. "How long have you been one?"

"We're not having this conversation."

"But you're letting me go, right?"

"Yes." I made my way along the pathway and over the ridge of the hill.

The lights of Penzance lit up the night sky, reflecting off the grey-crystal water. The tethered rowing boat bobbed on the surface.

"I thought Alex chopped the boat up for firewood." Sebastian said.

"Evidently he was joking." I checked the oars were secure and untied the rope, throwing it into the boat. "Get in."

Sebastian hesitated. "You told me that once on the other side of the island there was no going back."

"It was metaphorical." I pointed to the boat.

Amongst the clouds hung a low silver moon. Over centuries I'd observed its ceaseless wonder and come to know its dark and featureless lunar plains. Just as the moon nearly always showed its same face toward the earth, I too had hidden my darkest side. But clearly Sebastian was a remarkable man and I was finding it ever more challenging to hold back.

"How do you know I won't tell the world about you?" he asked.

"I trust you."

Now let him go.

He knelt and rubbed his calf out of habit as though his leg needed it.

"Get in the boat, Sebastian." I headed back to the castle.

"You followed me up that clock tower?" he called after me. "Didn't you? William, you knew I was once one of them?"

I paused and turned around, slowly.

"That's why you were on Big Ben?" he asked. "You were going to kill me, weren't you? After you got what you wanted?"

I broke his gaze, not sure how best to tell him that *yes*, his life had hung in the balance that evening and it had nothing to do with his fall from the tower.

The shame of what I might have done, too terrible to ponder.

"They insisted vampires were real," he said, "but I refused to believe it."

"Say their name."

"Stone Masters." He looked miserable.

"I'd obtained a list of their current members." I stepped toward him. "Your name was on it."

"Why am I still alive?"

I gave a slow deliberate nod, hoping that might serve as my

answer and turned quickly, heading back into the castle.

Sebastian's footfalls were close behind me, closing the gap between us. "Why not just force the answers out of me?"

"I didn't expect to like you quite this much," I said wryly. "Rather an inconvenience."

"What do you want from me?"

I headed on in.

Sebastian followed behind. "This is about my association with the Stone Masters then?"

I paused beneath the chandelier. "They're not what they appear to be."

Sebastian looked about for Alex. "How do you mean?"

"They murder vampires."

Sebastian came closer, proceeding cautiously. "Don't vampires murder people?"

"Rarely."

"You're like Count Dracula?"

"Not really," I said, amused with the way his thoughts were trying to make sense of this.

"But you can fly?" He reached out and squeezed my left arm. "You feel normal." He sucked in his breath as though riding the wave of panic.

"Take your time," I said.

"What else can you do?"

"Read minds."

"Seriously?" Sebastian leaned toward me. "What am I thinking?"

"Pretty much what you're saying."

Conscious that my attention was focused on him, Sebastian became wary again. "How old are you?"

I raised an eyebrow. "I've seen centuries come and go."

"Can't believe this is really happening." He stared up at the chandelier. "The things you must have seen."

I strolled over toward the central staircase and sat on the fifth stair up. "You became affiliated with the Stone Masters at Cambridge."

He sat beside me. "Being part of a secret society sounded intriguing. I thought it might help me get more dates."

"Your father was a member?" I made it a question, but knew the answer.

"And his before him." He bowed his head. "God, you're a bloody vampire."

"I'm hoping that during our short time together you've come to see I'm reasonable."

"More than that, you've been nothing but kind to me." He shuffled closer. "My leg?"

"I'm sorry about the way it was done."

He caressed his neck. "I thought that once you were bitten by a vampire you became one?"

"Myth."

"What about werewolves?"

"Never met one."

"What's to stop me from going to the Stone Masters and reporting where you live?"

"Seb, you're not that kind of man."

"How can you tell?" he asked.

"I'm an expert on the human condition."

"Huh." Sebastian scrutinized my face. "You're not going to kill anyone, are you?"

"Not unless they try to kill me."

"Can't blame you for that, I suppose." He scratched his head.

"What you witnessed during your initiation with the Stone Masters was real," I told him.

"There was a girl . . . they tortured her." He frowned, remembering. "I thought they'd hired some actress." His expression became strained. "What are you planning to do?"

"The Stone Masters have something I need." I studied him and then said, "Ancient scrolls."

"Why do you want them?"

"I'm afflicted with a condition that if left untreated . . ." I shrugged, indicating I didn't want to talk about that just yet.

"So whatever's written on these scrolls can help you?"

"Apparently."

"They are meant to have a collection of sacred scrolls." He stared off past me. "Though I've never seen them."

A part of me feared I too may never get to see them, these elusive rolls of parchment that were meant to have scribed upon them a guide to my way back. Perhaps, if it weren't for knowing about Paradom, I might never risk everything for such a tenuous chance to revert to what had once been.

These moments spent with Sebastian soothed my soul and as I observed the way he took in the foyer and then took me in, I realized why: Sebastian was free of judgment. He merely observed the world around him without offering criticism.

He leaned toward me. "Several of my friends were recruited and one of them put a good word in for me." Sebastian was momentarily distracted by the candle flames flickering in the chandelier.

"Your fathers' connection didn't help?" I asked.

"Still have to be found appropriate member material."

"Where were you initiated?" I asked.

"Not sure." He shrugged. "A car picked me up from Cambridge. I was blindfolded during the journey there."

"Go on."

"The rule of secrecy is sacrosanct," he continued. "The Stone Masters have a tier system. Seven levels. New members never get to know anyone from the above level."

"How do you communicate?" I asked.

"Through a designated Custodian. One member from each group communicates with him to get a message to the next level up."

"Tell me about your initiation."

"The things they did to that woman." He covered his face with his hands in shame. "I had no idea it was real." His hands fell to his lap. "When I arrived, a man dressed as the Grim Reaper met me at the door."

My expression shifted.

"Oh yes, skeletal mask, black robe and even a scythe that was all too real. I think it was meant to serve as a warning that this was serious. The Reaper gave me a black masquerade mask to wear and told me that under no circumstances was I to remove it. Once I got inside the grand hall, I realized I was joining about fifty other men, all of them wearing the same black masquerade mask. The place was dark. Everything lit with candles. Classical music played in the background. That is until the chanting began." He reached down and caressed his calf.

"I appreciate this is difficult for you, Seb. I'm thankful for your candor."

He hesitated. "How come you didn't go after someone more senior? As you can see I hardly know anything."

"You know enough."

"So that girl . . ." Sebastian knitted his brow.

"If her wounds healed no matter what they did to her, then she was most certainly a vampire."

He stared off at nothing. "I just stood there, watching . . ."

"The Stone Masters were watching you, gauging if you were suitable."

His eyes glazed over. "There were five senior Stone Lords acting out the ceremony. "

"And the girl?"

"Blindfolded and gagged." His face flushed with guilt. "It was meant to be a great honor to become a member."

"You didn't know."

He cringed. "It was barbaric. They drank her blood."

"I'm sorry you had to see that."

"What list was my name on?" he asked.

"Aristoi."

"Then the list you have is of new recruits."

"Ah."

"My old custodian from the society, Jeremy Montague, might know where the scrolls are," he said. "He buys up art and auctions it off to fund the Stone Masters."

"Interesting."

"So if we find him . . ." Sebastian puffed out his lips. "But he's not going to just tell us."

"Perhaps he might show us."

"There were probably hundreds of names on that Aristoi list," he said, "Why me?"

"You were homeless. You had nothing left to lose."

"Talking with you back in the Savoy . . . it really helped."

"You've seen how many bedrooms we have here," I said. "Shame they go to waste."

He turned to look at me. "You're saying I can stay?"

"Someone needs to help Alex improve his chess."

"Hate to break it to you, but this place has more spider webs than a haunted house. You need someone to manage this place." Sebastian lifted his trouser leg and examined his calf again. "To think I might even be able to dance again."

"That's who you are, Sebastian." I gave his back a pat. "And I'm excited for your future."

XVI

"FATHER JACOB ROCH is expecting you," said the short frail nun.

Escorted by the Sister we strolled down Salisbury Cathedral's North Quire Isle, and my attention was drawn to the gothic arched ceiling with its intricate curves masterfully bestowing the illusion of movement as though nature herself had forged the design.

We arrived in a second small transept where the cruciform church crossed between the nave and the choir at right angles. The nun gestured I was to proceed alone through the door before us.

I stepped inside Trinity Chapel, admiring the slender colorful columns rising up effortlessly and supporting an illustrious ribbed-vault. I took a moment to savor the craftsmanship imbued in the remarkable stained-glass windows.

Just ahead, Jacob was talking with Marcus and Rachel.

Rachel, who'd been turned at sixteen or so, looked weary, her paleness emphasizing her vibrant titian locks. Having disappeared over fifty years ago, it was good to see her alive. Marcus was talking softly with her, evidently relieved to have her back.

Jacob came over to greet me.

"I can understand why you like it here," I said, walking with him.

"It's peaceful," Jacob agreed.

"How is she?" I gestured toward Rachel.

"No better, no worse," he said. "The nuns watch over her when I can't."

Rachel's hands trembled though she didn't seem to notice.

Jacob sighed. "The quiet keeps her calm."

Rachel pointed to me. "Who's that?"

"A friend," Marcus told her, failing to hide his sadness.

She snapped her head round toward Jacob. "Is he one of us?"

"He is," Jacob reassured her.

"You've forgiven me then?" She tilted her head.

Jacob hesitated, and then said, "There's nothing to forgive."

"But I told you that your father Orpheus is a vampire?"

"Rachel, that's all forgotten now," Jacob reassured her.

Marcus glanced at his mobile, reading the text. "It's Anaïs. Belshazzar's is officially closed." He frowned miserably and shoved the cell back into his pocket.

"It's not permanent," I reassured him.

"Belshazzar's is living history," Marcus said. "I'm having a hard time with it."

"Is it my fault?" Rachel asked.

"No." Marcus kissed her forehead tenderly.

"What day is it?" she asked, bewildered.

"Wednesday," Marcus said. "You're safe now."

"Has she told you anything?" I asked Jacob quietly.

He shook his head. "And there was nothing unusual found in her blood results. Snowstrom's scientists were quite thorough."

Rachel's attention fell on me again. "Do you have any apples?"

Jacob coughed. "You can't eat apples, remember?"

She turned back to face him and rubbed her eyes. "I feel funny."

Marcus took her hands in his. "You and I, we've been through so much together and seen so many things."

"You always made sure I was safe." She snuggled in to him.

I approached Rachel and asked, "How long have you been back in London?"

She stepped away from Marcus. "A few days."

"Where were you?" Marcus asked.

She went to answer but the confusion on her face gave away that she didn't remember.

Marcus tried to get her attention. "I love you, you know that right?"

"You told me that every day." She waved her hands out by her sides, swinging them from side to side as though hearing some invisible music.

She balanced on her tip toes. "What's your name?"

I lifted the strap of her dress back up over her shoulder. "William."

Her hair fell into her face. "I wasn't the only one there."

"They captured other vampires?" Marcus asked, dismayed.

Rachel pointed to the door. "Can I go out?"

Jacob gave a shake of his head as though conveying she wasn't making any sense. "Orpheus always told us to be careful with doors." She pointed her right toe out and balanced backward. "Doors lead to places."

"Doors might lead to sunlight," I clarified.

She held my gaze for a while and then said, "Where's Sunaria?"

"Can you tell us where you've been all this time?" Jacob asked, trying to bring her focus back on us.

"In a cold room with no furniture." She pressed her fingers to her lips. "Aiden told me I was special because I knew Orpheus." She looked so frail, lost. "He dipped apples in blood and let me lick it off. It made him laugh."

"Who is Aiden?" Marcus asked.

Rachel pointed at nothing. "Aiden is Lord Crowther's son." She reached for Jacob's sleeve and pulled him closer, whispering. "Will it make them angry?"

"Not at all." Jacob smiled but it didn't reach his eyes.

Rachel seemed to remember something that scared her.

Entering her thoughts, I caught hold of the fleeting images she was reliving. "She was definitely captured," I whispered.

She ran her fingers over her collar bone. "Aiden told me I was his favorite."

"Did Aiden hurt you?" I held my breath.

Rachel's pale white fingers covered her mouth. "I escaped."

"Sweetheart, did they make you sick?" I knew to rush her might derail her. "Do you remember how they . . . poisoned you?"

Her head shot up. "Aiden fed me blood but it tasted funny." She looked up at Marcus. "Am I going to die?"

"No," he said. "We need you to tell us everything you can remember."

"Lord Crowther . . ." She stroked her long locks. "He's the one in charge of Sovereign. The Stone Masters and Sovereign don't get along anymore." She pointed at Jacob. "Isn't that true?"

Jacob pulled the edges of his lips downward hinting he had no idea what she was suggesting, though something in his eyes reflected guilt.

"Who the hell are Sovereign?" Marcus mouthed to us.

Jacob gave Rachel a nudge and that was all she needed to pirouette away from us; an ethereal titian vision of loveliness.

Jacob turned his back on Rachel, lowering his voice. "Sovereign is a faction of the Stone Masters." And on my reaction he added, "You're not the only ones spying and collecting names."

I resisted throwing him a look of distrust.

"Sovereign, what's their purpose?" Marcus asked.

"It's the conservative arm of the Stone Masters," Jacob explained, "Just as secretive, but rumored to hunt the supernatural with an unmatched ferociousness." He glanced back at Rachel. "Their symbol is a skeleton key with a snake wrapped from its handle, down and around to the blade. The very fact they let her go is a miracle."

Rachel danced her way back to us and rose onto her tip toes. She leaned into my ear. "I have a secret."

"What's that my darling?" I asked, my focus staying on Jacob, trying to read him.

She raised her forefinger. "Where's my ruby ring gone?"

"I'll get you another one," Marcus said. "Rachel, what more can you tell us about Lord Crowther?"

Rachel spun round. "Crowther wants to kill Dominion."

"Dominion?" Marcus asked, trying to keep up.

And then I remembered seeing it. "The name's written on one of the cells back at the Mount." I gave a shrug. "It's written in Latin, *Dominatio*."

"William, when did you see it?" Marcus asked.

I threw Jacob a wary glance. "I was unfortunate to spend a few hours in that very the cell."

"Huh." Marcus raised his eyebrows. "And you have no idea who wrote it?"

"No," I said. "Not sure how long it's been written there either."

"Who do you think Dominion is?" Marcus asked us.

"He's very dangerous," Rachel answered.

I took a step closer to her. "Do you know why Lord Crowther wants him?"

"Aiden's father told him that Dominion will wipe out Sovereign." Rachel covered her mouth. "I overheard them talking." She seemed to have a moment of clarity, her gaze falling on Marcus. "I overheard men from the Stone Masters arguing with Lord Crowther to let me go."

Marcus gestured his uneasiness to us and whispered, "What if they let her go in order to follow her?"

Jacob raised his hand to reassure us. "We used every precaution when we found her. No one knows we're here."

Rachel pressed her fingers to her lips. "When will I be able to see Orpheus?"

"Soon," I said.

Seeing '*Find Dominatio*' written on the cell was the first time I'd ever come across it. I wondered who might have written it and why. I recalled seeing Jacob's reaction when he'd seen it.

"You sure you don't know who Dominion is?" I asked Jacob. "Or where we can find him?"

Choir music carried into the chamber as Mozart's Requiem in D minor resonated, embracing us with its subdued intimacy.

"Jacob?" I pressed him for an answer.

Jacob loosened his clerical collar, his attention seemingly drifting off to another time, another place. "Rachel needs our full attention," he said. "Let's not get distracted by hearsay."

Marcus's grip on my arm broke my concentration and he guided me toward the back of the chapel. "I'm her brother," he said. "It was my job to keep her safe."

"You can't blame yourself," I said.

Rachel's always been ditzy but never made stuff up," Marcus defended her. "She really believes she was captured."

Jacob was close behind us. "Clearly the poison's affecting her," he told us.

Marcus rubbed his face in frustration, trying to ease the tension. "She's not making any sense."

I squeezed his shoulder, doing my best to comfort him.

"Rachel believes the Stone Masters aided her escape," Marcus continued. "She made it sound like the Stone Masters and Sovereign are now enemies."

"When was the last time you saw her?" Jacob asked.

"Fifty years ago," Marcus said. "That was the last time I heard from her. She wrote to me from Scotland.

I leaned back against the wall. "Paradom mentioned the Stone Masters too."

Marcus waved that off. "We have that list of names of new members."

"What list?" Jacob asked.

"How about telling us what you know, first?" I asked him.

Jacob gestured he knew nothing. "What's this list?"

"We obtained a flash drive with the names of new Stone Lords," I said, though wasn't sure I should have shared that with him.

"Where is it?" Jacob's tone was tense.

"Secure," I answered. "What do we know about the Stone Masters?"

"They still exist in a modest capacity." Marcus caressed his brow. "Are we missing something?"

Jacob's eyes softened. "We need to find out what's poisoning your sister. That's the issue here."

"If we can find whoever kidnapped her," I said, "perhaps that will lead us to the source of the poison."

"Rachel may tell us more," Marcus said. "We need to be patient with her."

I tapped Marcus's shoulder. "I agree."

"May I take a look at the names on your list?" Jacob asked.

"Yes," I said, trying to shake off this feeling that Jacob knew more but was failing to reveal it.

"Anything you can offer us from your days with the Stone Masters?" Marcus asked Jacob. "I know it was centuries ago, but you may remember something that can shed light."

Jacob paused as though thinking how best to answer.

"Any news from Lucas?" I asked him.

"He's ready to work on the scrolls as soon as we have them," Jacob said.

"Tell him to contact me personally," I said. "No more of this intermediary stuff, Jacob. Understand?"

"I'll certainly ask him," Jacob said.

"Can Snowstrom help us with any of this?" I asked.

"I'm meeting with him tomorrow," Jacob said, "If he has anything for us, I will of course share it."

"Now that's a meeting I'd love to sit in on," said Marcus. "Is Snowstrom really the Oracle everyone says he is?"

"He is," Jacob admitted. "The only downside, Snowstrom always tells you the truth."

XVII

THE SOHO ART GALLERY was currently closed.

Leiden, New Compton Street's private art house, was named after Rembrandt's birthplace. Although appearing rather modest in size, it honored the Victorian architectural tradition of extending back and generously accommodating a vast area of space with its high ceilings and simple lines, making it perfect to showcase paintings. The largest room was tucked away in the anterior and was currently hiding a grand collection of seven freestanding sculptures.

Having removed the last dust sheet, I took a moment to admire the collection, watched on by Alex who sat in the saddle of an enormous eighteenth century bucking bronze horse.

"What was Orpheus planning on doing with this place?" Alex asked.

"Needed extra room for these," I said, baffled as much as he was.

"So he never intended on this being open to the public?"

I cringed at the audacity of anyone keeping these huge sculptures for themselves and worse than that, the fact that all the pieces were all so ostentatious.

"What's wrong?" Alex asked softly.

"Let's open this room too," I said. "Sell everything."

"Someone's come to their senses." He pointed to the six foot Buddha head. "If someone pays thousands for that, doesn't it contradict what it's meant to represent?"

"Since when were you so philosophical?"

"I mean if someone gets crushed beneath it while moving the thing . . ."

"You have a morbid imagination."

"And yours spends most of its time thinking of her," he said.

"Who?"

"Ingrid."

I turned to see Sebastian heading toward us, thankful for his timing.

Alex kept his focus on me. "Can I have this one?"

"Where would you put it?" I asked.

Alex slid off and landed lightly. "The foyer."

"How about . . . no," I said.

"This place would be great to introduce you both back into society," Sebastian said. "Artists are known for being eccentric." He coughed. "Not that I'm calling either of you . . ."

"Eccentric?" Alex dropped his gaze.

"Different." Sebastian glanced at his shoes, suddenly finding them interesting.

"We're not planning on this place staying open," I said. "Just need a convincing front."

Alex headed toward the door and threw a smile our way. "I'll check on the hors d'oeuvres."

"Already did," Sebastian said. "Champagne's on ice."

"Looks like we're ready," I said.

Sebastian watched Alex leave. "He hates me doesn't he?"

"That was a smile," I said, amused.

Sebastian seemed apprehensive. "Then what's with him leaving the room every time I enter it?"

"I'm very impressed with what you've done with the place."

"Are you changing the subject?"

"You've done an outstanding job." I strolled over to him. "Everything looks authentic." I took in the Buddha, his calm expression exuding a serene presence.

Sebastian studied the Asian Master. "Quite something."

I motioned to Buddha's calm expression. "In Buddhism *Dukkha* is the first of the Four Noble Truths."

Sebastian crossed his arms over his chest. "All human experience is transient and desire brings suffering."

"Its philosophical meaning is more similar to *disquietude*."

Sebastian studied me. "You think I'm ready to dance again, is that it?"

"Only then will that voice within you be stilled, Seb."

"I'm not ready to leave here just yet."

"You'll always be welcome."

He chewed on his lip. "How come you're so damn calm despite

everything?"

"I'm surrendering to the presence of the moment."

This once internal warring seemingly having dissipated.

"After all," I sighed. "There is only *now.*"

"Looks like we're keeping the Buddha head then." He raised an eyebrow in amusement. "I came to terms with the idea I'd never dance again."

"Alex is in love with you," I said flatly.

"He knows I'm straight though, right?" Sebastian asked.

"Shall we open up?"

He hesitated, taken aback by the suggestion.

"The gallery."

"Oh . . ." He blushed. "Yes." He looked thoughtful. "Did Alex tell you that?"

"Didn't need to." I studied the Buddha again, envious of his timeless tranquility. "Champagne?"

"I need a minute."

I gestured my understanding and headed toward the door and though I wanted to glance back, I didn't.

The front gallery was cozier, despite the high ceiling and glass-fronted window that showed off the artwork and provided a modern feel. Red walls were complimented by the softest lighting, designed to eliminate shadows and best present each piece. I marveled at the variety, old masters and modern art complimenting each other in ways I would never have imagined.

Marcus stood across the room seemingly fixated on the 1745 oil painting by Francois Boucher, *Brown Odalisque.* The one that had once covered the safe back in Belshazzar's office.

Sharing Marcus's admiration, I took in the young half-naked girl in the portrait, her soul's yearning, her tender face, and pondered on her life as she carried me back with her all the way to the seventeen hundreds.

"How's Rachel?" I asked Marcus, breaking the silence.

"She's discovered video games," he said.

"God help us all."

"Still, it's keeping her entertained." He motioned to the painting.

"You're concerned this will end up in a private collection?"

"She's one of your favorites."

I gave a shrug. "Used to be."

"Mark her as sold. No one will know." Marcus surveyed the gallery. "I remember you buying this place."

Our first guests, three well-dressed women, had just entered, and were heading straight for the black-tied waiter holding a tray laden with Champagne flutes.

Marcus went to touch my shoulder and then drew back. "I miss looking into those hazel eyes of yours."

I gave his arm a squeeze.

Sebastian joined us and stared up at the *Brown Odalisque*. "Bit saucy, isn't she?"

"Art is about opening your mind," I said with a smile.

"Okay then." Sebastian turned his back on the painting. "Alex is keeping watch outside."

"We're right on time," Marcus confirmed.

"This place should fill up soon," Sebastian said. "I went to the pub opposite and discreetly mentioned free booze to the punters." He studied Marcus as though still uncertain of him. "Jeremy Montague has his VIP invitation. He was my custodian." Sebastian turned to me. "I'm no longer affiliated with them, Marcus knows that right?"

"He knows," I said. "You needn't worry."

"Sebastian, when Montague arrives you feel confident to handle him?" Marcus asked.

"I plan to use the fact we've met once before to gain his trust," said Sebastian.

"Hopefully he'll see something here he likes," Marcus said.

Sebastian relaxed a little. "Who wouldn't be intrigued with a gallery offering an undiscovered Gainsborough or the like?"

"Who is that staring at us?" Marcus asked, his frown deepening.

I turned to see two men carrying one of our larger portraits, supporting each side. When they finally passed by, my view to the other side was unobstructed.

James Lamont was staring right back at me.

Quickly I checked if Ingrid was with him and if it was possible to be relieved and disappointed at the same time, I was that man. With no other choice, I made my way through the crowd toward him.

"Well this is an unexpected pleasure." I wondered if it came out wrong.

Accompanying James was a young blonde woman wearing frosted pink lipstick, overdressed in a cream tweed suit and a little too much jewelry.

She shook my proffered hand and with an upper class accent introduced herself. "Lola."

"William," I said. "Mother a fan of the Kinks?"

She giggled and reached for a Champagne flute offered from a tray by a passing waiter.

"I've advised her to use her middle name for business," James said.

"You're also an attorney?" I asked, sensing the answer before she gave it.

"Yes," she said and took a sip of Champagne.

"I have a friend here who studied law. I'll have to introduce you." I saw Sebastian deep in conversation with Marcus and my attention fell back on James. "Where's the inspector tonight?" I flashed Lola another smile.

"Working, I imagine." James gave an uncomfortable nod. "William's an art dealer," he told her.

Lola replaced her glass with a fresh drink from another, younger waiter.

"We were in the neighborhood," James said. "Thought we'd check out the place."

"Planning on adding to your collection?" I asked, discerning just what James's relationship to Lola was exactly.

"How'd you hear about this place?" asked James.

"Well—"

"You know . . ." Lola viewed the small *Virago* hanging just in front of her. "The way I look at art is, if I can do something like that, why pay thousands?"

"You paint?" I asked.

"No."

I gave a polite smile but suspected it was more of a grimace. "There's several other *Virago* pieces you might like." I gestured to my left. "And over there we have a Trousseau. See how he captures light on the canvas?"

Lola took another sip. "It's not exactly the Tate, is it?"

"That's because *Leiden* is a private gallery," I said.

"And the Tate doesn't have a Trousseau!" Marcus appeared out of nowhere.

Lola seemed captivated with him and was subtly drinking in his shocking titian hair.

"This is Marcus," I said. "Marcus, may I introduce James and Lola."

"We have sculptures in the back." Marcus glanced my way for permission. "They're not on display to the public yet." He bestowed a spark of intrigue. "Fancy a peek?"

"Are we allowed?" Lola asked.

"This is William's gallery," Marcus said. "So yes."

"Oh God I'm sorry," Lola said.

"No offense taken." I gestured to the waiter to top off her drink.

Lola held out her glass, her cheeks blushing. James squinted at Marcus as though checking him out.

"Has the inspector settled in yet?" I asked, knowing how James would react.

He turned to Lola. "Why don't you go check out the sculptures?"

Sucking the Champagne off her lips, she headed off with Marcus. I gave a discreet warning he was to behave but Marcus ignored me and reached for her hand, guiding her away.

My attention was back on James. "Lola and Ingrid don't know about each other?"

"Lola's just a colleague." James peered over my shoulder.

When I saw the frosted pink smudge near James's left ear I suppressed my amusement. "So how long will Ingrid be in London?" I asked.

"She's consulting on a case here." He frowned when Lola disappeared from view. "Who's that fellow?"

"Marcus."

"Can he be trusted?"

"Absolutely," I lied. "So you and Lola?"

"We're just colleagues. We had dinner together to discuss a case." He cleared his throat.

"I understand."

"No really, Lola and I, we just . . . share the same chambers." Suddenly, he seemed focused on getting the attention of a waiter. "Work-wise of course."

"And you and Ingrid?" I immediately regretted asking, not wanting to hear the answer.

"She seems ready to take things to the next level."

I hated him.

"I never discuss my personal life with Lola," he said. "So I'd appreciate it if we don't discuss *things* in front of her." James reached for a glass of Chardonnay. "Champagne gives me a headache."

Outside the traffic sped by, the hum from the cars disrupting the classical music and staining Bach's genius with its modern din.

"Drink, sir?" The voice sounded far off.

I realized a waiter was offering me wine and declined it.

James peered into his glass. "Damn good collection you have."

"So where's Ingrid now?" I asked.

He seemingly realized our conversation was lingering on her. "At the British Museum."

My cell phone vibrated and I removed it from my pocket and

glanced at the screen, reading a message from Sebastian. *"He's here."*

"There was some kind of robbery." James studied me for the longest time.

"I'm sorry?" I asked, distracted.

"At the Museum."

"I see."

"How did you meet Ingrid again?" he asked.

The string quartet struck up and James turned round to watch the musicians.

I took advantage of the opportunity to slide away, navigating the crowd and trying to make it to the rear of the gallery before Jeremy Montague entered through the front door.

Strolling through the vast collection of marble and bronze lifelike sculptures, I heard high-pitched gasps and then turned the corner.

There in the very center was Lola, her skirt hoisted up around her waist, leaning forward over a reclining naked male, stone statue. The sculpture reminded me of Auguste Rodin's *Thinker*, only this flawless model lay on his back upon numerous marble pillows, his arms leisurely by his sides.

I was astonished at how fast Marcus had seduced her and couldn't help but wonder at what kind of girl Lola was. Marcus was introducing Lola to an uncommon pleasure, dangling her over both the statue and a lust filled edge, threatening to shove her over at any moment.

He saw me and grinned.

I gave an incredulous smile and then gestured that Montague had arrived.

Marcus splayed out his left hand, indicating he'd only be five more minutes with her and then leaned forward, gently grasping Lola's blonde curls, nudging her face lower.

I turned to go but hesitated briefly, admiring the sculpture's masterfully chiseled face, my attention caught by his heavy-lidded rapture.

* * * *

Within twenty minutes Marcus and I were driving with Sebastian, who was at the wheel of the hired blue Mini Cooper. We'd just made a swift left at Great Newport Street.

Sebastian squeezed on the breaks in time to let several Japanese tourists continue their journey across the street, seemingly oblivious to the fact we'd almost run them over.

Just ahead, ensconced in the passenger seat of the Hackney carriage was Jeremy Montague, his taxi disappearing round the corner onto Charing Cross Road.

"I don't remember mentioning anything about a Mini." My knees were scrunched up against the front passenger's dashboard.

"You wanted fast and nippy," Sebastian said.

I grabbed the handrail. "Had a Jag in mind."

"Can't believe you sold Montague the *Brown Odalisque*," Marcus said from the backseat.

Sebastian crinkled his nose. "You never told me it was off limits."

He navigated the car onto Bow Street and there we watched Jeremy Montague exit his taxi and head up the steps of the Royal Opera House with the painting tucked under his left arm.

"What's that other thing under his arm?" Marcus asked.

Sebastian peered though the windscreen. "Some kind of material?"

"Pull up here." I gestured to the curb.

Montague quick footed it inside and Marcus and I were out of the Mini and right behind him. We entered the grand foyer with its illustrious white arched windows overlooking the finely polished pinewood floorboards. Rising on either side of us were thin ornate pillars.

Montague was well ahead of us. He swept a long black cape around his shoulders, still hugging the painting snugly beneath his left arm. With a nod of permission to enter the theatre from a male usher, Montague slipped out of sight.

Marcus and I followed, though when asked for our tickets we merely had to trance out the young man to make it past him and into the grand amphitheatre.

Above us spread out an endless dramatic ceiling with opulent colorful circles and on either side were golden lit three-tiered private booths, throwing rich textures of yellow light into the center and illuminating the stalls.

The stage was set for a performance of *Phantom of the Opera*. This audience, however, mingled amongst the seats, all of them wearing late eighteen century attire and all of them masked.

And we'd lost Montague.

XVIII

BELSHAZZAR'S, THE ONCE THRIVING haunt of London's elite, was now a shell of its former place, stripped bare of everything and everyone that had made it one of England's most exclusive clubs.

For centuries discreet nightwalkers and privileged mortals had mingled here, enjoying the grandest refuge the city had to offer, placing aside their innermost fears and exploring the darkest recesses of their imaginations and crossing over, immersing themselves completely in the underworld.

Echoes of the past were fast fading.

Within Orpheus's private domain in the deepest chambers of the club, I'd rolled up my trouser legs and was sitting on the far edge of the thirty-foot swimming pool, soaking my legs in the crystal blue water. Light reflected off the surface, shimmering along the walls and providing a relaxed aura to the low ceilinged chamber.

But I found no peace here.

After losing Montague, I'd spent an entire evening searching for Paradom again, braving another attempt to see him in hope of finding the Stone Masters' library. But the night had been wasted.

I sensed Ingrid's presence, angry with her for defying me, and was in no mood to deal with anyone but myself.

With no bouncer to prevent her entrance, Ingrid strolled alone down the corridor leading to the main nightclub. The sweeping chandeliers that had lit this dramatic entrance were gone, leaving wires hanging from their sockets, the red carpet that had once guided visitors in now ripped up revealing bare wooden floorboards.

From the lowest depths of the club, I continued to psychically follow her every move.

She stepped up her pace and pulled on the handles to open the double doorway into the main club. Once inside she turned around and around trying to process what she was seeing; no tables or chairs and the bar empty.

Belshazzar's was deserted.

Ingrid approached the elevator and punched the down button.

I considered slipping away without being seen and heading out to rejoin Marcus and Alex, who were waiting for me back in the gallery. They'd promised they weren't giving up and had tried to convince me I shouldn't either.

Ingrid was standing in the doorway. "There's no record of any funeral," she called over to me.

"Orpheus was very private," I said.

"And he liked swimming by the looks of things?" She headed in.

I leaned back using my hands to support me, leisurely kicking my legs and enjoying the sensation of the water.

"This is the last thing I'd have suspected to find down here." She knelt and dipped her hand in. "What's this, your last swim before it's drained?"

"Something like that."

She rose. "Where is he?"

"You do realize you're trespassing *again*?" I asked.

With a wave of her hand she dismissed my remark, strolling down the right side of the pool. "Did you close this place because of me?" Her cheeks were flushed from the cold. "Let me take a wild guess, if I was to bring in a team of forensic scientists they'd merely find traces of cleaning agents?"

"The underworld has existed long before you were born and it will exist long after you're dead."

She stepped closer. "You're destroying evidence."

"Ingrid—"

"Two girls were murdered and those responsible have gone unpunished."

"If I knew I could explore this subject more with you in confidence, you might just get the answers you want."

"Having trouble manipulating me?"

"The door's closing, Ingrid. Any last words?" I lifted my feet out of the water and stood up.

She came closer, close enough to touch. "Those responsible for these deaths will be brought to justice."

I clenched my jaw trying to hold back. "What do you know of punishment?"

She hesitated.

"Jadeon died trying to save your life," I snapped. "Isn't that the ultimate punishment?"

"I don't believe you." She frowned her confusion. "You told me he's in Italy."

"Look around you. Is this not proof enough that Orpheus is dead too? Belshazzar's was Orpheus."

"More lies."

"Don't look at me like that." I didn't care how it sounded.

"See, you do this. You give me a glimpse into what you are but then you pull back."

"Goodbye, Ingrid."

She raised her forearm. "I took another look at the photos from Gillian's autopsy. The girl we found dead at Stonehenge. Gillian had this exact same brand on her arm." Her voice broke and she studied the brand as though for the first time. "You ask me to forget and then give me this."

Staring at her lips, I tried to stop myself from tasting them, tasting her.

"Do you know the difference between a brand and a tattoo?" Ingrid's expression became fierce. "A brand goes deeper and it's permanent."

"You think it represents shame?"

"If not, then what?"

"You're the detective, you work it out."

Pain surged though my chest and snatched my breath away as the electric shock jolted me backwards, and I plummeted with my arms out and splashed into the water.

I sank to the bottom.

Stunned but relieved to get all feeling back, I saw Ingrid's distorted silhouette moving above. She'd kicked off her boots and was undressing.

Muffled by the water, I questioned why I'd not thought about coming down here before as I settled onto the bottom of the pool, actually enjoying the stolen serenity, savoring the sensation of being wrapped in warm quiet blueness.

There was a loud splash.

Ingrid's hands scrambled to lift me. I grabbed her, pulling her into a smoldering kiss. We made our way to the surface like that, spiraling until we reached air, and I let her go.

Ingrid splashed wildly, spitting out water. "You almost drowned me!"

Treading water, I went to help her. "You just tasered me."

She slapped me across my face, hard.

I grabbed her wrist, twisted her round and hugged her. "I'm trying to help you."

"Let me go."

I released her and turned, swimming toward the opposite side. She thumped my back and I fended her off.

Her nails scratched my face. "You branded me his whore!"

I tried to push away from her.

"That's what this circle actually means, doesn't it?" She wriggled and her right hand got free from my grip and her fingernails slashed my cheekbone.

I wiped blood off my face and grabbed her right arm and swam, dragging her along toward the poolside. "This is not exactly the goodbye I had in mind."

She spun round and went to slap me again. I thrust her against the edge, pressing up against her and using my weight to hold her still. "That's enough."

Her knuckles whitened as she gripped the slippery ledge. I caught her hand before it struck me again.

Leaning into her, kissing her passionately, opening her mouth with mine. She bit my lip and I tasted my own blood. Ingrid tasted it too and she sucked in her breath, startled by the sensations surging through her veins, electrifying her senses. She grabbed the ledge with outstretched arms. "What is that?" Her head fell back and she let out a protracted moan.

I hugged her into me. "Just say the words and I'll let you go."

Ingrid rocked against me, slowly, surely, responding to the sensations bestowed by the blood, holding my gaze as though hoping to understand her arousal.

I kissed her forehead. "Because of that brand, no vampire will touch you. It keeps you safe when I'm not there."

Ingrid's lips were quivering.

I rested my forehead against hers, studying her every response, each delicate nuance to my ministrations, taunting her with gentle caresses. "We're going to do this my way, understand?"

She moaned her answer.

Kissing her throat, working downward and lower still, her sighs begging me to snatch her breath from her.

As I did now . . .

Responding to the way she pulled me into her, bestowing a multitude of pleasures to every part of her.

Together we swirled around and around, waves encircling us as we neared the center, sharing our tenderness with delicate strokes, the gentlest affection. Ingrid's soft sighs echoed and the delicate blush arose on her neck.

Her tremors of her surrendering, an uncommon enchantment unlike any other; I lost myself in these rare precious moments with her, savoring her softness, her true mortal perfection.

Ingrid's gasps rose and fell as she planted more kisses to my cheek, wrapping her legs around my waist and clutching me into her, blue water lapping around us.

Finally, she buried her head into my chest.

We stayed like that, embracing for the longest time, both of us enjoying the lingering ripples of pleasure.

The water now still.

I assisted her out of the pool, and offered her a towel from the freshly stacked linen nearby.

Ingrid took it from me and dried herself off. "That bottle of wine you gave me?"

"French farmers protected it during the Second World War and named the Bordeaux *Liberté* which translates to—"

"*Freedom.*" She took a deep breath. "Yours or mine?"

I slipped into some fresh clothes. I'd wash off the chlorine later.

Ingrid turned away.

"This is just us taking a swim," I said.

"We did more than swim." Ingrid's wet hair was tussled and tumbling over her droplet covered shoulders, her serious expression reflecting worry. "Is Jadeon really . . . dead?"

"It's complicated." I moved away from her, hoping the distance might make her more comfortable.

"What just happened between us?" she asked.

I wanted to tell her she was beautiful, her presence a welcome change from the drama of my own private world, with darkness seeping into each moment threatening to devour me. But I couldn't say it and as my thoughts searched for the right words, the silence lingered.

"We must never do this again." She bit her lip as though fighting the memory of us.

"That's probably a good idea."

"I've been asked to consult on a case here in London," she said, trying to inject normalcy.

I feigned I didn't know. "Not a permanent move then?"

"Not at this point."

I didn't want her to know that James and I had spoken, fearful it would lead to more questions.

I pulled on my shirt. "How are things between you and James?"

"Fine." She watched my reaction. "Are you inside my head?"

I reached into her mind trying to extract what she was up too. "Absolutely not."

Ingrid turned away from me and continued dressing.

Suddenly I wanted to be anywhere but here, coaxing my thoughts out into the night, allowing my imagination to entertain an endless array of possibilities, and if I dared, allow my true nature its freedom; blood was calling my name.

"You didn't ask me," she said.

"Ask you . . . ?"

"About my new case." She squinted my way.

Faint blue veins arose on her neck and beckoned, inviting me to share their mystery.

"Belshazzar's is history," I said. "As in you and I history."

Ingrid scanned the floor, feigning she was looking for an item of clothing she'd already gathered.

"You understand why?" I asked.

"I'm going to take a peek around."

I moved closer and grabbed her arm.

"A girl's got to try." She pulled out of my grip and buttoned her shirt.

"My world has nothing to offer you." I fought the urge to thrust her against the wall and take her properly this time.

And drink from her.

"I don't believe you're capable of hurting anyone," she said, perhaps having caught my eyes devouring her.

"Hurry up."

She grabbed her bag.

I reached for Ingrid's arm, pulling her toward the long corridor, leading her toward the elevator.

"Déjà vu," she whispered.

"As I recall that time didn't go well either." I searched her thoughts for any evidence she was ready to put this place behind her.

"Something tells me I'm getting to you."

I nudged her into the lift and waited for the doors to close. We jolted upward.

She gave a crooked smile. "You don't like small spaces, do you?"

"It's not that."

"Then what?"

My attention fixed on the digital count of each level we passed and I willed it to go faster.

"As far as I'm concerned this never happened," she said.

After what seemed like a decade, the doors slid open and I followed Ingrid into the bar.

Ingrid's face fell. "Blake?"

Blake was sitting on one of the stools, leaning over the bar, resting his head on his arms.

"What are you doing here?" she asked.

Blake twisted round to face us. "I have to talk with you."

"How did you know I'd be here?" she asked.

He shrugged.

"You look dreadful," she said. "Are you alright?"

"You have to know," Blake said. "I can't hide it from you anymore."

Ingrid looked nervous. "What are you talking about?"

With a subtle glance, I told Blake he didn't need to do this.

Tension was etched into the lines on his face. "Rumor is Orpheus has disappeared."

"Blake, his promise will be honored." I didn't care how cryptic it sounded.

Ingrid tried to process our interaction. "Promise?"

Blake raised his left shirt sleeve, revealing a small circle branded on his inner forearm. "I'm a Gothica."

Ingrid slumped onto the bar stool next to his. "And what does that mean?" Her words fell out, the intensity of her scrutiny boring into Blake.

"I'm a servant of the undead," he admitted.

She pressed her fingertips to her lips.

"Orpheus told me he needed someone to watch over you," Blake said. "That's all he ever asked of me. And I wanted to do that anyway."

"How much did he pay you?"

"Ingrid, please."

"How much?" she pushed.

"It wasn't about money," Blake snapped.

She shook her head, not believing him. "That's why you supported my move to London?"

He turned to me for support, his energy waning. I gestured he must show her more than just his circled brand. Blake now peeled back his other sleeve, lifting it further up his right arm, revealing a white square dressing in the bend of his elbow, out of which poked a thin flexible tube.

Ingrid jumped off the stool. "What the hell is that?"

Blake ran his fingers over it. "It's a PICC line."

"And why is it in you?" she screeched, thinking the worst.

"I have Hodgkin's," he said flatly. "I get my chemotherapy through it."

She shifted her stance. "What?"

"The reason why I wanted you to move to London," Blake added, "was so that I could go on sick leave without you knowing."

"Blake, I'm so sorry. You should have told me."

"Keeping it from everyone was relatively easy until I started this damn chemo." He ran his fingers along the edge of the mahogany bar. "You introduced me to Belshazzar's. I didn't believe you at first. Thought you were crazy to be honest." He looked roguish. "But then I decided to check out the place."

"You came here?" her voice rasped. "Without me?"

"Mentioned Orpheus's name," he said, "and walked right in."

"What did he offer you?" Ingrid asked. "Tell me it's not what I think it is."

"Please listen to him," I said.

"How long have the doctors . . . given you?" she asked softly.

"Not long enough," he said. "Ingrid, I don't want to die."

Ingrid realized. "No."

"What would you do, Ingrid?" he asked. "Wouldn't you fight to live?"

"They have amazing scientific breakthroughs," she said, panicked.

Blake gestured that was naive.

"Orpheus is dead," she said. "He can't turn you now."

Blake's focus slid over to me.

Ingrid caught it and said, "Blake, we need to talk about this rationally away from this place."

"I've had plenty of time to consider this," he said. "I want to see Italy. I want to ride in a hot air balloon." His face lit up. "Paris, I've never seen the Eifel Tower—"

"The Taj Majal," I murmured.

"You think this is helping?" Ingrid snapped at me. "All you're doing is confusing him."

"Let's hear your plan," I said.

"Blake, you're the one who tampered with evidence aren't you?" Her tone was nervous. "All this time I thought it was Vanderbilt."

Blake was spotted in perspiration. He rested his forehead on the bar. "I'm sorry."

"Orpheus tried to kill me!" Ingrid said. "You do realize that?"

Blake reached for a discarded napkin and wiped his brow. I gestured my reassurance to him.

"What was that?" Ingrid glared my way. "Tell me that wasn't what I think it was?"

I ignored her. "Blake, go lie down."

Using his last remnants of energy, Blake headed over to the lift and punched the down button.

"He knows where he's going?" she asked anxiously. "I thought this place was stripped bare?"

"Not quite," I said. "Not yet, anyway." I waited for the lift doors to close behind him. "I'm afraid Blake has a hard road ahead."

"How dare you decide what's right for him!"

"Ingrid, how about we make it your decision then?" I asked. "You always like to have the last word."

XIX

SEBASTIAN REOPENED *LEIDEN* the following day.

I returned to the gallery that evening and found him still hard at work, sorting through boxes of business supplies.

He'd actually gone out of his way to organize the back office and with its modest bookcase, swivel chair, desk, table lamp and silver plated pen holder as well as all the other tasteful accoutrements, it easily inferred this was a working gallery. And the Big Ben paperweight made a nice touch.

Sitting behind the desk, I took a moment to give normalcy a try, peering into the teacup and cringing before sliding it out of the way.

I'd spent hours mulling over the map spread out before me, studying where the fifty red crosses had been marked indicating where vampires had been supposedly poisoned. That, as well as the other documented cases, left me feeling frustrated that we really had nothing.

"Someone drove over my bloody bicycle," Sebastian said appearing in the doorway.

I looked up at him and leaned back in my chair.

"My bike is sticking out the back of the chassis of some twit's jeep." He stormed on in.

I folded up the map. "Alex's driving leaves much to be desired."

"Alex?" The veins on Sebastian's neck bulged.

"Consider it a goodbye gift." I reached for the small box on the desk and slid it over to him.

"I need more time." He moved closer. "Where's Alex?"

"Open it."

"Your brother needs his head checked." He picked it up and

flipped open the lid. "Car keys? A Jeep?" He ran his thumb over the key ring. "The same one that's squishing my bike?"

"We're not comfortable with you cycling through London."

"Oh."

"Blame Alex. It was his idea."

"Thank you."

"Thank him," I replied.

"But he did crush my bike."

"Well, I could say we'll replace it. But we won't." I pointed to the teacup. "What kind of impression am I meant to be making exactly?"

He shrugged. "We've only got one mug."

"Why can't I have that?"

"It's not like you're actually going to be drinking from it. Anyway, the Inspector's got it."

Ingrid strolled in, her hands wrapped around the mug as though drawing warmth from its heat. I threw Sebastian an annoyed frown for not warning me.

He acknowledged my silent criticism. "That's for my bike." He headed out and edged passed Ingrid.

"An art gallery?" she asked. "You never fail to surprise me."

I pointed to the chair. "You've spoken with Blake?"

She gestured she wanted to stand. "We argued. He hung up. I've left him several messages."

"Try to see it from his perspective, Ingrid."

"As opposed to whose, yours?" She saw the map. "What's that?"

I tucked it away in the desk side drawer.

She gave a suspicious frown. "Sebastian makes lovely tea. What else does he do for you?"

"You mentioned something about an investigation on the phone? Didn't say anything about popping in."

She pulled the chair out and sat. "There was an incident at the British Museum." She hovered the mug over the desk. "Do you have a coaster?"

"We need a new desk anyway." I beamed a smile.

She hesitated, set the mug down and then said, "There was a break in."

"I see."

She looked tense. "My case has no evidence."

"Surveillance cameras?"

"Disarmed."

"What was stolen?"

"A mummy." She lifted her mug and took a sip. "How much do

they run for on the black market?" She pulled a face. "Just wondering."

"I wouldn't know." I sat up. "What about your other case back in Salisbury?"

"It's ongoing."

"You were taken off it?"

"My expertise was needed here." She shifted uncomfortably.

"Vanderbilt placed you on this case?"

"This is another high profile crime." She crossed her legs. "Do you or someone you know have anything to do with this incident?"

"Sebastian," I called out.

He appeared in the doorway holding a copy of *The London Times*.

"The museum wants their mummy back," I said. "Have you unwrapped it yet?"

He raised his eyes to the ceiling and walked away.

Ingrid spun round and pursed her lips.

"It's probably gone to a private collector," I offered.

"We've considered that." She narrowed her gaze. "Sebastian mentioned something about sculptures? Not collecting Egyptian artifacts as well are you?"

"How long have you been on this case?"

"Why?"

"Just wondering why you're bringing it up now. We've seen each other several times since you started your investigation."

"It's been a need-to-know case."

I sat back. "Go on then, let me see it."

"What?"

I gave her a look.

She removed the piece of paper from her handbag and placed it on the desk before me. "It's the museum's photocopy of the missing parchment," she said. "The writing's Aramaic but a form they're unfamiliar with."

"I have a friend who can interpret this." I slid it back to her. "Can I have a copy?"

"Of course." She seemed to relax a little.

Rain struck the windowpane and water pooled on the ledge.

I rose and strolled over to pull the latch closed.

Ingrid came around the desk and stood close, seemingly trying to gauge the reason for my disquietude.

My gaze rested on her lips. "Looks like you'll need an umbrella."

"William."

The moon reappeared from behind grayish clouds and sopping

leaves tumbled off down the street.

She came closer. "Thank you for offering to help me on this."

"Did I?"

Ingrid gave a long sigh and took in the office. "You have some lovely paintings here."

"Thank you."

"I want you to trust me."

"You can have mine."

"Huh?" she asked.

"Umbrella."

"Oh, yes of course. Thank you."

I checked the window latch though it didn't need it. "If you want to wait in the gallery until the weather breaks, that would be fine."

Clouds glided longingly, caressing the night sky with soft puffs of white, though further away darker clouds threatened to close in.

She broke the silence with a sigh. "James is a good man."

I went to reply but the words didn't come.

"He's always been a good friend to me," she added.

I faced her, trying to read the truth in her eyes.

"He gets ticks in most of the boxes," she said wistfully.

"Ask Sebastian to make a photocopy."

"I'm sorry?"

"Your evidence," I said. "We'll make sure it gets into expert hands."

"I appreciate your help on this." Ingrid headed toward the door and turned slightly. "No one will ever know about you, I promise."

"I appreciate that."

She hesitated, waiting for me to say something else.

I wanted to offer reassurance that she was making the right decision with James but instead turned away, not wanting her to read doubt in my eyes that she'd find happiness with him.

Though Ingrid had left, it felt as though some part of her still lingered.

The rain didn't let up, striking with such insistence it sounded as though it was warning me to go after her.

I sensed Sebastian in the doorway.

"Would vampires ever be caught dead in Wellington Boots?" he asked and glanced outside.

I gave a crooked smile and pulled the long drapes to shut out the world.

"So what's this evidence I photocopied for Inspector Jansen?" he asked.

"I offered to show it to a friend who can read hieroglyphics," I said.

He grinned. "Surely there's experts at the museum that can do that?"

"He's a renowned Professor of ancient Egyptian." I threw Sebastian a wary look. "Don't say it, Sebastian."

"I see the way she looks at you. And the way you look at her."

I rested against the ledge.

Sebastian twisted his mouth as though mulling over his next words. "Overheard her ask your opinion about James."

"What could I say?"

"You're not planning on telling her then?" he asked. "About Lola?"

I peered over at the half empty mug resting on the desk. "This is her chance at a normal life."

"Who are you trying to convince?" He came closer. "Why are you afraid of your feelings for her?"

"It's a matter of pain now or pain later."

"Funny, you strike me as someone who goes after what they want."

With a flash of thought, I was sitting back down at the desk.

"I'll never get used to that," he said in a high-pitched tone.

"Yes, you will."

"You once told me that what we love is worth fighting for."

"Sure that was me?"

"You're terrified of needing her." Sebastian stepped closer.

"It's complicated."

"Love often is."

"Have you any idea of the will power it takes not to bury my fangs into her?" I rose and came round to his side. "It's my natural inclination. That's what I'm up against."

Sebastian sat on the edge of the desk. "You don't seem to mind me being around."

"I don't want to . . . do things to you."

"Really? I'm offended." He leaned toward me. "She's in love with you. Are you really going to just stay locked up in here—" He scanned the office— "with your precious paintings by men long dead and let life pass you by?"

"So what's next?"

He paused and then said, "I could always visit Cambridge University. Go back to find other students who are still members?"

"Too dangerous."

"The list you found my name on. I may recognize some of the other names."

"I'll get it for you."

"Oh, I almost forgot." Sebastian pulled a post-it note from his pocket. "A gentleman by the name of—" He read the note— "Lucas Azir phoned while you were out. He wants you to call him." Sebastian handed it to me.

Reverently, I studied the scribbled phone number.

Sebastian picked up the mug. "You and Ingrid, you're both the same." He gave a knowing nod. "You're both trying to save the world one person at a time."

I can't even save myself.

"There's something about her that's haunting," Sebastian whispered.

I looked up at him and gave a sigh. "Seb, I'm not sure there's any more room for any more ghosts."

USING THE FRONT DOOR had been out of the question.

And yet entering via the bedroom window of James's flat felt wrong too. The idea of having to engage in small talk with him was mildly annoying, and I was well past trying to come up with a convincing explanation of why I'd come here again at this time of evening.

Sounds from the kitchen carried and a rich aroma of spices filled the apartment. With my supernatural hearing, I picked up the pasta bubbling on the stove as well as the highly seasoned sauce being methodically stirred in another pan; a rich Cabernet was currently being enjoyed.

Ingrid strolled into the bedroom carrying a long stemmed wine glass. Taking a sip as she walked, she suddenly saw me and halted, the burgundy liquid swooshing, threatening to spill.

Quickly, she closed the door behind her and said, "What are you doing here?"

"I don't have your number."

"I work at Scotland Yard, you could have phoned me there." She placed her glass down on the Elmwood chest of drawers.

"I've arranged the meeting."

"What meeting?"

"With my friend, the Egyptologist. He's deciphering your parchment."

"You needed to tell me that *now*?"

I tried a smile.

"Meet me outside," she said.

The door opened.

Ingrid spun round and came face to face with James. "I can explain."

"I'm not that anal, Ingrid." James lifted the glass and reached for the silver coaster, resting the glass on it.

Ingrid shot round and saw I'd gone.

"Dinner's almost ready," James said.

"I have to go out."

He let out a long irritated sigh. "It's nine o'clock."

"Sorry."

"Of course you are." He slammed the door shut behind him.

Leaning against my red Ferrari, I waited for her.

Ingrid, now dressed in jeans and a black coat, stormed out of the building toward me. "What the hell were you thinking?" she snapped.

"Grey walls in the bedroom, really?" I asked.

She eyed up the Ferrari. "This yours?"

I pointed to the manila folder she was holding. "What's in the file?"

"You're about to find out."

I opened the car door for her.

"You had no right to come here." She strolled round to the front and checked the number plate. "Anyway, I thought you had to be invited in?"

"Now that would be boring."

"We're using mine." She headed off toward the long line of parked cars.

I shut my car door and headed after her. Ingrid slipped behind the wheel of her Rover. Once inside with her, I slid back the seat. She revved the car more times then it needed and steered us away from the curb, quickly picking up speed.

I peered into the back seat and saw the numerous discarded empty sweet wrappers.

"Been under some extra stress lately?" I gestured to the tell-tale evidence.

She glanced at her side view mirror. "Don't always get time for lunch."

"I visited the scene of the crime," I said.

"You went to the museum?"

"Watch where you're going!" I pointed to the road. "One of us is undead let's not make that two."

She grabbed the clutch and changed gears with verve. "The museum's still cordoned off."

"I was careful."

"Well?"

"It was a professional job."

"I assumed that."

"You did ask me to help you."

She shot me an annoyed look.

"At some point you really should talk about it," I said.

"Talk about what?" She shook her head and shifted the gearstick with brute force.

"I want to help you." I reached for the handrail above the window.

Her eyes went wild. "You mean manipulate me?"

"Your fear of abandonment, shall we explore it?"

Her fingers clutched the steering wheel.

"If you marry someone you don't love," I continued, "and he leaves you, there'll be minimal pain. Am I right?"

She steered wide on Sloane Street. "You had no right to visit James's flat." She adjusted her seatbelt. "I think I'm starting to hate you."

My fingers slipped off the rail. "Pull over."

"Driving helps me think."

"You call this driving?"

"All I'm asking is that you call ahead, and don't go around trashing crime scenes." She raised a finger. "Don't turn up uninvited."

We drove on in silence, with Ingrid seemingly in a quiet rage and I trying to fathom her indignation.

She swerved toward the pavement and the car jerked to a stop.

"Why do I get the sense that your recklessness isn't reserved just for your driving?" I asked.

"You want me to have a normal life, well this is me having one." She reached for my arm. "It was only natural I would be drawn to you. Blake was right, you did swoop in and save me."

"What are you saying?"

"Promise me something."

I waited for her to continue, hoping she'd come around and see it from my perspective.

Her cheeks blushed. "You must never touch me like that, ever again."

My mind raced to remember those intimate moments we'd shared, exploring each instance to disentangle the truth and recall if I'd truly be the one to initiate them.

Without waiting for my answer, she was out of the car. There was something in her expression as she looked up, studying one of the taller Edwardian buildings.

I exited the car and joined her, gazing up at the ornate brickwork, searching for the right words until I found them. "I'm sorry if I offended you."

"In my line of work there can be no distractions," she said.

"That explains James."

She folded her arms. "Blake and I were locked out of our investigation." She stepped into the arched entranceway of a building, shielding herself from the cold. "I conducted my own inquiry."

I followed her, taking the one step under the archway. A shot of fear ran up my spine as soon as I saw it. Engraved into the stonework above the enormous double doorway was a skeleton key with a snake wrapped from its handle down and around to the blade.

Sovereign.

Jacob's words resonated. *"They're ferocious."*

"That folder you asked about," she teased, "it contains some pretty interesting stuff."

I wanted to tell her she'd gone mad, but as she considered me with that wide-eye intensity I knew she had no idea of the danger she was putting herself in.

The danger she put me in.

"Your face just told me everything I needed to know." She reached for the brass door handle.

I pulled her back, terrified that Stone Lords might pour out of there any minute and drag us both inside.

"This is Vanderbilt's." She waved the file. "In here he mentions this place." She looked triumphant.

I grabbed her arm and the folder dropped from her grasp. I spun her around, forcing her hands above her head, pinning her against the brick with my body.

"Interesting reaction." She tried to twist her wrists out from my grip. "I'm going to find out just what it is they get up to in there."

I tried to extract her words before she spoke them. "You're delusional," I whispered. "Go in there and you're in serious trouble. If I go in there, I'm dead."

"Don't be ridiculous. It's secret handshakes and golf tournaments."

"That sugar's gone to your brain." I pointed above the doorway. "Do you know what that symbol represents?"

"They're men of law, scholars and scientists." She glanced at the handle. "I've done my research."

"We're leaving." I picked up the manila folder and pulled her away along the pathway.

With a flick of her wrist she unlocked the doors to the Rover and climbed in.

I quickly joined her. "Start the engine."

"You're probably right." She adjusted the rearview mirror. "I should have given this more thought."

I threw the folder onto the back seat.

"Just give me a minute to explain, okay?" she said. "The museum's surveillance cameras were disarmed, but the ones from a building across the street were working just fine. The thief's number plate is registered to this address."

I gestured for her to hurry up and start the engine.

Ingrid placed the key in the ignition but didn't turn it. "Chief Inspector Vanderbilt was conducting a subversive investigation on my case. Inside that file—" she pointed to the back seat— "I found his invitation to attend a meeting here."

"Vanderbilt was being summoned," I realized.

"Looks like my boss is a member of a secret society." She raised her chin high.

"And Vanderbilt's the one who put you on this new case?"

"He convinced me that the Salisbury case might be connected to the one at the museum."

"Is he using you or trying to distract you?" I asked, glancing back up at the building nervously.

"Are we talking about Vanderbilt or you?"

Waving off her comment I said, "But you came to London despite your doubt?"

"I wanted to be near Belshazzar's."

I paused, giving her the silence that she deserved.

Ingrid's door flew open and she leaped out onto the pavement and slammed the door shut. A loud click signaled she'd locked me in with her remote.

I fiddled with the lock and flung my side door open and flew after her.

When I reached the empty arched entryway, the front door was ajar.

XXI

GETTING PAST THE SECURITY guard at Sovereign's reception desk was relatively easy.

Though stopping my hands from shaking took a little more effort.

The tranced-out officer pointed at an elevator on the other side of the foyer when asked which direction the Inspector had gone. I left him staring out at nothing after our short discussion, where I'd convinced him he hadn't seen me and that handing over the elevator key was a good idea.

It wasn't only the premier real estate of the building but also the remarkable luxury of the interior that reflected its vast wealth. Euclidean geometry was incorporated into both the marble flooring and wall designs, with a well orchestrated arrangement of the circle, rectangle, octagon, square and hexagon all tied together in a richly designed three dimensional effect. An enormous silk Persian rug in the center offered up the only color.

The credit sized card slid down the security panel and the lift doors glided apart.

Hesitating briefly, I questioned the sanity of stepping in.

If what Rachel had told us held any truth then these recent poisonings in London were connected to this band of ruthless men, and as I stepped into the lift with my hands balled into fists, I readied myself to confront them.

Despite the smooth descent the lift felt endlessly suffocating. The last time I'd felt this panicked was when Jacob had locked me in that coffin back at the Mount.

Had I really been such a threat?

The doors opened to a cherry paneled office. A little way in Ingrid was sitting at a desk opposite a forty-something smartly dressed man. They both rose to greet me.

"He was parking the car," Ingrid explained, then discreetly threw me a look of surprise that I'd actually followed her in here.

The man, wearing a pinstripe suit, proffered his hand. "Alistair Smith."

I had no choice but to shake it and reply, "William."

Behind the desk there was a walnut bookshelf stacked high with leather bound books, their bindings marked with numbers, not titles. The incandescent lighting was so natural it made me want to step back into the elevator.

"Do take a seat," Alistair offered with an upper class accent, gesturing.

I sat next to Ingrid.

"Members will be arriving soon," he said, glancing at his wristwatch.

"Men only?" asked Ingrid.

He gave a long sigh. "Our culture is being decimated by a society that sees no value in our heritage. We merely desire to preserve our unique history."

"Women were part of history too," she said.

"Ah, a feminist."

"You misunderstand—"

"Ever enjoy a night out with the girls?" he asked casually. "That's all we chaps want. Just a chance to smoke our cigars and keep the conversation on a steady course." Alistair leaned back and then turned to me. "Isn't that so?"

I offered a smile though it hurt to hold it, and Ingrid's head snapped round to look at me.

Unable to pick up on any of his thoughts, my reason for not wanting to enter here was being realized. Mind closing was only practiced by certain kind of men, the kind who wielded wooden stakes.

Or worse.

Ingrid seemed oblivious. "May I have a list of your members?"

"Quite out of the question." His heavy-browed focus slid my way. "Would you like an application? Our stipulation is merely an acceptable profession. A reasonable income."

"And what would that be?" Ingrid asked.

He ignored her. "If you have a friend who's already a member, a good recommendation goes a long way."

I played out in my mind how it would go down. The way in

which I'd grab Ingrid and fly back into the lift, quickly ascending, making our escape and living long enough to argue about it later.

Ingrid sat up straight. "There's evidence to suggest that one or more of your members are involved in a crime."

"Probably hooligans." He rested his elbows on the desk. "Did they vandalize something?"

"These weren't hooligans," she said.

"We conduct thorough background searches to ensure our members are of the finest caliber. Our political members are ensured their reputations will never be tainted."

"What's the name of your club?" She sat back.

"We don't have a gym. We don't have a pool. We don't call it a club."

"I'd love to have a look around," Ingrid said. "We have time."

"I'm afraid that's not up to me."

Resting on the right of his desk, the antique black rotary phone rang.

"Excuse me." His eyebrows twitched as he listened into the receiver. The phone chimed its disapproval when he hung up. "I'll be right back." He rose and headed for the door behind his desk.

Ingrid waited for him to exit and then shifted in her seat to face me, lowering her voice. "What do you think?"

"About what exactly?" I asked, annoyed.

"Well, what is he—"

I snapped my hand up to stop her question and whispered, "We're probably being watched."

"You're paranoid."

"He was recalling with fondness how it was once legal to hang, draw and quarter."

"Really?"

"No, wait . . . that was me." I pulled her up and out of her chair and nudged her across the room into a corner and gestured she must whisper. "You'll get us both killed and by the looks of things you're going first." I glanced over toward the glass of water on the desk, poured by Alistair for Ingrid upon her arrival.

"You're not seriously suggesting—"

"Drink it and let's find out," I said.

"You still haven't told me what he's thinking."

"He blocked his thoughts."

"What does that mean?"

"What do you think it means?" I snapped.

"See, this place is important." She headed toward the leather recliner and reached for the briefcase leaning up against the chair and flicked the latches. She rummaged, nudging his spectacle case out of the way. She removed a leather bound book.

I grabbed it from her and flipped through the pages. I glanced at the door. "He's coming back."

Ingrid snatched the book from me and shoved it into her coat pocket and then sat again.

Alistair strolled in, his mind so quiet that I questioned whether he was thinking at all, and his expression so blank he'd have seemed serene if it weren't for the way his eyes burned with suspicion. "Looks like a tour won't be possible, I'm afraid."

"Why?" asked Ingrid.

"We have a visiting dignitary and apparently he's running early." Alistair glanced at his wristwatch again.

Ingrid rose. "I'll be back with a warrant."

"I think you'll find one hard to get, my dear," he said.

She rested her fingers on the desk tapping away half-distracted. "And why is that?"

His lips thinned. "You'll have a challenge getting anyone to sign it."

She threw me a glance. "We'll see."

"Next time make an appointment," he said.

"Tell me, Alistair," she sounded fierce, "what would your members want with an Egyptian mummy?"

"Are you familiar with the term etiquette?" Alistair's tone was scathing.

Ingrid's hands shot to her hips.

He strolled toward the lift and pressed the button. "Do give Chief Inspector Vanderbilt my regards when you see him, won't you?"

The lift doors slid open.

Ingrid and I ascended in silence.

As we passed the guard stationed at the front desk he peered up from his newspaper and showed surprise, having no recollection of me entering.

Once outside I sucked in air not caring that it was smog filling my lungs.

"Well that seemed to go well." Ingrid patted my back. "See, I told you we had nothing to worry about."

I glanced back and scanned the windows, hating the feeling we were being watched.

"He's protecting his members." Ingrid's expression changed. "Not the first time I've had to deal with chauvinism."

I removed the keychain from my pocket and flicked the car key and a little way down the curb a blue Porsche convertible flashed its lights.

Ingrid came after me. "What are you doing?"

"Thought I'd check out Alistair's car." I opened the driver's side door and climbed in.

Ingrid glanced back to confirm we weren't being watched and joined me, sitting in the passenger seat. "Where did you find his keys?"

"In his briefcase."

"I didn't see them."

I reached over to her side and opened the glove box, rifling through it, I quickly found a folded map.

I handed it to her. "Something tells me this isn't Alistair's day job."

She peered at it, taking note of how it had been folded. "East Sussex." She shoved it back into the glove box.

The key slid smoothly into the ignition. "Did you know the same company that makes these cars also designed tanks during the second world war?"

"Interesting. Now . . . turn it off."

"Oh, one more thing," I said. "If I ever mention you mustn't go in somewhere, you'll listen."

"What are you doing?"

I steered the car away from the pavement. "Making a point."

"You'll get me arrested!"

"That would happen only if they found us *in* the car." I shifted into second gear and then quickly into third.

"What are you talking about? Slow down!"

"Trust me my driving skills exceed yours on all levels." I buzzed open the roof. "Apparently it's bad to let down the top when driving over 70." I glanced up. "Seems to be handling it well."

"Okay, I get it, I'll never put you in that position again."

"What was that?" I shifted the Porsche into fourth.

"I'm sorry." She eased her seat belt round and clicked it into its socket.

I beamed a smile, steering the car slightly right onto Margaret Street, admiring the images in the rearview mirror, enjoying the world flashing past and blurring the scenery that fell away quickly.

Ingrid edged down in her seat. "We have to go back. I left my bag in my car."

"You won't need it where we're going."

"Car thefts are on the rise." She shuffled uncomfortably and grasped the handrail. "Where are we going?"

"It's a surprise." I pointed left to the Italian restaurant we were fast passing. "Cafe Nero. Apparently they have the best coffee." I released her seat belt and directed the Porsche toward the corner of Westminster Bridge. "How well do you swim?"

"Not funny. Pull over, William." Her hair whipped across her face. "We're heading for the Thames. We'll go in if you're not careful . . ."

I checked the speedometer. "Why look at that, we're approaching 100." Using telekinetic force, I sent a shockwave of destruction at the bridge wall ahead and it crumbled, leaving a gap large enough for a car to pass through.

Ingrid's scream filled the car and we shot up and over the bridge, the engine revving and the wheels spun against nothing.

Enjoying the sensation, I sat back as the car arched in the air, picking up speed, the seat heavy beneath me with nothing but a view of the starry night sky.

We nosedived toward murky water.

With my arms wrapped around her, I lifted her out of her seat, flying skyward. The Porsche slipped away beneath us. Hugging her tightly, Ingrid's face was buried into my chest and her body was rigid against mine.

Below us, there was a loud splash.

In the center of a dark alley, next to *Ye Old River Thames Inn*, I eased Ingrid away from me. She was shaking, her eyes wide with terror, her right hand pressed over her mouth and her left still gripping hold of my jacket.

Peering over her shoulder, I caught the Porsche sinking.

I guided her around to the front of the Inn. "This place was built in 1720," I said. "Back in the day it was a working class tavern."

Her eyes were wide, her face frozen in fright.

Standing in the doorway, still clutching Ingrid's hand, I took in the scene. Restaurant staff as well as twenty or so customers had gathered at the long window which ran the entire length of the restaurant overlooking the Thames, and everyone was staring out at the river.

With no concierge to guide us to our table, I picked up a wine menu and led Ingrid through to one of the cozier burgundy leather booths. She plopped down into her seat. I sat opposite and leafed through the wine menu. Ingrid was seemingly fixated on her shaking hands.

I peeked at the wine list. "Looks like you could do with a drink."

XXII

INGRID WAS EARLY.

I sensed her ascending *Leiden's* gallery stairwell.

When she finally stepped onto the roof I was caught off guard. Her red dress accentuated her figure and her hair was styled up with curls spiraling over her shoulders. She held her coat over her shoulder casually.

"How are you?" I handed her a tall glass of Champagne.

"Having nightmares about falling." She took it, considering the glass as though deciding whether she wanted it. "I'm assuming you invited me here to apologize." She laid her coat over the stairwell railing.

"You look . . . stunning," I said.

"James and I are having dinner." She watched my reaction, tilting her head with a mischievous glint. "Can't stay, I'm meeting him in half an hour."

I feigned disinterest.

"It was on the news." She took a sip. "You driving a Porsche into the Thames. Someone filmed it with their phone."

"Saw the footage. We'd exited the Porsche by then."

"You're reckless!"

"Actually, that's the word I keep in reserve for anyone who wanders into the heart of a secret society's headquarters after being *clearly* informed of the danger."

"Nothing happened."

I gave her the look that deserved. "Yet."

"Why did you ask me to come here?"

"More Champagne?" I offered.

"Unlike you, I haven't got all night."

I shook off her remark. "May I introduce my friend Lucas."

He stepped out of shadows half lit by the tea lights, his striking features bestowing a Middle Eastern descent; a typical woman's man, thirty-something, tall, dark and ridiculously good looking. "What's this about a Porsche?" asked Lucas with a glint of amusement.

Ingrid studied him.

"Lucas is a good friend." I pretended not to notice her reaction. "He's here . . . for you."

She rested a hand on her chest as though trying to work out what I'd planned for her.

"I thought it was time you two met," I teased her, speaking slowly and emphasizing my words to make a point. "Ingrid, you're *ready* for this."

She turned toward me slowly in an accusatory manner.

I motioned to Lucas. "There's no one quite as skilled as you."

He lowered his chin and those deep brown irises of his caused Ingrid to freeze. She shook herself out of the trance he had her in and turned back to me, unable to surrender her presumption.

I took her drink from her and glanced over at Lucas. "She wants this."

Ingrid's lips parted as though trying to speak but unable to find the words.

"Are you alright?" I feigned concern and wrapped my arm around her waist.

She shook her head. "I'm not sure . . . what this is?"

"Perhaps you should call James and tell him you'll be late." I moved away from her.

Her eyes begged me to stay.

"This is about you finding the answers you need," I whispered.

She was taking small breaths, her anticipation rising with each second that I used the silence against her.

Finally, I said, "Lucas spent his entire life digging around Egyptian burial sites." I leaned back against the railing next to her. "I promised to arrange a meeting with the Professor. Well, here he is."

Ingrid tried to save the moment. "Well that's marvelous."

Of course I wasn't going to bring up the fact that Lucas was also a vampire. She didn't need to know that, and by the way she relaxed a little, she didn't seem to detect it either.

"You've seen a copy of the parchment?" She glanced at the glass sitting on the tray which I'd moments ago taken from her.

Lucas picked up the Champagne flute and handed it back to her.

"The parchment is over two thousand years old."

"How can you tell?" she answered.

Lucas glanced at me. "These hieroglyphics were used predominantly around 60 B.C."

Ingrid reflected eagerness for him to go on, her feeling of awkwardness fading.

Lucas removed a piece of a paper from his inner pocket. "This is the copy you gave William." He nudged up against her right side and pointed. "This first hieroglyphic represents the symbol for balance. This next one," he slid his fingertip down, "Moon God." His finger slid to the next symbol. "Thoth." He smiled at me. "The wisest of the Egyptian Gods."

"Thoth?" Ingrid asked.

"An Egyptian God," Lucas told her, "famed for keeping a great library of ancient scrolls written by the Gods themselves. The goddess Seshat was one of his wives, the goddess of writing, and collector of mysteries. The son born of their union was called Hornub and he was associated with literature, arts, and learning."

"What does this symbol mean?" Ingrid pointed to it.

"Blood," Lucas said. "And if this scroll really did come from his tomb, never separated from the body, then this suggests the mummy stolen was Hornub, Toth's son."

"Hornub was meant to be magical," I said. "Apparently he overcame death."

Ingrid gave me a sideways glance. "How much would something like that fetch?"

"I doubt it was for the money," Lucas said.

In agreement I said, "Two exhibition cases down from Hornub's was a solid gold statue of Osiris."

"Perhaps a corrupt collector?" Ingrid asked.

Lucas shrugged. "There's always illicit activity associated with these kind of artifacts. When ancient Egyptians found out that foreign buyers would pay a king's ransom for their dead, they created fakes. Imagine the little bastards working away on the kitchen table, scooping out their late relative's organs and then wrapping the body in linen. All to turn a profit."

"Taking advantage of people's ignorance," Ingrid said.

"Despite its repulsive nature," I said, "they look at it as just another way to make a living."

Lucas slid his finger downward. "This is the symbol for the underworld."

"Which means?" Ingrid asked.

"It's expected," Lucas said, "after all it was their obsession."

Ingrid chewed her lip thoughtfully.

"The heart was traditionally the only organ not removed from the body," he said. "That's not a common known fact. When we find the heart intact we're usually looking at an authentic mummy."

"Why do you think thieves might want this one?" Ingrid asked.

"Hopefully we'll find out when we get him back," Lucas said. "I'd very much like to see Hornub restored to his homeland."

"You don't approve of him being on display?" she asked.

"Conflicted," he replied. "Honor the dead. Respect the dead. Learn from the dead."

Ingrid was riveted. "Where does that come from?"

"A people who know that the line between this world and the next is as fine as the veil that separates them."

"Your people?" she asked softly.

"The world is full of mystery, Ingrid," he said. "Once your heart is as open as your mind, then the book of truth will open before you and all your questions will be answered."

She seemed to be holding her breath, wooed by his words.

I turned to Lucas. "I appreciate your time."

"I'm looking forward to checking out your collection," he said. "I hear it rivals the Getty."

"Hardly," I smirked. "Sebastian will give you a tour."

"It was good to see you," Lucas said to me. "I hope to have answers for you soon on that other matter." He took my hand and squeezed it with affection. "Let's have dinner tomorrow night?"

I gave his back a pat of reassurance. Lucas strolled toward the top of the stairwell and disappeared down it.

"How do you know him again?" Ingrid asked.

"An old friend," I said. "That's how I know we can trust him."

She frowned. "Ever since finding Vanderbilt's file I've not trusted anyone."

"So you're the only one allowed to sneak around?"

"I was conducting an investigation."

"On your boss?"

She folded her arms. "He was acting suspiciously."

"And you're never guilty of that?"

"You better not be trying to read my mind."

"I try to avoid chaos," I said. "Did you find anything in that book you pinched?"

"It was blank." Her hand slid to her necklace and she fiddled with her chain. "James has invited me to go away on holiday with him."

A dove landed a few feet away, flapping its wings before settling and then pecking at nothing.

She looked up at me. "He wants us to go to Scotland. I'd rather go to Paris."

Two more birds flew down to join the first, displaying their entitlement to the roof.

"I've always dreamed of going barefoot in Paris," she sighed.

I turned away. She took my hand and we braved to hold each other's gaze, sharing a moment that should never have happened.

"My driver will take you," I offered.

"I'll catch a taxi." She placed her glass on the tray.

My hand rested in the arch of her back and I guided her toward the stairway. "I'm going to stay here for a while."

She hesitated by the top of the stairwell. "That ruse you pulled on me with Lucas." She gripped the narrow rail ready to descend. "Wasn't funny. See, not laughing." She raised an eyebrow.

Stunned with the mind message she sent me, I quickly headed back her way.

"Something wrong?" she asked casually.

"Sebastian merely runs the gallery," I said. "Arrest him?"

"I was *thinking* that, yes."

"On what grounds?"

"I was hoping he'd tell me more about you."

"What do you want to know?" I tried to suppress my disquiet. "Sebastian's been through enough."

"You're referring to his car accident?"

"You've been investigating him?"

"He was on his bicycle when a car hit him?" She tried to read my expression.

Which I was trying desperately trying to control.

Standing right behind Ingrid was Anaïs, her long black locks trailing over her face, her chin low, and her still demeanor eerie.

"It does sound awful," Ingrid broke the silence. "His accident." She clarified to get my attention back on her.

"Sebastian made a full recovery," I said, hoping Anaïs would respond to my telepathic command to meet me somewhere else, some other time.

Yet the fledgling just stood there, staring like a haunting phantom, her lips slightly parted as though readying to speak, defying me.

"Does Sebastian know what you are?" Ingrid asked.

What you are? Ingrid's words sliced into my mind and I wasn't sure if it was the way she'd said it, or her tone.

"Master," Anaïs finally whispered.

Ingrid spun round to look at her.

Anaïs knelt and bowed her head. "Status Regal, I am your obedient servant."

I resisted the urged to roll my eyes. "Rise."

Anaïs did so with a supernatural ease.

"Status Regal?" Ingrid made it a question.

I nudged passed Ingrid and grabbed Anaïs's arm, guiding her to the roof edge where I hoped she'd take the hint.

"I have a message," Anaïs blurted.

"Not a good time." I avoided the urge to shove her over. She could fly after all. Or if she hadn't yet, she soon would.

Anaïs's long black locks caught in the breeze. "He wants her."

I leaned into her ear. "What are you talking about?"

Ingrid followed us over, seemingly rattled by the way I held Anaïs precariously close to the ledge. "William, what's going on?" she asked.

"These feelings are natural," I told Anaïs. "My commitment to you is unwavering, but you must obey."

Anaïs frowned up at me.

I scanned the other rooftops hoping to glimpse Marcus, or even Zachary, who might just be tracking this newbie and making sure she didn't mess up too much in her early days. After all they'd promised just that. Anaïs tried to ease out of my grip.

I tightened it.

"You've been summoned by Fabian Snowstrom," Anaïs said, her free hand reaching inside her coat pocket. She withdrew a cream envelope with *F.S.* initialed into the wax stamped seal. She offered it to me. "You both have."

XXIII

NAVIGATING THE RED FERRARI along Edward Street, I glanced over at Ingrid. "How did James take it?"

She flicked her mobile shut. "Right now I'm seriously questioning my judgment for getting back in a car with *you*." She buzzed her window down and strands of hair blew over her face. "How loud does my internal screaming sound?"

I steered the car westward.

"I'm hoping you've grown bored of driving into rivers." She rested her stiletto heels upon the dashboard.

"Where's the trust?" I asked.

"Yet to be earned."

Reaching inside her mind, I realized she'd twisted the truth a little about meeting James for dinner. Ingrid had dressed up for me.

I feigned interest in my side view mirror, hoping she'd not catch my boyish grin.

She twisted in her seat to face me. "Who was that girl?"

I pulled back on the smile. "Anaïs."

"How is she connected to you?"

"The question you should be asking is, who's Fabian Snowstrom."

She removed the note from the envelope. "Well?"

"Someone you don't keep waiting."

Ingrid read the note from him again. "*Meet me where the past, present and future meet, beneath the once shadow of Nonesuch House. -F. A. Snowstrom.*"

"He wants us to meet him at London Bridge," I said.

"I've never even heard of Nonesuch House."

"In the late fifteenth century a four-story house was built on top of London Bridge."

"Nonesuch House, meaning no other house like it?"

"Exactly. The building was an unprecedented workmanship of its time." I steered the car around the traffic circle, taking the third exit toward St. Martin's Le Grand. "It was originally built in the Netherlands. Later it was dismantled and shipped to London and reassembled piece by piece."

"What happened to it?" she asked.

"It was torn down in the eighteenth century."

"What about the past, present and future bit?"

I glanced at the note. "Still working on that."

"So this is Fabian's way of using code?"

"Just in case his message didn't reach us. Or if it got into the wrong hands."

"Does he have enemies?"

"Fabian's one of the oldest of my kind. He's sought after."

"Why does he want to see me?"

"Not sure." I shot her a look. "Consider this a privilege. This is where history gets interesting."

* * * *

Screams echoed down the long, black corridor.

The strobe lighting made us blink. When the axe swung dangerously close and the man wielding it let out a maniacal laugh, Ingrid nudged up closer to me.

We were standing with a crowd of twenty other people and that made it fairly easy to dissolve into the background of the London Bridge tour group.

Trevor, our young cockney guide, made a sweeping gesture and said, "Those who dare to enter London's Tomb will find the secrets to its past."

Together the crowd meandered after him through the brass gates, seemingly enjoying the first part of the tour.

Trevor jangled a large bunch of keys, continuing. "In the year 60 B.C. Queen Boudicca gave the order for the bridge to be burnt down."

I whispered to Ingrid. "She was Queen of the Brittonic Iceni tribe."

"Once her command was given," Trevor's voice boomed with rehearsed passion, "the slaughter ensued. Bodies were lain to waste across the city, and others could be seen floating down the river. The stench of death reached every part of London."

My gaze slid to Ingrid's stilettos, the tips of her shoes resting upon a faded terrazzo tile, upon which a faint hourglass was etched. I took Ingrid's left hand and held her back, waiting for the last tourist to disappear around the corner.

Ingrid followed my gaze and knelt, tracing her fingers over the etching.

I knelt beside her and pointed to the drawing's lower compartment, symbolizing where the sand gathered. "Past."

Ingrid gestured to the upper compartment. "Future." Her forefinger slid to the thinnest part. "Present."

Together our eyes moved up to the brick wall.

"Excuse me!" the cockney voice reached us.

We stood to greet the young woman with *Staff* printed on the front of her black shirt.

She hit us with her flashlight. "You need to keep up with the others."

I approached her. "Niki. You didn't see us." I projected a wave of energy that struck her right between her eyes.

Niki's head jolted. "How do you know my . . . name?" Her eyelids fluttered.

Ingrid moved closer, fascinated, though probably questioning her moral obligation to stop me.

"Niki, go back to work," I said. "You didn't see us. You don't remember seeing us." I motioned for her to turn around.

In a lazy hypnotic state she scratched her face, lost in a sea of thought and then headed back.

Ingrid folded her arms. "Have you ever used that on me?"

"Of course not," I said. "Getting inside your noggin is far too dangerous."

High on the brickwork was an antique brass torch sconce. I reached for it and twisted it sideways. The wall scraped open.

After checking it was safe we entered, trekking down a stone stairwell and onward. At the very end another door greeted us. Once inside the ten by eight foot room we both took a wall, eager to find the next clue to advance our mystery tour.

The door slammed behind us.

Ingrid tried to open it. "It's locked!"

"This is Fabian's modus operandi." And then I saw it. There, resting on the floor in the far corner, lay a rolled up piece of cream paper.

I unraveled it.

Ingrid peered from behind my shoulder. "Tell me you read—"

"Latin, yes."

"Well?" Ingrid reached for my shirtsleeve and tugged it.

I dropped the piece of paper and went straight for the door handle, desperately trying to turn it. When that failed I shoved my right shoulder up against the frame.

Ingrid had picked up the note and was reading it. "We have to tell each other our deepest fear?"

I rested my forehead against the door.

Ingrid read on, "Only then will Fabian let us out?" She looked confused.

I knew why, and I hated him for it.

With concentration I focused on the door, ready to send a jolt of force at it. Pain exploded in my skull and I fell against the wall, stunned.

Fabian had just sent a warning right into my frontal lobe, commanding me not to try my trick in here; and evidenced by my pounding head, he was insisting. I turned round and slid down the wall.

The paper slipped from Ingrid's hand and spiraled to the floor. "What's going on?"

"He's not letting us out," I whispered.

"But I need to pee."

"We have a bigger problem," I said. "You're trapped in here with a vampire."

Ingrid sat and wrapped her arms around her knees, hugging them into her. "Tell me this isn't you manipulating me?"

"No."

She reached for her cell and stared at the screen. "No signal. Do you think they'll hear us if we scream?"

I shook my head, dazed.

She gave a shrug. "I'm willing to share my deepest fear." She gave me a look of reassurance. "James and I went out to dinner the other night. He ordered us dessert to share. Vanilla ice-cream."

I raised an eyebrow, fascinated with where she was taking this.

"It's not that I don't like vanilla." She shifted her position. "It just suddenly dawned on me that I don't want my *life* to be vanilla." She turned to face me. "Domestic drudgery terrifies me."

Silence ensued filling the small chamber, leaving us quiet with our thoughts.

"I suppose it goes deeper." Ingrid broke the silence again. "My dad was a Sergeant in the Army." She pulled the end of her sleeves over her hands so that only the tips of her fingers were showing. "I got to travel quite a bit. Europe, mostly." Distracted, she examined her fingernails. "My dad got posted to the Middle East. You know, I'm still not quite sure why they call it friendly fire?"

I realized what she was saying. "Your father was shot?"

"He recovered. But then they sent him back. Right into the center of combat. When he returned home from that second tour . . ."

"Post Traumatic Stress?"

She seemed far away.

"Ingrid, how old were you?"

"Thirteen," she murmured.

I followed both Ingrid's thoughts and her words, daring to reach her in that darkest place within but not able to go there.

"Your father took his own life," I whispered, having read her mind, barely able to grasp the fading images.

"I have this reoccurring nightmare that I'm standing at my parent's bedroom door. But I don't go in."

I tried to find the words that might lesson her pain, but there were none.

Her face was flushed with grief. "My dad survived two wars and yet he couldn't survive the one raging inside his head."

"I believe this is Fabian's way of helping us," I said, hoping this was true. "Having us open up to each other like this." I chastised myself for not seeing this coming.

Ingrid wriggled round to face me. "William, go on then, what's your biggest fear?"

Staring straight ahead, I silently begged Fabian not to do this.

Quietness ensued, the small chamber stiflingly still, punishingly claustrophobic. Fabian's answer was evident.

"You can trust me," Ingrid said. "We're in this together, right."

I looked over at her. "Your memory was wiped by Fabian."

"What?"

"You witnessed something unspeakable in the dungeons of St. Michael's Mount. So Fabian removed those memories."

"How?" She looked horrified. "What did I see?"

I rested my head back against the brick, doubting Fabian's method of having me finally reveal to Ingrid who I really was.

XXIV

THE WORDS TUMBLED OUT and I'd almost choked on each one, glancing over at the door, hoping Fabian would end my trial and this terrible fear of losing Ingrid forever.

And by my own hand, no less.

The truth had no choice but to find its way, sparing nothing.

Ingrid's back was pressed up against the far wall. "I don't believe you!"

"It happened at Stonehenge," I continued, trying to get through to her.

"You're lying."

"Afterward, Alex took you back to the Mount. You actually witnessed my transformation."

"I didn't, William."

"Fabian really did wipe your memory." It sounded fantastical, convenient even.

"Stay right there!"

I made a gesture to reassure her I would.

She pressed her hands to her face trying to hide her terror. "There's no Fabian Snowstrom."

"You're holding back something, Ingrid."

"What?"

"If you'd have shared it with me we'd be out of here by now."

She was staring, full of mistrust.

"I know how this sounds," I said. "I don't expect you to believe me."

She slammed her hand against her mouth stopping any further words from spilling.

"I told you Orpheus is dead because I didn't know how to explain *this* to you," I said.

"Please, William, let's leave now."

"I'll do what I can."

The end wall shifted and shoved me forward and I turned round to see it advancing toward us. I pushed up against it trying to slow its advancement.

Ingrid screamed.

"Fabian!" I yelled, pressing my shoulder against the advancing brick.

"Do something!" She reached out, pushing against the wall with me.

The space was closing rapidly.

Ingrid backed up against the end wall and I turned to face her, pressing my body against hers, trying to protect her. "Ingrid . . ." I said. "What's your biggest fear?"

She clutched my forearms realizing. "I want to enter your world and know it completely." She glanced over my shoulder, her eyes wide.

I shook my head. "Ingrid, say it."

"William, my biggest fear is that I'll fall in love with you."

The wall pressed against my back and crushed us together.

She screamed. "I've fallen in love with you!"

The wall stopped.

And then it started its seemingly effortless journey back. Both of us reached out into the freedom of the space that now surrounded us. The wall reached the end of the room and kept on going.

We dashed to our right, quickly entering a larger chamber.

There standing before us was Fabian Snowstrom. "Real freedom is from yourself," he said calmly. "What other entrapment is there?"

"You could have killed us," Ingrid said.

"Fear's more likely to do that," he answered.

"The wall was metaphorical," I said.

"And you overcame it." He pointed to his right. "Powder room."

I gave Ingrid a signal it was safe and watched her head off in that direction.

The low ceiling and fine brickwork gave the place a closed in feeling. At the far end of the chamber were three office chairs positioned to face each other. Next to one of them rested a leather flask.

"The journey back is waiting," Fabian said.

The wall shifted, returning to its original position behind me. I turned to face Fabian again, still unsettled that he'd forced my hand. "Was that really necessary?"

"You were worrying too much about what she'd think of you," he said. "Wasting time, William."

I gave a shrug. "Is it really possible to separate?"

"We believe so," he said.

"How long do I have?"

"The sooner you revert the easier it will be on you in the long run."

"Are we talking weeks, months?"

"Days, hopefully."

I was stunned. "I've yet to find the scrolls."

Fabian glanced in the direction of where Ingrid had disappeared. "That's why you need her."

"I'm not sure getting her any more involved is a good idea."

"That's not up to you."

I hesitated, shocked by his bluntness. "Do you know what's poisoning us?"

He gestured for me to follow him toward the chairs. "We know who it is. But not what. Not yet, anyway."

"Are the Stone Masters responsible?"

"Sovereign. They're poisoning themselves."

I sat on the edge of the chair opposite his. "And Sovereign transfer it to vampires who drink from them."

Ingrid reappeared and Fabian gestured for her to sit with us.

"Why did you want to see me?" Ingrid asked nervously.

"You don't base all of humanity on the sole act of one," Fabian said.

"You're saying not all vampires are bad?" She crossed her legs, getting more comfortable, still shaken.

"Ingrid?" Fabian spoke her name with affection.

She shook her head as though coming out of a daze.

He leaned toward her. "So now you know about William."

"How am I meant to wrap my head around something like that?" she asked. "I don't know who or what to believe anymore."

"The truth always surfaces." He glanced back at me. "William is the balance of the two now."

"Why didn't you tell me?" Ingrid asked me, her frown deepening.

"You wouldn't have believed me," I replied.

She shook her head in disbelief.

"Ingrid, you were with Jadeon just before it happened to him," Fabian said.

Her shoulders slumped. "He told me that, but I . . ."

"You witnessed William's resurrection," he offered. "His formation."

She shook her head again. "Fabian, is it true you wiped my memory?"

"I did." He rose and gestured for her to approach him.

"Why did you do that?" she asked.

"You weren't ready," he replied.

Her brow furrowed. "How did you do it?"

"You were given a little of his blood to drink," I said.

Ingrid slammed her hand to her mouth.

"Quick and painless," Fabian reassured her. "But you're ready now."

"For what?" she asked.

"The knowledge of us," he told her. "Come closer, my dear."

Ingrid glanced my way for support and then took a wary step toward him.

Fabian reached for her left arm and slid up her sleeve, running his fingertips over her brand. "This encircles a birthmark, see?"

Ingrid peered closer.

"This circle with a small dot in the middle symbolizes a circumpunct," Fabian continued. "The balance of female and male energy. William marked you his equal." Fabian kept his attention on her. "Balance is sacred." His forefinger circled.

Ingrid's frown softened.

"Change. We fear it but cannot live without it," said Fabian.

"Why did you put us through that?" She pointed back toward the small chamber.

"To help you face your fear," he explained.

"Of falling in love?" she murmured, shaking her head, realizing. "That's . . ."

"Tragic," Fabian finished her words. "Let me ask you this—" He placed his thumb on her forehead and pressed in-between her eyebrows. "Do you want to know?"

"Know?" she asked.

"The night your father died," he said.

"I don't understand," she murmured.

"You went in, Ingrid." Fabian pressed harder.

She looked puzzled. "No I didn't."

"Oh but you did," Fabian said. "And we need to get that little girl out of there."

I stood up, daring to defy the ancient who was about to push

Ingrid too far.

Fabian detected my reticence but kept his attention on her. "The memory is repressed. If she can't see it, William, neither can you."

"What happened inside that room?" I asked.

"Shall we see?" asked Fabian.

Ingrid gave a subtle nod, not really understanding what she was consenting to. Fabian closed his eyes and pushed harder.

Ingrid's mouth gaped, her jaw slackened, her eyes glazing over as though Fabian had sent a jolt of energy right into her frontal lobe.

Something crashed.

Glass.

A thirteen-year-old girl standing before a closed door that towered over her. Her small hand resting on the doorknob.

"Turn it," came Fabian's voice.

On the other side of the door was a man dangling in the center of the room from an open attic. He was strangled. The chair kicked from beneath him, tipped over. A family photo smashed into pieces.

A thirteen-year-old Ingrid turned to see Fabian standing there in the corner. He gave a supportive gesture for her to continue . . .

Searching for the scissors she knew her mother kept in one of the upper linen drawers, Ingrid's hands shook as she reached in and pulled them out, guilt ridden for disobeying her mother for even touching them. Righting the chair that had fallen, she stepped up onto it and reached for the rope around her father's neck, cutting furiously . . .

"He's already dead, Ingrid," Fabian said softly.

The scissors fell.

All this time Ingrid had suppressed this memory, never once facing her childhood pain, never standing still, perhaps unconsciously afraid it might one day find her. And it had, in the form of the underworld, in an altogether different kind of pain promising to drown out her torment.

With her small hand in his, Fabian led her out, pausing in the doorway, allowing her a moment to glance back and see that the room was now empty.

Ingrid broke away and staggered back, finding her footing, spinning awkwardly as though expecting to find herself in her childhood home.

The spell broke.

Ingrid let out a sob.

"It's over now," Fabian said, trying to comfort her.

Ingrid's tears stained her cheeks. "All this time I didn't think . . ."

I wrapped my arms around her, kissing her forehead again and again until she calmed. "You did everything you could," I whispered.

Fabian picked up the flask, unscrewed the lid and poured a light brown liquid into it. He handed Ingrid the cup.

She took it and sniffed the contents.

"Tea." Fabian gestured we were to sit again.

Something told me Fabian had put some thought into our meeting.

He pointed upward. "How was the London Bridge Tour?"

"We missed most of it," I said, taken with how swiftly he'd moved on, and glanced over to check on Ingrid.

"But not the important stuff," Fabian continued. "Boudicca, Queen of the Celts."

Ingrid sipped her drink; steam wafting.

"History, isn't it intriguing?" Fabian directed the question to Ingrid. "Everything we do has a consequence." He waved his hand through the air. "Better now?"

"Better," she replied, though she was still clearly fazed.

Fabian's face crinkled into a smile.

"Why did you leave after I was transformed?" I asked the question that had been burning a hole in my heart.

"Jadeon knows why," he said. "Look deep within you and all questions will have the answers you seek."

I sat back, sure I'd never know.

Ingrid was staring at me, searching for any evidence that I was indeed the Jadeon she'd once known, desperately trying to grasp an impossible concept.

"Jadeon was to become the next Stone Master," Fabian continued. "Before Orpheus turned him."

"That was a long time ago." I glanced at Ingrid, uncomfortable to discuss this in front of her, and not even sure she was up to it.

Ingrid leaned forward, intrigued.

"Jadeon never did study our origins," Fabian said. "All those books of your father's and you never read them."

Fabian's words reached some part of me that had seemingly lain dormant.

"Boudicca was the first Stone Master," Fabian said. "The first Stone Master was not only a woman but also a vampire."

"Boudicca was a vampire?" Ingrid asked, "But I thought the Stone Masters were vampire hunters?"

"Vampires were once ruled by a joint alliance of immortals and mortals," he said.

"This is documented?" I now knew why Fabian wanted to meet us here.

"Boudicca's husband Prasutagus was mortal," he said. "Together they ruled the underworld."

"An allegiance between vampires and mortals?" I tried to fathom it.

"Until Boudicca led an uprising against the Roman Empire," Fabian explained. "She died in battle. Her husband inherited the title. After that only men became Stone Masters."

I sat back, astonished.

"Much has changed." Fabian waved a finger. "Within the last fifty years the Stone Masters have struggled to control Sovereign."

"Who are Sovereign exactly?" I stood, too restless to remain seated.

"Guardians," he said, "of Dominion." He held my gaze. "They guarded the one destined to become the grand ruler of the Stone Masters."

I was amazed I'd never heard of this until now.

Fabian made a gesture that he understood my reticence, but nevertheless turned to Ingrid. "That secret society you payed a visit to in London is Sovereign. They were once members of Stone Masters. Sovereign's new directive is to wipe out every last vampire."

"How?" Ingrid asked.

"They're poisoning them," I told her. "Rendering them confused."

Ingrid looked horrified.

"Vampires wander into daylight," I said, gravely.

"The Stone Masters need Dominion to take back control." Fabian offered a reassuring smile. "He will stop this annihilation of our kind."

"That's why the Stone Masters severed their allegiance?" I realized. "They disagreed with Sovereign on how to manage the vampires."

"The Stone Masters are ready to return to joint rule," Fabian said. "Vampires and mortals governing together."

"I need those scrolls," I said.

Fabian looked solemn. "Sovereign has them now, I'm afraid. Several years ago they raided the Stone Masters library and stole them."

"Any idea where they may be keeping them?" I asked.

"None," said Fabian.

"I'm having a hard time putting the pieces together," Ingrid admitted.

"That's because a piece is missing," Fabian said.

"We need Dominion," I said. "Where do we find him?"

Fabian lowered his gaze. "I'm afraid there's an issue even more pressing."

Ingrid caught our interaction.

Fabian gave her a sympathetic look. "I'm afraid your friend Blake has been poisoned."

Ingrid became panicked and leapt to her feet.

Fabian rose. "He's safe at the Mount. Alex is watching over him."

"Is there a cure?" her voice sounded frail.

"The poison eventually dissipates," Fabian said. "Metabolizes. Though until then, if left unobserved the vampire forgets the threat of daylight."

"Fabian, can you return my memory?" She glanced my way. "I want to help but I can't do it unless my memory's restored."

"I'll allow it." Fabian appeared thoughtful. "William, she imbibes an abundance, less than needed to turn her, but enough to kindle her. And then you keep her awake."

Ingrid's face flushed with excitement. "Will it be returned completely?"

Fabian's full attention stayed on me. "Maintenez arousal sensuel continu."

"Was that French?" Ingrid asked.

I sighed, and gave her a look of the obvious.

She blushed wildly, realizing.

"Both of you can discuss this later, perhaps?" Fabian said. "Your first step of this journey should be taken at the Mount." Fabian strolled away, nearing the far corner.

"What does that mean, exactly?" I asked.

"Keep Dominion safe." Fabian paused and peered back to me. "The truth will out."

XXV

THE NIGHT AIR CHILLED my bones, and I turned my attention to the cloudy night sky, banishing the moon if only for a moment.

Waiting for Ingrid on the castle roof, I stared out over the ocean admiring the way Marazion's city reflected bursts of light off its surface. The Mount felt like home again, and this once stagnant melancholy was now lifting. Though I still didn't feel ready to take on that which seemed cruelly daunting.

Sensing Ingrid's approach I continued to direct my attention toward the horizon, not quite ready to see what she might convey.

Standing side by side with nothing but the sound of the rolling waves caressing the shoreline, Ingrid and I shared a moment of calm and eventually she snuggled against me. I wrapped my arm around her, feeling her warmth as she relaxed.

"Jadeon," she whispered at last, squeezing me tighter.

I realized I'd been holding my breath.

"How does drinking your blood help me get my memory back?" She looked up at me.

"Apparently for a mortal," I began, "blending imbibed blood with your augmented arousal initiates a biochemical reaction, and a transformation naturally induces a heightened state of awareness."

"And afterward I'll remember everything?"

I gave a reluctant smile.

She sucked on her bottom lip, her gaze drifting.

Affectionately I rubbed her back. "How about you just believe everything I've told you?"

She gave what looked like an unconvincing nod. "I've been trying to work out who's the dominant one." She lifted her head away from my chest and peered up. "Orpheus had a penchant for terrorizing people." She watched me carefully.

"Jadeon's tamed the dragon."

"I can see that." She took my hand. "Do you really believe those ancient scrolls hold the key to reversing this?"

"They're my only hope, apparently."

"I'll help you find them."

I squeezed her hand, wanting to tell her that through her strength I was finding mine. Though facing death terrified me, virtually incapacitating me from finding my way back.

She turned to see my face clearly. "How does it feel?"

"I've almost managed to still these clashing thoughts. I feel normal." I gave a shrug. "Perhaps normal isn't right. Centered." I searched for the words. "It feels like William was always here."

"I wish you'd have told me who you really are, William."

"There were so many times I wanted to." I shook my head. "You still doubt it, even now." I gave her a nudge. "Can't blame you."

She gazed out over the ocean. "On more than one occasion I'd have sworn I caught sight of Jadeon in your eyes." She shook her head.

"I'm sorry for everything I've put you through."

"You've been strong for me. Now it's my turn."

I went to answer but was too choked up to let the words find their freedom.

"Your friends adore you," she said, "so you must be doing something right."

I coughed, clearing the emotion from my throat. "Trusting the word of a vampire?" I pulled a face. "Foolish at best."

She softened as though her thoughts had returned to those last few hours we'd shared.

"You take my breath away, Ingrid Jansen." I reached just below her right eye using my thumb to wipe away smudged mascara. "I'm grateful you're hanging in there with me."

Marcus strolled toward us and stopped short a few feet away as though trying to judge whether he'd interrupted something.

"Marcus," I said, warmly inviting him to join us.

"Nice evening," he responded.

"Small talk?" Ingrid asked. "So unlike you."

"Glad to see we're all still friends." He raised an eyebrow.

"Your actions don't go unnoticed." She pointed at him. "One misstep . . ."

Marcus shrugged. "Look, we all want the same thing. Let's get over our differences and work together."

"Don't ever leave me alone with him," Ingrid whispered to me.

Marcus was evidently amused by her remark. "Right then, everyone's gathered." He tucked his hands into his pockets. "Alex, Sebastian and Anaïs."

"Can I see Blake?" Ingrid asked. "How is he?"

"Doing well," Marcus said. "Alex has him set up in his bedroom. The windows are already blacked out. Just a warning, we keep the door locked. With Blake's consent of course."

I quickly added, "If he becomes confused it'll prevent him from wandering out of the castle."

"Blake's excited to see you, Ingrid," Marcus said. "Go easy on him, okay?"

"Of course," she said.

Marcus stepped closer. "William, we've come up with a plan."

"Let's hear it," I said.

"We find Dominion, and hopefully he'll help us find Sovereign. We get the scrolls and give them to Lucas to do his thing."

"Sounds simple enough." I gave a crooked smile.

"What if I go back to Sovereign," Ingrid said. "Persuade Alistair to tell us where the library is?"

"I'll consider it," I said.

Ingrid turned to Marcus. "Fabian told us we'd find clues here."

"That was generous of Fabian." Marcus shook his head. "I'll meet you downstairs."

Ingrid watched him walk away.

"Are you sure you can trust him?" she asked.

"Marcus is a loyal friend," I replied.

She let my hand go. "Orpheus's friend."

I resisted the urge to turn away, not wanting her to see my darker side.

"Jadeon, I'm going to save you." She gave my sleeve a tug of reassurance.

With my arm wrapped around her waist, I guided her toward the stairwell.

"I'm so relieved you're alive," she said.

This probably wasn't the right time to tell her that I was having second thoughts about going back. Until now death had never been on the agenda, for me anyway. Together, we made our way along the sweeping corridors.

"I'm sorry about your father, Ingrid," I said.

She wrapped her arm around my waist and hugged me closer. Even though her grief still lingered, there was the subtlest shift in her presence, a promise of resolution for a lifetime of being weighed down by guilt. And I caught a brief glimpse of Ingrid's authentic nature, the tranquility of her femininity surfacing.

We soon found Blake lying on Alex's bed and he was reading the *Daily Express* newspaper. Ingrid hesitated in the doorway, preparing to see him for the first time as a vampire.

She rallied the courage to go in and rested on the edge of his bed, reaching for Blake's hand and kissing it.

"Hey you," he said, shoving the paper to the side and straightening his back up against the oak headboard. "Well, what do you think?"

"You look the same," Ingrid said. "Paler perhaps. Can I get you anything?"

He shook his head. "How long can you stay?"

"As long as I'm needed," she said.

"Ironic isn't it?" Blake said. "I become a vampire to cure myself from an incurable disease, and then go and get poisoned." He gestured toward the blacked out window. "I'm meant to be out there somewhere, wearing leather pants and jumping off roofs."

Ingrid suppressed a smile. "I'm not going to stop until I find the answers."

"I'm so sorry I messed up," he said.

I waved off his remark.

"Do you remember who you bit?" Ingrid asked. "We're thinking the poison came from members of a group called Sovereign."

"They're purposefully ingesting poison," I explained.

Blake cringed. "It was a bit of a crazy night. I went out on the town with Marcus's friend Zachary. Though he's fine. No one got hurt, honest. I can promise you that. Zachary was teaching me the art of the *little sup* technique."

"Meaning no one died," I said for him.

"I get it," she said.

"Zachary and I went bar hopping in SoHo," Blake added. "We were kind of wild." He ran his fingers through his hair nervously.

"Well, let me know if you remember anything that you think might be relevant." She looked over at me. "Does Blake know?"

"About me?" I asked. "Yes. Everyone does now."

"William met with me, Sebastian and Anaïs earlier," Blake explained, "and dropped the bombshell about what really happened to him."

"How's everyone taking it?" I asked.

"Pretty well," Blake said, "though Sebastian's having a hard time with it."

"Me too," Ingrid said.

"William's been nothing but amazing," Blake told her. "It's important you know that."

"He's helping me too." She turned her head toward me. "In so many ways." Ingrid's deep brown eyes held mine. "You always did remind me of Jadeon. I just couldn't shake that feeling."

Blake scrunched up his nose, gesturing his unspoken thoughts.

"I know," Ingrid said, picking up on them, "Orpheus is in there too."

"Great vote of confidence." I folded my arms. "For the record I feel like me, whatever that means."

Ingrid turned back to Blake. "Can I get you anything?"

"You've already asked me that," he said, "and the answer's still no."

"He can't stay locked up in here all day," Ingrid said.

"We need to keep track of him," I said.

She frowned. "This room is so bare it'll drive him crazy."

"I'm here!" Blake waved his hand and beamed a cheeky smile. "I could cut the sexual tension with a knife."

I shook my head, quietly amused.

"So what now?" Blake asked, as though changing the subject would undo his last words.

"We're all going to be working on this," she said. "We have our work cut out, but nothing we can't handle."

"Isn't Vanderbilt hounding you?" Blake asked.

"I've taken some personal days," she said. "He seems okay with it."

"Must be his imminent promotion keeping him happy." He winked her way. "We're lucky to have you, Ingrid." He glanced over at the chessboard, the pieces set in their opening positions. "Tell Alex to prepare to be conquered."

Ingrid kissed his forehead. "You're family, you know that."

He scooched down the bed and pulled the blankets up and over his head, his voice muffled from underneath. "Go find those bastards who are doing this, and stop being so uncharacteristically sensitive."

Ingrid feigned being offended, resting her hands on her hips, smiling affectionately at Blake who was still hidden beneath the bedspread.

"Let's join the others," I mouthed.

She stared off at nothing, her thoughts seemingly racing. "How's Alex going to react when he sees me?"

"He'll be fine," I said. "I've had a long chat with him."

"I'm going to hang out here for a while." Ingrid sat again. "Just need to gather my thoughts." She reached for Blake's hand and pulled it from beneath the sheets.

Even my unspoken words felt out of place.

Blake reappeared from beneath the sheets. "Can I have my hand back before you break it?"

She cringed. "Sorry."

I left and gave them the privacy they needed.

Within minutes of entering the library, I was met by a worrisome Alex who seemed as equally anxious about being in the same room as Ingrid as she was with him.

Sebastian, Marcus and Anaïs were riveted, waiting for me to answer his question.

I said at last, "Yes, Alex, we can trust Ingrid."

The table was stacked high with books, some opened at random pages, some waiting their turn to be read or follow in the same fate as others and become discarded and thrown to the floor.

I picked up one of them, reluctant to step over it. "Careful, some of these are antiques."

"There's more at stake than your beloved library," Marcus said.

"Jadeon's library," Alex mumbled.

I peered down at the table, wondering how long it would take for us to read all of them.

"Ingrid's agreed to help us?" Anaïs asked, raising an eyebrow.

"How do you know she won't use everything she learns against us?" Alex asked.

"Because I do," I said flatly.

"She's invested in helping Blake," Marcus reassured Alex.

"That's great!" Sebastian opened his hands. "Isn't it?"

"Are we still friends?" I asked Sebastian.

He changed his stance. "Is there anything else you're keeping from me? I mean, it's hard to keep up with all your fanciful secrets, William."

"I've told you everything, Seb, you have my word." I addressed the others. "We all proceed with complete honesty from here on in, understand?" I put down the book and reached for another. "Any mention of Dominion in any of these?"

"None," Anaïs answered.

"What if Fabian is Dominion?" Marcus shook his head.

"He's not," I said. "Apparently Dominion was in his twenties when turned. Fabian insisted the answers could be found here."

"No other clue than that?" Alex asked, astonished. "Why is

Fabian always so elusive?"

Sebastian asked the obvious question. "Why doesn't Fabian find Dominion?"

"He's asked us to," I said.

Ingrid entered and headed straight toward us. "What've you got so far?"

"Books," Marcus said. "A library full."

"I've got a feeling we won't find the answer here." She rested her fingers on her mouth, thinking. "What about those books in the anteroom?"

"How do you know about those?" Alex asked.

"They're just religious text," I said.

Ingrid's brow furrowed. "Wouldn't a secret society have a safe place to keep their prized documents?"

"I've lived in this castle for over two hundred years," Alex said. "I know every inch, intimately."

"Jadeon told me that the Mount has a number of secret staircases," Ingrid said.

On Alex's nervous glance I said, "Didn't show them to you though."

"Bet I could find them." Ingrid grinned.

Marcus snapped his head round to look at Alex and smiled his way. "Inside voice, Alex."

Alex shrugged. "I was merely going to suggest we stop wasting time."

Ingrid moved over to the large bookcase to our left. "What's behind there?"

"A wall," Alex said.

"And you know that for sure?" Ingrid asked.

Marcus and Alex heaved the bookcase forward, their supernatural strength making easy work of it.

Alex peered behind. "Well, look at that!"

Ingrid peered at him suspiciously.

"A wall," he said.

Sebastian reached for one of the books on the table. "We have to split up the rest of these."

"Why not just go after Sovereign?" Anaïs asked.

"We must find Dominion first," Marcus said. "That's our priority."

"Dominion will bring down Sovereign," I added. "Fabian's confirmed they're responsible for the poisonings."

Ingrid strolled over toward the bookcase and peeked behind it.

Marcus sat on the edge of the table. "I'll use the network to send word out we're looking for Dominion."

"Slow down," I said, "We don't want to send him underground."

"I've gathered all the books I considered relevant." Sebastian leaned over the table. "One hundred, give or take. That's twenty each." He started stacking them into five piles.

Ingrid knelt close to a canvas leaning against the wall and turned it round, dusting it off. It was one of my discarded paintings of Alex that I'd never finished. Alex had become bored posing for it and walked off halfway through a sitting. I'd never found the time to revisit the canvas.

"Where are the other secret tunnels?" Anaïs sounded excited. "I'd love check out those."

"Privileged information." I winked at Alex.

Ingrid approached him. "You look just like your mother." She raised an eyebrow. "Jadeon just like his father, but neither of you have his temperament."

"Jadeon told you that?" Alex asked.

"He did." Ingrid's face lit up.

"Go on Ingrid," Marcus said. "I know you're dying to tell us."

"Lord William Artimas must have had a contingency plan. In the only way the Master of a secret society can." Ingrid headed out of the library.

We followed her into the foyer toward the east corridor leading toward the dungeons.

She paused halfway and stared up at a portrait of the late Lord William Artimas. The artist, Italian painter Alberti Garbodar who'd been commissioned to paint this great nobleman, had done an exemplary job using tempura and oil on wood to capture his intensity; the weight of his responsibilities skillfully etched into the lines of his face. Lord Artimas's posture was proud, his left hand casually but somewhat awkwardly resting on the long armrest, his forefinger pointing to the floor.

"That's your father?" Anaïs put her arm through Alex's. "Scary looking."

"You have no idea," he said.

I nudged up toward Ingrid. "His pose?"

"Maybe Artimas was trying to get a message to you," she said. "Perhaps just in case he died before he passed on his legacy?"

"We didn't catch it," I admitted.

"We didn't like looking at him," Alex said.

"Where did this painting originally hang?" Ingrid asked.

"It's been here for decades." Alex leaned in. "Before that the anteroom."

An uncomfortable quiet ensued as Lord Artimas's steely-eyes judged us from the portrait.

"Really does look like he's pointing to the floor," Anaïs said softly. "What's the insignia on his ring?"

"The Stone Masters crest." I lifted the painting off the wall and carried it toward the anteroom.

The others followed, all as eager as me to see if our hunch was right.

Alex was particularly pensive.

"I'm not planning on arresting you, Alex," Ingrid said, catching his trepidation. "I'm concentrating on helping both Blake and William now."

"Why the change of heart?" Alex asked her suspiciously.

"William's convinced me you had nothing to do with those girls' deaths," she said.

"And you believe him?" Alex asked, surprised he was off the hook.

"Yes, I really do," she said. "Now, can we be friends?"

"No," Alex said bluntly.

Marcus pointed to Alex. "Don't worry about him, he has father issues."

"Lord Artimas threatened to slit my horse's throat." Alex clenched his teeth, remembering. "And there was nothing wrong with her."

"Seriously, Alex," Marcus said, "that was two hundred years ago. Is that the average time you hold onto a grudge?"

"He was also ready to bleed me to death. Mustn't forget that."

Anaïs cringed. "That kind of stuff stays with you."

The anteroom hadn't changed in two hundred years, and by the looks of things neither had the dust. Marcus and I knelt before the fireplace and unraveled the worn rug back into the room. Dust powdered up.

"We renovated some of the castle but never touched this room," I said, balancing the painting on one of the four high-backed armchairs.

"Because no one ever came in here," Alex said.

"Which tile do you think Artimas is pointing at?" Ingrid asked.

I lifted up one of the chairs and placed it in the exact position as the one in the portrait, aligning the background fireplace in the painting exactly with the one in the room.

Kneeling, I examined the tiles. After my third attempt one of them gave and I lifted it out. Sliding my fingers into the hole I felt something hard and grabbed hold of it, removing a small metal box.

Everyone gathered around to watch me open it.

Inside lay a large, rusty key.

A flash of inspiration came over me and I headed out of the room, making my way back along the corridor. Taking two steps at time I descended into the dungeons.

I burst into the torture chamber.

Footsteps approached, signaling the others were right behind and Marcus, Alex, Anaïs, Ingrid and Sebastian flooded in to join me.

Sebastian was holding the halogen lamp he'd grabbed from the stairwell. It threw shadows around us.

"I was eighteen the first time I came into this room." I turned around. "Followed my father Lord Artimas down here. By the time I got in here, he'd gone."

"Jadeon's perspective," Marcus said, studying me.

They immediately went to work, Sebastian taking the far wall, Alex the left, and Marcus the right. Anaïs examined the table top.

Ingrid went for the table too, kneeling low beside one of the four table legs. "If I know one thing it's blood stains." She pointed. "See how this one's trickled beneath this tile?" Ingrid's smile of exhilaration beamed back at me.

"What were they doing in here?" Anaïs glanced up at me.

I swapped a wary glance with Alex.

Ingrid ran her hand up the table leg. "Looks like this is the mechanism."

Marcus leaned in beside her and twisted the upper rounded edges in the opposite direction of each other.

Upon the floor, stone scraped along stone as a central panel rose up several inches and slid outward revealing a winding stairway twisting into the darkness.

"Maybe we don't want to know where this leads," Alex said.

"Aren't you intrigued?" Anaïs asked. "Who's going first?"

"That'll be you, Anaïs," Marcus said. "Just in case there's a death trap."

She rolled her eyes. "What do you think is down there?"

I ducked under the table and eased myself into the square entryway. "Only one way to find out."

"Here you go." Sebastian held up the halogen light.

"Um. We can see in the dark," Anaïs said. "We don't really need that."

Sebastian lowered his arm. "Oh."

"Wait here," Marcus told Ingrid and Anaïs. "You too Sebastian."

"Why?" Anaïs asked.

"Just in case," he insisted.

"If you're not back in five minutes—" Ingrid spread out her fingers— "we're coming after you."

Marcus threw her a smile. "Now I really feel safe."

Alex, Marcus and I descended into blackness.

XXVI

IN SILENCE ALEX, Marcus and I descended further.

The secret stairway continued endlessly, spiraling into the earth. My thoughts drifted back to the chamber we'd just come from, where Ingrid, Anaïs and Sebastian were waiting for us.

Within that room two hundred years ago the Stone Masters had held their so-called sacred ceremonies, torturing vampires before transporting them to Salisbury for their final punishment. Death by daylight, a cruel and terrible condemnation for merely being different.

I hoped I'd have the courage to face whatever lay ahead.

Alex's footfalls paused a little way behind me. "Orpheus murdered my father."

I too stopped and glanced back down at the steps yet to be discovered. "You're bringing this up now?"

"Alex, I thought you hated your father?" Marcus's mouth twitched and he seemed to regret saying it.

"Lord Artimas, your father, was a Stone Master," I reasoned. "He hunted vampires."

"This feels wrong," Alex said.

"We're just taking a look," I said. "Perhaps there's a chance that whatever's in that room can help us find Dominion."

"Alex?" Marcus studied him. "What's going on?"

"I'm not sure if I want to know what's down there." He leaned against the wall.

"We're here with you," I said. "You don't have to face it alone."

"I found a stack of letters from father," Alex explained. "Missives between mother and him. In them he expressed his disappointment in me."

Marcus motioned for me to answer.

I let out a long sigh. "I was the one who was destined to carry on the family tradition," I said. "Become the next Stone Master. I was the disappointment. Not you."

Marcus shrugged and then on my subtle glance of disapproval at him, he turned back to Alex. "You don't have to come."

Alex shifted his footing as though taking his time to think it through.

"Demons are meant to be faced," I said.

Alex shook off his reluctance and slid past Marcus, pressing his back against the wall to squeeze past me.

"*He still doesn't trust us*," I mouthed to Marcus.

Marcus patted my right arm and headed after Alex.

The lower we trekked below sea level the lower the temperature fell. The stairwell curved to our right and we soon reached the last step.

Before us rose a wide oak double door, upon which was a faded painting of a winged Saint Michael the Archangel artfully portrayed across it. Michael's presence was serene, majestic even, his gaze averted as though he too shared the secret of what lay beyond.

"The prince of light." I ran my fingertips over Michael's wings. "Leader of the forces of God against the darkness of evil."

"And we're the evil," Alex murmured.

"Take a breath, Alex," Marcus said and tried the handle.

The door was locked.

I reached into my pocket and removed the large key we'd just found, and slid it into the lock and turned it.

Alex nudged up against me. "What if everything in this room is just an affirmation of how much father hated us?"

"What if it's not?" I said. "Alex, I will never let anything happen to you."

He gave a reluctant gesture he was ready.

I clutched the brass circled handles, pulling the doors open with a shuddering creak.

A gust of cold air burst forth and puffs of dust danced around us; the scent of incense and stale wax wafted. All three of us took a moment for our eyes to adjust to what lay ahead.

We stepped back in time . . .

The expansive cathedral opened up before us with its high vaulted ceiling inlaid with intricate frescos, dramatic scenes portraying the Book of Genesis featuring the creation of Adam at its center. The marble flooring appeared flawless, seemingly never caressed by time, decorated with ancient symbols, some of which I recognized as emblems used by the Stone Masters. Dark green and gold baroque volutes kissed the walls bestowing a Romanesque air and a rare supremacy, making it difficult to guess its age.

We strolled down the central isle with carved pillars looming on each side of us, guiding our way.

Majestically rising out of the floor where one would expect to see an altar was a solitary fifteen-foot high standing-stone, reaching reverently toward the golden leafed ceiling dripping honeyed tinges of light down upon it.

It was as though a stone had been plucked out of Stonehenge and was now resting here.

Marcus nudged my right arm. "How the hell did they get that—"

"Down here?" Alex shook his head in disbelief.

"It must weigh at least four tons," Marcus said.

"They built the castle around it." I saw this as the only reasonable explanation.

"Do you think it was dragged all the way from Stonehenge?" Marcus asked.

"Perhaps." Taking the three short steps toward the enormous granite Goddess, the room seemed to disappear. I rested my hands against the rock and closed my eyes, caressing her coldness, her perfect irregularities as though reacquainting; my long sigh finding its way back to me as if the stone itself had sighed in response to my touch.

Silence soaked into my very bones.

When my trance eventually dissipated and the room found me again, I was greeted with confused expressions from Marcus and Alex who were staring at me.

"Isn't she magnificent?" I asked, unable to comprehend their lack of emotion at being in her presence. I stepped back, once more admiring the megalith.

A ray of light flashed across us.

Ingrid was sweeping her pocket-flashlight our way and Anaïs and Sebastian were close behind her. Sebastian was clutching the halogen lamp as though his life depended on it.

Ingrid climbed the three steps toward the stone, her face a mixture of excitement and awe. "What a remarkable contradiction," she said. "All this opulence and then this."

"Do you think they performed ceremonies down here?" Alex asked.

"I can see them worshipping the stone," Sebastian offered.

My fingers caressed the megalith again, sweeping down and along her base. "There's a room below." I turned and examined the area behind the stone, fingering the eight wooden panels on the back wall.

"How did you know to look for that?" Alex asked.

"I'll show you." I tapped the panels until one of them gave.

A doorway opened up before us. The thin corridor led us down further. Ingrid threw me a look of excitement, seemingly thrilled to be sharing this adventure. At the end of the stairwell were simple wooden doors so ancient I feared they'd crumble if touched. Gently I turned the handles and eased the doorway open.

The walls of the small chamber threw off a dark blue hue.

There, at the end of the room was the base of the enormous megalith we'd seen above, the other half of it disappearing into the ceiling. Positioned in front of the stone was a long marble sarcophagus.

Reverently, we entered.

Alex approached the marble sarcophagus and ran his fingers over the limestone lid upon which was inscribed with the name *Guardian*, and just above it was engraved a circle of golden leaves in the shape of a Celtic crown.

"Do you think Dominion's in there?" Anaïs whispered, her eyes wide in wonder.

"Let's find out, shall we?" Marcus asked me.

Alex, Marcus and I approached the tomb and all three of us took a side, sliding the slab across the base, the sound echoing around us. An open onyx coffin lay within.

"William?" Ingrid's whisper brought me back into the room.

I shook my head, gesturing the coffin was empty.

Ingrid knelt before the front of the sarcophagus. "William, what does it say?"

I joined her. "Dominatio's Tomb." I explored the rest of the inscription.

Alex came closer, he too reading the Latin. "According to this, Sovereign were once monks sanctioned by the Stone Masters to guard over Dominatio."

"Dominatio is Latin for Dominion." I rose and strolled over toward the base of the megalith, resting my hand on her. "This is the guardian stone."

"Do you think father knew who Dominion was?" Alex asked.

"Perhaps," I said.

"Look at this." Ingrid pointed to the other end of the tomb.

I strolled around to join her and together we studied the engraving of what appeared to be a ritual at Stonehenge, where seven monks surrounded the central stone.

"A vampire on the altar," I said, trying to make out why he wasn't restrained. More striking still, two of the monks were kneeling at either side of Dominion, each drinking from his wrists. "Dominion is willingly feeding them," I said, amazed. "He's crowned with the same Celtic wreath engraved on the lid." And then I realized. "They're worshiping him."

"Worshiping Dominion," Ingrid agreed.

"Why?" Marcus asked.

"I thought Sovereign hunted vampires?" Anaïs said.

"Maybe he was special in some way," Ingrid offered.

"But why would Sovereign now want him dead?" I pondered on their change of heart.

Ingrid leaned precariously over the edge of the coffin, examining something she'd seen inside. She wiggled back up and pretended to be fascinated with the side of the tomb again. She dropped whatever it was she'd found into her pocket.

I gestured to the engraved Stonehenge scene on the tomb. "Look at the monks' expressions."

"They're all tranced out," Marcus agreed.

"That's bliss." I ran my fingertips over their faces, tracing their rapture. "The monks are high from drinking blood. Only the Stone Master himself is permitted to drink, but if you're a member of Sovereign, it's permitted."

"To motivate members of the Stone Masters to transfer over to Sovereign," Ingrid suggested.

"And keep them loyal," I added.

"Something happened for them to change their mind," Marcus said, "and turn on Dominion."

"And turn on the Stone Masters," Ingrid agreed.

"They found out about the Stone Masters' plan to initiate joint reign," I sensed this as the only explanation. "Vampires and mortals ruling together. Dominion went from deity to threat. Maybe they hated the idea of him ruling them."

All of us stared at the empty sarcophagus, fearing the worst.

"Do you think they killed him?" Anaïs bravely whispered the words we were all thinking.

"Fabian would know that," Alex said. "Wouldn't he?"

I wanted to believe that. "Perhaps we'll find more answers in London." I pointed to Anaïs and Sebastian. "I need you to search every corner of this place. See if you find anything else." I threw Alex a glance that he was to assist them.

"You're not planning on going back to Sovereign?" Marcus asked nervously.

"Ingrid, up for a trip to London?" I asked her.

Marcus approached and steered me into the corner, lowering his voice to a whisper. "It's too dangerous. Remember what Jacob told us about them?"

"I'm not going alone," I said.

Marcus shook his head. "I'll come with you."

"I need you to get word out to every vampire," I told him. "Warn them."

Marcus shook his head. "I wish we could just get those scrolls and get this over with."

"Sovereign once watched over Dominion," I said. "They must know something."

"You're sure you can handle them?" he asked.

I opened my hands and then closed them into fists, gesturing. "Once we have what we need, I'm going to annihilate the bastards."

"I'll miss you, you know." Marcus glanced over at the others. "When you revert back to Orpheus."

I stopped my flow of thoughts, afraid they'd reach him.

Marcus frowned having already caught every last one. He grabbed my forearm with an ironclad grip.

"Not now, Marcus," I whispered.

He blinked in astonishment and said, "Tell me you haven't changed your mind about separating?"

"I need you to find Jacob," I said, "find out if he's come up with anything. And check on Catherine. Tell her . . ." Yet the words wouldn't come.

Marcus's intense focus was burned through me. "Why did you react like that to the stone?" he sounded fierce.

"She's familiar . . ." I tried to remember why.

Marcus frowned, his gaze falling on the megalith and lingering there suspiciously.

I turned to Ingrid. "Ready?"

Ingrid removed a notebook out of her handbag. "We found this in Alistair's briefcase at Sovereign." She offered it to Alex. "It's blank but I bet there's something written in there."

"And why are you giving it to me?" Alex asked.

"I know you'll be able to find out if there's anything written in it," Ingrid said. "I doubt it's blank." She glanced over at Anaïs. "You'll help him?"

"We'll take a look at it," Anaïs said.

Alex softened and he accepted the book from Ingrid.

"Take care everyone," I said. "I'm counting on you."

Marcus was desperately trying to hide his alarm from the others. "Don't do this to me, William," he said. "We agreed."

"Nothing's decided," I said.

Marcus gripped my shoulder. "You want to look like Paradom, is that it?"

"Is everything okay?" Sebastian called over to us.

"Oh yes," I said, casually easing Marcus's hand off. "We were just discussing where to go from here." I turned to face them. "Marcus is in charge. He'll guide you. Everyone alright with that?"

Alex gave a signal of acknowledgment, though I doubted he meant it.

I gave Marcus's arm a pat. "Keep Sebastian safe."

Ingrid headed toward the door.

I followed her out, feeling Marcus's stare locked on me until I was out of his sight.

XXVII

INGRID AND I TOOK a moment of shelter beneath the park trees.

I nudged her up against a tall cedar, avoiding the low lying branches, making sure we were out of Alistair's line of sight.

He was heading toward the northeastern corner of Ravenscourt Park.

We seemed to be the only ones taking the night air in this twenty acre garden located in the London borough of Hammersmith, and it wasn't surprising considering the late hour.

We'd spent twenty minutes in her Rover, parked opposite Sovereign's HQ, trying to agree on the best way to enter the building. When Alistair had exited via the front door, heading off down Sloan Street, we'd both breathed a sigh of relief and set off on foot after him.

Within the hour he'd led us to Ravenscourt Park.

"Ingrid," I whispered, "you weren't in the room when I demanded the utmost truth from the others."

She twisted her lips, showing her guilt.

I leaned toward her and slid my right hand into her coat pocket. She cringed.

I removed the small object. "You extracted this from Dominion's tomb." I rolled it between my fingers, studying the engraved symbol on the cufflink. "A pictogram."

"I was going to show it to you." She looked sheepish. "My methods are a little guarded, I admit."

"We're working together. Let's not forgot that." I glanced off toward Alistair.

She followed my gaze. "He's just standing there. Do you think he's waiting for someone?"

Sensing danger though unable to define why, I tried to reach into his mind. He'd shut down his thoughts.

Ingrid pointed to the cufflink. "What do you think that symbol represents?"

"Not sure. It's Newtonian."

"Sir Isaac Newton?"

"Yes. Newton used planetary symbols for metals and standard symbols for common substances." I handed it back to her.

She tucked it back into her pocket. "What if it fell off one of the members of Sovereign?"

"They were the only ones allowed in that chamber," I agreed.

Alistair headed into the midst of a small clearing and turned in our direction. "Inspector Jansen!" he called out.

I tried again to slip past his mind's defenses but his thoughts were still closed down.

I grabbed hold of Ingrid's arm. "Follow my lead, understand?"

"I was about to say the same thing to you," she said and strolled off toward Alistair.

Warily, we joined him in the clearing.

"I'm assuming you're not following me to discuss joining our society, William." Alistair said.

"We just want to ask you some questions," Ingrid began.

"Then why not just come to the office?" he asked, his tone scathing.

I scanned the area trying to confirm we were alone.

"What are you doing out here?" Ingrid asked.

He buttoned up his coat. "Since when did police officers start associating with the undead?"

She stood her ground.

"William, if that really is your name, when you came to my office you hid your affliction well."

"Affliction?" Ingrid asked.

"Vampirism," he said flatly. "Immediately after you left my Porsche was stolen. Only a vampire would survive crashing a vehicle into the Thames."

"Perhaps we could explain," Ingrid said.

He gave a look of annoyance. "One can only assume you've tasted your friend here, Inspector." He gestured to me. "Which would explain your wayward behavior."

Ingrid tried to hide her reaction.

"I can see you have from your expression," he said. "Taste the blood and you taste the power. Vampires must be annihilated. They threaten humanity like no other contagion."

"But the Stone Masters don't feel that way," I said.

Alistair ignored me. "William seduced you, Inspector. You didn't stand a chance. Don't blame yourself."

"It's not like that," she insisted.

"He's designed that way, you see," Alistair continued. "His ability to lure so exquisitely makes him the perfect predator. His victims are actually grateful when he takes them into his arms and drains them."

"That's why Sovereign broke their allegiance with the Stone Masters," I persisted, ignoring his rant. "You hate their plan to bring back joint vampire and mortal rule."

"A significant disagreement." His smile thinned. "Inspector, shall I give you a moment to say goodbye to him." Alistair held out his hand to her. "I'll help you escape him. That's what this meeting is about. We've been waiting for you to return to us, so that we can save you. An opportunity has arisen. I'd take it if I were you."

"I don't need rescuing—"

"William's brainwashed you." Alistair wasn't letting up.

Ingrid folded her arms defiantly.

Alistair seemed calm, too calm considering the circumstances and the arrogant air he wore so well seemed out of place.

"We'll get you to a safe house," Alistair said. "You'll never have to see him or his kind again."

"Within this very hour you've imbibed vampire blood," I said. "Something tells me you're addicted."

His right eyelid flickered, though his expression remained unfazed. "A small perk."

"Your ethics are skewed," I said.

"What do know about Dominion?" Ingrid asked.

I shot her a look but it was too late, the words were out and she'd stepped toward him, insistent on getting an answer.

"Why do you think the Stone Masters are a dying breed," he asked, "and yet Sovereign are thriving?" He made a sweeping gesture to make his point. "We evolved."

"Sovereign's sole purpose was to protect Dominion," I said. "Your reward for keeping him safe was his blood?"

Alistair shook his head. "We were promised that, yes."

"I don't understand," Ingrid said.

"You're not meant to," he replied. "None of this is your business."

"Let me share with you what we do know," I said. "Members of Sovereign were commissioned with the task of watching over

Dominion. And then someone messed up."

Alistair snapped. "And yet not one member of Sovereign tasted Dominion." He raised his head high.

"You took your blood from other sources," I said, "other vampires."

"But never once drank from the promised fountain of bliss," he said.

"Dominion himself," I murmured.

Ingrid and I must have been sharing the same thought, remembering the engraving of Dominion on his tomb, the image portraying the vampire feeding two members of Sovereign. Though we weren't going to share that knowledge with Alistair.

Alistair seemed distracted by something far off along the tree line. "Two hundred years ago," he said, "my predecessors discovered a terrible revelation." He shook his head. "The monks guarding Dominion's sarcophagus gathered the confidence to open it after their brothers had watched over it with a blind obedience. They cracked the seal, breaking their vow to protect it. And when they peered in . . . what they saw changed everything . . . forever."

The realization touched me like a blade. "The tomb was empty. Dominion . . ."

"Was gone." Alistair took a shallow breath.

"So all that time they were guarding nothing?" Ingrid asked, her tone confused.

"Nothing but a lie," said Alistair. "Have you any idea of the lives that could have been wasted standing watch?"

"What became of the monks?" Ingrid asked.

"They knew they'd be blamed for Dominion's disappearance. They fled Cornwall."

He was telling us too much, and I was plagued with the distinct impression we weren't the only ones in the park.

"We were betrayed," Alistair continued. "By the very men who'd commissioned us to guard over Dominion." His eyelids widened. "The Stone Masters stole our beloved Dominatio. Though we had no idea of when. Then, they turned him against us. The Stone Masters threatened that Dominion would slay every last member of Sovereign. The very servants who'd offered their lives to protect him. The threat went further. Once we were all decimated, the job done, Dominion would be crowned the next Stone Master." Alistair spat the words. "An abomination."

"That's why you're hunting him?" I asked. "To get to him before he gets to you?"

Alistair's lips formed a sinister smile. "When we find him he'll regret his betrayal. Dominion will beg for forgiveness. None shall be given."

"Why are Sovereign poisoning vampires?" I asked.

"And with what?" Ingrid asked.

He tapped his temple. "The answers."

Alistair flew backwards with my fangs lodged in his neck and my lips pressed against his throat, blood bursting into my mouth . . . The taste peculiar.

I'd attacked him too rashly; fulfilling his will.

I shoved him back. The metallic tang reached my throat and raged on into my nostrils causing me to wretch. Having not swallowed I'd barely saved myself from the poison.

Alistair looked surprised. "How old are you?" he muttered, nervously.

Hinting that the older the vampire, the more likely they'd be to taste the blood was tainted. But not the younger ones, the more vulnerable.

I wiped my mouth with my sleeve, staining the cuff scarlet. "You're trying to control vampires before they control you?" I asked, having stolen the answer.

He stared at me as though hoping the poison would take effect. Though soon realizing that wasn't going to happen, he slid his right hand into his jacket and removed a small pistol.

Terror shot up my spine when he pointed it at Ingrid.

"Inspector, you're coming with me," he said. "I'm here to save you from yourself!"

"Put the gun down." She raised her hands in defense.

"Are you refusing?" he asked, his demeanor insistent.

"I won't go with you," she said.

"William." He glanced my way. "Let her go."

"That's not my decision," I said.

"Please, Alistair," Ingrid tried to get through to him, "let's discuss this."

"My orders were clear," he said, "no negotiation." His finger squeezed the trigger.

A shot rang out.

I swept Ingrid up and dived to our left, shielding her, twisting my torso, but the bullets found me, piercing between my shoulder blades, burning holes on their way through. Ingrid had slipped from my grasp rolling several feet way. I crashed to the ground and lay motionless, paralyzed.

Stillness filled the air.

Stunned, I stared up at the low lying branches vacillating in and out of focus, the warmth of pooling blood beneath me.

Alistair loomed over me and said, "Silver bullets. Very reliable." He wiped his neck and studied his blood stained fingers.

My words gurgled and made no sense as wave after wave of agony gripped me, snatching my breath away. My mind slipped into darkness and the futility of consciousness mirrored my fear that my body was giving up.

Or giving me over.

Death, I'd faced it before. Not a mortal's passing but something altogether different, a miraculous transcending of time and space as though reaching the very edges of infinity, only to be dragged back, pulled by some immortal coil and snapping back into flesh and bone, reanimating my being with a fierce pulse.

I could feel my legs again and the sensation rippled upward allowing me to fill my lungs and take a breath. The contractions where the bullets had left were settling.

Ingrid was sitting up on her heels staring wide eyed into the barrel of the revolver that Alistair was pointing at her.

I grabbed his gun and threw it. "Silver bullets only work if they stay embedded."

Alastair staggered backwards, his face twisted in fear. I shoved him up against a tree.

"What's your blood poisoned with?" I wrapped my hands around his throat.

He curled his top lip into a grimace, his face reddening as he muttered. "You didn't swallow any of it. So you may be unaffected, but that also means you saw nothing."

"I saw enough," I said, bluffing, "You stole an entire collection of scrolls from the Stone Masters."

His face twisted in misery. And I read from his expression that Sovereign had no idea what was on them.

Westminster Abbey leaked from his mind, a momentary lapse in an otherwise secure mind.

"Are the scrolls in Westminster Abbey?" I tightened my grip.

His furrowed brow deepened. "Why are they of any interest to you?" His expression changed. "That's all you saw. Useless." Drops of spittle came with the words. "You have only one value and that's to serve *us*."

"The scrolls," I snapped, "where are they?"

A whipping sound flew past my ear and a warmth sprayed

against my face, but there was no pain . . .

Alistair slumped to the ground, his head matted with blood and skull fragments. He'd been shot through his right eye with an arrow.

XXVIII

SHIRT OFF I LEANED over the sink, washing off Alistair's blood.

Ingrid was silent, leaning against the far wall with her arms crossed over her chest, her thoughts racing.

This small, modest sacristy paled in comparison to what lay beyond the door at the far end of the room, London's thousand-year-old Gothic monastery Westminster Abbey.

Buttoning up the clerical black shirt, I fiddled with the dog collar.

Ingrid approached and assisted me to position it correctly, her hands still shaking. "I thought vampires had to steer away from anything religious." she said.

"You're thinking of Bela Lugosi." I took her hands in mine, trying to still their trembling. "You're still shaken from flying."

"Were they aiming that arrow at us?" she asked.

"I'm not sure. Alistair failed his mission to persuade you to go with him. Maybe Sovereign didn't approve."

Her face was flushed with horror. "We just witnessed a murder."

She seemed too shaken for me to bring up I'd almost seen hers.

"Westminster Abbey flashed through Alistair's thoughts," I said. "There's something significant here. I have to find out what that is."

"Are the scrolls here?" she asked. "Is that what you saw?"

I shook my head. "His thoughts were too blurry to get anything of substance."

"What if he was trying to mislead you?"

I picked up the soiled shirt and shoved it to the bottom of the corner wicker hamper. "Let's find out."

We headed into the Abbey.

"How old is this cathedral?" Ingrid asked, her gaze wandering.

"Over a thousand years old. It's the resting place for history's artists, poets, kings and scientists."

In any other circumstance she'd have found the medieval coronation throne fascinating, or perhaps she'd have paused longer before Charles Dickens's memorial, or taken time to pay homage to William Shakespeare's sepulture; but neither these nor any of the other veritable monuments of English History could shake Ingrid from her disquiet.

Finally she spoke again, her voice a whisper. "We just left his body lying there."

"We had no choice," I said.

"I shouldn't have left the scene."

"Then the next arrow might have found you," I reasoned.

"Alistair worked for them." She shook her head. "And they killed him in cold blood." She stepped back, shaking her head woefully. "What am I caught in the middle of?"

"Perhaps now you understand why I wanted to keep you at arm's length."

"What if Alistair thought of this place merely as a ruse?"

"I know what I saw," I insisted. "There's something significant here."

"What did his blood taste of?"

"Metal."

"Obviously it disgusted you enough to make you spit it out." She sighed deeply. "Sure it wasn't garlic?"

I gave her a look. "He's deliberately ingested or injected something."

"Something that poisons vampires but doesn't harm mortals?" She grimaced. "We could be in here for a week and not find anything." She threw her hands up in frustration. "He was our only lead."

"I'm sorry." I ran my fingers through my hair, sharing her frustration.

"Oh no!" She grabbed my shirt sleeve and guided me back the way we'd come. "Alistair's blood." Her pace sped up.

Twenty or so school children flocked around us, slowing our return to the vestry.

Once inside I went straight over to the linen basket where I'd discarded my shirt soiled with Alistair's blood.

It was empty.

"How could I be so stupid?" Ingrid cringed. "It was right in front of us." She threw her hands up in the air.

Lost in our own thoughts we headed back out into the Abbey.

Taking a seat in the front pew, Ingrid looked miserable. "I need to focus," she said.

I tried to find the words to reassure her.

"We can't afford any more mistakes," she continued.

We sat in silence, watching the crowds swarming each monument only to move on again, though soon replaced by other tourists, all eager to experience a small piece of England's history.

"Look at them," Ingrid said, "they have a living relic in their midst and they have no idea."

"That's the way I like it." I peered down at the bibles stacked along the back of the pew.

"And yet here sits the most remarkable artifact!"

"Not sure I want to be considered a relic," I said.

She turned to face me. "You've probably met half the buried men in here."

"Not exactly."

"Had I not seen your transformation myself, witnessed it firsthand . . ."

I broke her stare.

"I fell in love with Jadeon," she said softly, "loved him more than I've loved anyone. And I don't think I've ever hated anyone as much as Orpheus."

My focus turned to the ceiling with its intricate design and I wondered what it must be like to paint upside down.

"Does Jadeon still exist?" she asked. "Does he know it's me?"

I took her hand. "Yes."

"You invited me back to your castle. Remember? God it was so romantic."

"I opened up to you in a way I'd never done before," I admitted.

"I feel like I'm betraying Jadeon in some way." She gave a shrug. "Do you really believe there's a way to reverse this?"

I braved to reach inside her mind, daring to find the answers that seemed to linger on the lips of everyone close to me: that I, William, was temporary, merely waiting in some kind of metaphorical no man's land, half-loved, half-hated, with everyone eager for me to die.

With me out of the equation this situation might just be better for everyone.

Ingrid squeezed my shoulder. "We need you, William. I need you."

Her intuitive words struck me to my core.

Such tenderness was too much, her affection burning through me like the sun I no longer knew, and unwilling to surrender to this moment and to her kindness that I didn't deserve, I eased her hand off.

"Are you going to break my heart?" Her voice was barely a whisper.

I leaned over to kiss her forehead.

She softened as though that was all she needed. "We have a case to solve." She rose and edged left along the pew.

I followed, trying to push away the feeling of futility of finding anything here, powerlessness seeped into my bones.

We strolled beneath stone columns, reminding me of the ones we'd seen back in the Mount's secret tomb, recalling that ancient bluestone seemingly luring me back; that rare megalith safely ensconced in the lower chambers of a Cornish castle, bestowing a supernatural seduction.

The answers seemed just out of reach.

Gothic arches swept up, elegantly curving along the dimly lit corridor toward the north side of the nave. I paused to appreciate David Livingston's tomb. His epitaph stated he was a Doctor and Missionary who'd spent much of his life exploring Africa, and I remembered him fondly as one of Victorian Britain's most popular Heroes.

I caught up with Ingrid again.

She was riveted by Sir Isaac Newton's tomb. The monument was grandiose, a sculptured Newton lay upon a black-marble sarcophagus, an uncanny younger version of the man elaborately carved reclining back onto his beloved books as two child angels nestled close, guarding over both him and his scientific discoveries. Above, a giant orb was decorated with heavenly bodies and upon that sat the goddess of astronomy.

Ingrid turned to me at once. "The cufflink." Her hand slid into her pocket and she held it in her palm, studying it again.

I studied the monument. "Newton was one of the most influential men in history."

"He was a physicist." Ingrid placed the cufflink in my palm. "Discovered gravity when he saw an apple fall."

I pointed to the orb. "An astronomer."

"An alchemist?"

"That's right."

"We need to find out what this symbol represents." She turned to face me. "I know this sounds crazy . . . "

"Go on."

"What if Dominion was never even in the tomb that Sovereign

watched over?"

"What makes you say that?"

"Sovereign guarded it with their lives. If members of the Stone Masters tried to move Dominion, then it wouldn't have gone unnoticed. Men talk. Rumors circulate. And the Stone Masters never accused Sovereign of stealing him."

I was stunned. "Why would men guard a tomb with nothing inside?"

Ingrid stared off. "Exactly."

Two choirboys strolled toward us and we waited for them to pass.

Ingrid's mobile vibrated in her pocket. She removed it and read the screen. "It's my boss." She strolled away from the nave to take the call.

The choirboys began lighting candles, diligently carrying out their duties as altar boys.

Ingrid rejoined me. "That mummy I've been trying to find . . . it just turned up."

"Where?"

"Back at the museum. Placed in its original case."

"That's odd."

"Forensics are on the scene." She studied Newton's likeness. "Was he ever a member of a secret society?"

"There were rumors, yes."

Ingrid rubbed her forehead. "Why would Westminster Abbey be in the forethought of Alastair's mind?"

"Maybe he was meant to meet someone here?" I asked.

"The thieves who stole the mummy led us to Sovereign."

"And Sovereign led us here."

"It's all connected. But how?" Ingrid slid her phone back into her pocket. "I have to get over to the museum." She looked thoughtful. "Very often a clue presents itself as an intuitive lead."

"Via Harrods," I said.

She frowned.

"I need a new shirt," I explained and then leaned back, wondering why Ingrid was fiddling with my clerical collar.

She eased out the white dog collar and tucked it into her coat pocket. "There."

* * * *

Escorted by the young male curator, Ingrid and I strolled down the well lit endless corridors of the British Museum's underbelly, admiring the artifacts, stealing glimpses at some pieces that may never be viewed by the public and taking in others that had been replaced by more alluring sights.

When the curator opened the door to the examination room the scent of ammonia hit us.

Lucas Azir was already here, having agreed to meet us, and was predictably in the middle of an intense conversation with the museum's senior scientist Dr. Amy Hanson.

Other than the row of mummified cats lined up along the back wall shelf, the laboratory was simple; decked out in chrome and well lit. Laying in the center of the room upon an examination table was our man of the hour, the newly returned mummy.

Dr. Hanson barely acknowledged us. "There are discrepancies between the dates." She peered over her silver lenses at Lucas. "Manchester's results attributed the bones to at least 1000 B.C. and yet the cloth was estimated at 380 A.D."

"It was assumed to be an older shroud." Lucas threw us a welcoming gesture.

"Radiocarbon dating has come a long way since 1979." Hanson peeled back the thin mesh covering the mummy, and took a moment as though running through a checklist in her mind.

Lucas approached me, explaining, "We're discussing an old case of my father's."

"It's an honor to finally meet you, Professor Azir," Hanson said. "Your father's work was extraordinary."

"The pleasure's all mine." Lucas gave a slight bow which might have seemed out of place given his age of twenty-seven, but his Egyptian heritage excused such a gentlemanly gesture.

Hanson peered over at Ingrid. "Professor Azir's father was a renowned Egyptologist. But that's why I imagine you invited him."

Ingrid hid it well that she didn't know about Lucas's father.

Hanson glanced down at the body. "Apparently you're not the one I should be thanking for returning our friend here."

"He just turned up this evening?" Ingrid asked.

"The guard was doing his rounds," Hanson said, "and reported that at 7:15 p.m. the case was empty and at 7:25 p.m. Hornub was back in it. Our guard saw nothing."

"Your cameras might have caught something this time?" Ingrid made it a question.

Hanson sighed, frustrated. "Same camera interference, apparently." She turned her attention back to Lucas. "Your father's work is impressive. Big shoes to fill." She nudged her spectacles up her nose. "Did he really only work at night?"

"The desert sun is cooler," Lucas said. "Tourists are asleep. Only the most dedicated assistants are willing to toil during the late hours."

I wondered if this was his tried and tested speech delivered on so many other occasions to excuse his nocturnal existence.

Lucas turned his attention on Ingrid to take it off himself. "Those are real cat mummies."

Ingrid neared them. "Seriously. What's with that?"

"Kittens," said Lucas. "Around 332 B.C. cats were bred for the purpose of mummifying."

She pulled a face. "You mean they didn't die naturally?"

"Four month old kittens fitted into the mummy's container better," he said.

Ingrid's face fell.

Hanson realized Lucas had hit a nerve. "You prefer animals to humans, Inspector?"

"It all boils down to motivation," Ingrid said. "Humans know better. Or should."

"I imagine you've seen quite a bit of death?" The doctor peeled off her latex gloves and tossed them in the bin.

Ingrid stared at her as though frozen in the memory of Alistair sitting slumped up against the tree stump, an arrow protruding from his right orb.

Ingrid quickly shook off her trance. "We both have that in common, Dr. Hanson." Ingrid gestured toward the mummy. "From what I understand, the belief that you'd need a body in the afterlife was why they mummified their dead."

"At first it was merely reserved for Pharaohs," Lucas said. "Later it became fashionable and nobility were mummified. Before long everyone wanted in on the act."

"Did our forensics find anything?" Ingrid asked.

"They let me do the honors," Hanson said. "I am after all his keeper." She looked my way. "I've not been able to sleep since he went missing. The guilt weighed too heavily."

"You developed a bond," I said.

"There's a theory that a nation can be judged on how they treat their animals. The same can be said for how we honor our dead."

"You consider their remains sacred," I acknowledged.

"A once living temple." Hanson scratched her collar bone with an un-manicured fingernail. "Whoever took him had no respect. They still have his sacred scrolls."

"His map to the afterlife?" Ingrid said, remembering what Lucas had told her.

"Shameful." Lucas shook his head.

"But surely he's made it to the afterlife by now?" Ingrid asked. "Maybe he doesn't need the map anymore."

"Please excuse her," I said. "She doesn't mean to be so pragmatic."

Ingrid threw me a look.

"And what's your background?" Hanson asked me.

"Historian," I answered.

"Inspector, you have quite the team." She turned to me again. "Then you'll know the sacred scrolls placed with him at his death included incantations that would guide his soul on its perilous journey to the edge of the land of the dead." She peered at Ingrid. "His scrolls were unique. They actually depicted a spell of resurrection back into this life."

"Reincarnation?" Ingrid asked.

Hanson shook her head. "Eternal life."

"You mentioned scrolls." Ingrid asked, "There was more than one?"

"Yes," said Hanson. "The first scroll depicted directions on how to survive immortality."

"I never got to see that," Ingrid said. "I missed it."

"That was probably my fault, I'm afraid," Hanson admitted, "There was a lot of confusion that day and I wasn't myself."

"May I see your copies?" Lucas asked.

"Of course." Hanson opened up a beige folder and rifled through the papers within and handed them over to him.

Lucas held them respectfully as though studying the originals.

Hanson folded her arms and leaned back against the edge of the chrome shelf. "We've yet to fully interpret them."

Lucas glanced up. "He was a hunter."

Hanson seemed impressed. "Anything else?"

"Just his obsession with immortality," Lucas answered, avoiding the question.

"You really believe this is Hornub?" Hanson asked, warily.

"According to the scrolls it is," Lucas said. "He was rumored to have fractured his left ankle as a child, but made a full recovery. Anything on his X-rays?"

Hanson raised her eyebrows in surprise. "We found a hairline fracture on his left tibia." She shook her head. "This changes everything. We're talking of a groundbreaking finding." She signed deeply. "Of course more tests will need to be done. To think we almost lost him."

"I imagine those who stole him didn't know either," Lucas said. "Otherwise he'd never have been returned."

Hanson's face lit up. "Perhaps you'd consider coming on staff, Professor?"

"I'm always available for consultations," said Lucas.

"I'll hold you to that." Hanson turned her focus back onto the mummy. "Even after all these centuries, Hornub—" she paused, still seemingly astonished with the possibility of it being him. "Hornub still speaks to us. Our advancement in mass spectrometry allows us to learn so much about past civilizations. The way he lived and the way he died is evidenced within his very bones." The doctor's face changed. "His DNA tells us two things. First, he was alive circa 100 B.C. and second, he suffered from severe anemia."

"Impressive," Ingrid remarked.

"His story is far from over," Hanson said. "It seems we're not the only ones who are interested in him on a scientific level."

"How do you mean?" Ingrid said.

"See this puncture mark here." Hanson pointed to his outer thigh. "Someone with expertise seems to have taken a sample. Perhaps a DNA specimen."

"Why not just ask to see your findings?" I asked.

"That's what we don't understand," she said. "Our findings are public knowledge."

"Why not just take a hair sample?" Ingrid asked.

"Now that's a good question," Lucas said. "We'll make a scientist out of you yet."

Hanson gestured her point. "Firstly, it's not accurate and second, he's bald." She lifted the veil covering Hornub's head to show Ingrid.

Ingrid strolled around the table toward her. "Would you happen to know what this symbol represents?" She held the cufflink in her open palm and reached over the table.

Hanson frowned.

"It's a cufflink." Ingrid raised it higher.

"I can see that," Hanson said. "Where did you find it?"

"Cornwall," Ingrid said.

Hanson peered over her spectacles. "I take it you're not going to tell me where, exactly?"

Ingrid gave a tilt of her head as a polite way of saying that *no*, she'd not be sharing that information with the doctor today.

Hanson glanced my way. "High levels of hydragyrum were found in Hornub's DNA."

"Mercury?" I clarified.

"It's found throughout the world." Hanson studied the cufflink. "This pictogram was Newton's symbol for mercury. Interesting, don't you think?"

"Why's that?" Ingrid asked.

"After Newton died high levels of mercury were found in his body." Hanson turned back to Hornub. "Looks like the dead know something we don't."

XXIX

TWENTY TOURISTS OR SO meandered through the museum's Egyptian Gallery.

Lucas, Ingrid and I hovered by the gilded Cartonnage mummy mask, presented on a thin, black stand and dated: *late 1st century B.C. - early 1st century A.D.* The description stated the mask was a depiction of the head and chest of the princess who once wore it.

Ingrid nudged closer to me, keeping her voice low. "If it's mercury poisoning, why stamp the symbol onto a cufflink?"

"Newton's world was so different to the one we know today," I said. "They had no idea such knowledge would one day be shared."

"Accessible to everyone," Lucas agreed.

"Do you really believe Sovereign are ingesting mercury?" she asked.

"It would explain the taste," I said.

Lucas looked horrified.

"I spat it out," I said.

"But high levels of mercury would harm them in the long run," he said. "They couldn't sustain that for long."

I shrugged. "The ultimate sacrifice."

Lucas looked thoughtful. "Unless they've found a way to alter the way they metabolize the element."

All three of us scrutinized the sad face of the gilded mask.

"Hornub was a vampire hunter," whispered Lucas.

"Perhaps he was taking mercury to protect himself from a vampire attack?" Ingrid suggested.

Lucas considered her words and then sidled up to me saying, "William, the scrolls we're looking for are written by the same hand."

He gestured his explanation. "Sovereign won't be able to interpret them either." He checked no one else was listening. "Hieroglyphics are a phonetic language corresponding to sounds. The hieroglyphics on Hornub's scrolls are uniquely written partly in cuneiform. They're from Mesopotamia."

"What does that mean?" Ingrid asked.

"They're written in Coptic code," he said.

"Making them even more complicated to interpret," Ingrid realized.

"According to Hornub's two scrolls, there were seven in total," he said thoughtfully.

"And Hornub was buried with two of them?" asked Ingrid.

"Yes," Lucas said. "And it seems that Sovereign have the others."

"Is that why they stole Hornub?" Ingrid asked. "Why not just take the scrolls?"

"Their interest lies with Hornub," Lucas explained, "the scrolls just happened to come with him. They took everything in the presentation case."

"Then it must be the fact he'd digested mercury," I said.

"They're trying to perfect the right amount," Lucas said.

"Enough to deter vampires," I added, "but not seriously affect the one who ingests it."

Lucas became even more enthused. "Hornub inherited his father's scrolls otherwise known as the Book of Thoth. Anyone who reads these are predicted to become the most powerful magician in the world." Lucas's eyes lit up. "The words written by the god of wisdom. 'The secrets of the gods themselves'. When the scrolls come together they form a book. They were rumored to have been separated and buried with several mummies to protect the knowledge. They were meant to take them over to the afterlife."

Ingrid's quizzical expression softened. "But as the mummies were discovered so were the scrolls."

Lucas shook his hands with excitement. "And they're all now gathered in one place."

"And on them is written my way back . . ." This well overdue epiphany took my breath away.

"We're so close," Ingrid said.

"Call Marcus," I said to Ingrid, "tell him to test his sister and Blake for mercury poisoning."

"It's consistent with their symptoms," Lucas said. "I only wish I'd seen it sooner."

I followed the direction of where Lucas was staring.

Two male nightwalkers had entered the room and were pretending to be fixated on one the exhibits.

I took Ingrid's hand and guided her into the next exhibit hall.

Lucas was right behind us. "Are they following?"

"Well we'll soon see." I glanced back. "Probably nothing. Vampires have a thing for history too." I winked at Ingrid.

"Diplomacy is always the best way to deal with our peers," Lucas said. "I've dealt with their kind before."

"Who are they?" Ingrid asked.

"No one we can't deal with," he reassured her. "I'm always wary for thieves. Tomb raiders. I try to stay one step ahead of them. It's been my life's work. I know I seem paranoid but I've seen too much. Back in Egypt, thieves wait until it rains and then go looking for dents in the sand that reveal hidden tombs beneath. These men desecrate the burial site and then sell the artifacts." He shook his head. "Decimating history without remorse."

"Dr. Hanson mentioned your father?" Ingrid said.

He gave her a look of the obvious.

She shook her head, realizing. "Of course."

"I've used my fake lineage to remain prominent in his field without arousing suspicion," he admitted.

"So when Hanson was talking about your father," Ingrid said, "she was actually talking about you."

He let out the longest sigh as though still coming to terms with his lifestyle.

"I'm afraid we are being followed," I said.

Lucas pretended to be interested in the one of the glass cases containing a mummified rat. Ingrid stood close and feigned she was reading the description of the shriveled specimen.

I slid Lucas the credit card sized room key. *"Take Ingrid to the Savoy."*

He shoved it into his pocket. "Sure you can handle them?"

"What's going on?" Ingrid peered through the cabinet at me.

"Go with Lucas." I tried to get another look at their faces.

Lucas grabbed Ingrid's hand and guided her away.

Strolling leisurely through the exhibit, the two well-dressed vampires disappeared behind a black curtain. I headed after them, quickly entering the museum's fifty seat theatre, reassured to see we were alone.

Playing upon the large screen was the film *Ancient Egyptian Book of the Dead*.

The two nightwalkers sat in the back row and I edged along the one in front of them and sat.

Both of them were dressed in jeans and blazers and they were easily two of the most ridiculously pretty twenty-something vampires I'd seen in a while. They'd easily pass for aristocracy.

The dirty blond sat forward. "William, we need your help," he said.

I detected his sincerity but not so much in his dark haired friend who seemed impatient.

I locked on him. "How do you know who I am?"

"We saw you at Belshazzar's," the blond said. "With Marcus."

I sincerely hoped it wasn't the night I was covered in blood. "You know my name, how about you tell me yours?" I said.

"Raven," the darker haired one gave his name, dismissing the way his friend had started. "Where's Orpheus?"

"You assume I know?" I looked over at his friend.

"You're well acquainted with Belshazzar's." The blond sat back.

I went quiet waiting for his name.

"Angus," the blond said, sounding like he regretted telling me.

"Belshazzar's closed down," I said.

"On whose authority?" Raven asked.

"Orpheus, of course," I replied flatly.

Raven seemed reassured. "We must speak with him."

"Why?" I asked.

Angus became agitated.

"I'll pass on your message," I said. "What is it?"

"So he's not dead?" Raven asked.

I gave a bored sigh. "You've interrupted my visit to the museum. Can we hurry this up?"

"You're good friends with Lucas Azir," Raven said. "As is Orpheus."

"And Marcus," Angus added. "Orpheus's closest ally."

I folded my arms. "What's your point?"

"We can only assume you're in contact with Orpheus?" Angus asked.

"He's in Italy," I lied with panache.

"How might we persuade you to help us?" Raven leaned forward and pouted, sending a wave of pleasure between my legs with merely a thought. He sat back and his lip curled upward triumphantly.

I used the same trick he'd just thrown my way, only mine penetrated his solar plexus and jolted a shocking frisson directly into his spine and downward, staying there, vacillating.

Jaw slackening, lips quivering, Raven dug his fingernails into the armrests, clearly taken by surprise.

I arched an eyebrow. "You were saying?"

Raven's back stiffened and he blushed wildly, gesturing he needed a moment.

Angus pretended not to catch his reaction. "We need to get a message to Orpheus."

"Why?" I asked.

Angus glanced at Raven.

Raven sucked on his lips still seemingly recovering, and then said, "We need his permission." His shoulders slumped. "Marcus refused to tell us where Orpheus is. This is the first time anyone's mentioned where we can find him."

"Where in Italy, exactly?" Angus asked.

I emphasized my impatience.

Raven lowered his chin in a gesture of respect. "We can't advance with any action until sanctioned by the ruling Status Regal."

"Proceed with what?" I asked.

Raven hesitated and then said, "Killing him."

I tried to read him. "Who?"

Raven swapped a glance with Angus. "Dominion of course."

"You want that?" I kept my tone even.

"Don't you?" Angus asked, surprised. "If he's allowed to take up his position of authority with the Stone Masters . . . we're all in serious trouble."

I glanced away.

"If Dominion sides with the Stone Masters," Raven said, "We're all vulnerable."

Angus sat back, questioning my reticence with a frown. "So you'll help us find Orpheus?"

"I'll see what I can do." I turned to Raven. "How many are there of you that want Dominion dead?"

Raven looked surprised. "All of us."

THE TIP OF THE KNIFE pressed against Ingrid's neck.

"Please put the knife down, Sunaria," I said casually and threw my jacket onto the back of the armchair.

Sunaria glanced over at Lucas.

My gut wrenched to see him lying face down on the carpet, unconscious, his throat slit and blood oozing, staining the hotel room's plush carpet, scarlet.

Telling Lucas to bring Ingrid back to the Savoy had been a terrible mistake. From the disarray in the hotel room, Lucas hadn't gone down without a fight. With my mind closed down, Sunaria wouldn't know just how full of panic I really was.

To save my friends, calmness was needed; a clear head.

I took a seat in the high-back chair. "How are you?"

"What a ridiculous way to begin," Sunaria snapped.

"You do realize Ingrid's one of your descendants," I said.

Sunaria sighed and her fingers loosened around the handle of the knife.

I reached for the copy of *Time Magazine* resting on the coffee table.

"Ah." I threw it down. "Last month's."

Suspicion burned in Sunaria's eyes. "You're taking too long to find a way back."

"We've been looking for the scrolls." I glanced over at Lucas. "You do realize he's the only one who can interpret them." I grimaced. "Lucas is my only way back."

Sunaria's attention slid back to Ingrid. "Why her?"

"She's helping us." I gave a shrug. "Simple."

The knife lifted off Ingrid's flesh leaving a tiny ooze of blood.

Ingrid was begging me with her eyes to save her.

"Sunaria," I said, "Lucas really was looking forward to meeting with you." I rose from the chair and strolled over to him. "He's obsessed with all things Sumerian."

"He refused to tell me where you were." Sunaria sounded bitter. "And then he refused to leave me with her."

"He was obeying my order," I said.

Sunaria pressed the knife deeper against Ingrid's throat. "What is she to you?"

There was no other choice but to look at Ingrid and hope I'd not give anything away. "How was Cornwall?" I asked.

"I never went," she said.

Sunaria reminded me of an Egyptian goddess and the memories I'd held at arm's length flooded in, and I shared them with her, using the mind gift so that she too could relive those daring moments of our once-love burning brightly; torturing each other with our obsession for each other . . .

"You don't love me anymore." It sounded more like a question.

Raising my chin, I persisted to woo her . . .

Recalling our tempestuous relationship, during those neverending nights when I'd provoked her, shown her nothing but affection.

"I want that again," Sunaria whispered, her eyelids fluttering in response.

"It was you who left me, remember?" I took a step closer. "I begged you to stay at Belshazzar's."

"It was all too much." Her lips trembled.

"I understand."

"I lost you," she said, "lost everything."

"We're close to a resolution," I told her. "I need you to hang on for just a little longer."

"Orpheus?" she asked desperately.

"Sunaria, please don't do this."

Voices carried from outside the door; other guests were deep in conversation, strolling toward their hotel room with no idea of what was unfolding in this one.

It fell quiet again.

Kneeling beside Lucas, I bit into my wrist and rested it against his lips, giving a little blood at first, just enough to heal his gash, before he came round and realized the state he was in.

"Get rid of her," Sunaria's tone was scathing.

One wrong move on my part and Sunaria would slice Ingrid's throat.

"The London Eye is over four hundred feet high," I said. "It's an observation wheel on the Thames." I glanced down at Lucas who was clutching my wrist to his mouth, sucking furiously.

"So?" asked Sunaria.

"I want to show it to you," I said, easing my arm away from Lucas and ruffling his hair with affection.

Sunaria caught my tenderness toward Lucas and threw me a disapproving look.

I knelt in close to Lucas's ear and whispered, "You always did prefer Piccadilly."

He squeezed my hand that he'd understood.

I headed for the door and opened it.

Ingrid tumbled forward, burying her face into the carpet and though I didn't wait to see her cry, I knew she would.

As Sunaria and I left, I wrapped my arm around her waist and said, "I hear the view from the London Eye is spectacular."

* * * *

When we reached the London Eye it was closed to the public for a private event. Undeterred I led Sunaria into the crowd of thirty late night party goers before we were guided through to the landing zone.

The gigantic Ferris wheel loomed over the River Thames from Parliament Square, situated between Hungerford Bridges and Westminster. What might once have been considered a modern day monstrosity had become a beloved city landmark.

And this was the first time Sunaria had seen it.

Cursing myself for choosing this location so hastily, I'd seemingly forgotten my fear of heights.

It was too late now.

Sunaria and I stepped into our own private pod and sat upon the central wooden seat. We took off effortlessly, gliding upward in its seamless rotation, its glass panels allowing a magnificent, if not terrifying, panoramic view.

Just beyond this small closed-in space, life was suspended, if only for a while.

Both of us were awed by the dramatic nightscape that unfolded beneath us, brilliantly showing off Big Ben, Parliament and Westminster Bridge and then reaching out farther, unveiling all the way to the vast dark horizon.

"You'd have told me anything to have gotten me out of there," she said.

"What you did to Lucas was despicable," I said.

With a turn of her head she brushed off my statement.

I wondered if anything good could come from this meeting, questioning my judgment for locking myself in here with her.

"Well, you saved him, didn't you?" She faced me, her silhouette lit brilliantly by the city lights.

"How can it be fair that Orpheus is lost to me?"

"That's not exactly true."

"You're moving on." She caressed her hands, full of angst.

"I've been trying to find a way back." I leaned forward, resting my elbows on my knees, trying to cope with the words as I spoke them. "Facing my mortality . . . is challenging."

"Did you ever grieve for me?" she asked softly.

"I punished everyone including myself for losing you. Pushed everyone away. Marcus and Lucas stood by me when everyone else was too scared to even be in the same room as me." I rose and joined her by the window. "This," I clutched my chest, "is the result of my self-hate."

"Don't say it."

"I'm also Jadeon Artimas." I took a breath. "Everyone seems to forget that."

"You blame me for this?"

I pressed my hands up against the glass. "I'm done blaming."

She shook her head. "I don't believe you."

"Haven't you heard about the poisonings? Vampires have been dying."

"And why is that my concern?"

I threw her a look of disapproval.

She acknowledged her regret for her words. "Lucas told me you know what's causing it."

"And then you slit his throat?" I snapped.

She folded her arms defiantly.

"A faction has broken away from the Stone Masters," I continued, hating the silence. "They call themselves Sovereign. They have the scrolls I need, apparently. And I need Lucas to interpret them. Ingrid's using her detective skills to help us."

"You're in love with her?"

I pressed my forehead against the glass. "My relationship with *everyone* is skewed."

"What's in Piccadilly?"

I stared dead ahead.

She folded her arms. "Jacob's been lying to you."

"About what?" And then I saw it in her eyes. "You met with him?"

"I needed answers."

"Where is he?"

"I don't know and I don't care."

I backed away, unwilling to see her pain; the agony of how much Jacob's betrayal had hurt her.

"I needed to hear the truth," she whispered.

"Jacob saved you from the Stone Masters."

"With no intention of ever waking me." She shook her head. "I'm not the only one Jacob's betrayed. Your beloved Lucas is Jacob's eyes and ears. He's been watching over you and reporting back to Jacob."

"Why do you say that?"

"Jacob convinced you that Lucas would assist you, but what he's really doing is keeping you distracted."

"What?" I studied her, not wanting to miss a single nuance she might give away.

Her eyes widened. "Jacob is *still* a Stone Lord."

"Impossible, they killed his wife!"

"Seems he forgave them." She lowered her chin. "How do you think Jacob knew about Paradom's existence?"

"Lucas told him about him."

"Why do you think Jacob is so obsessed with protecting Paradom?"

I shook my head, annoyed with what she was insinuating.

"Paradom is Dominion," she said.

As her words spilled out, I tried to comprehend them.

All this time I'd fought my rising doubt that I was doing the right thing, my mind so muddled that I'd struggled with making the right decisions, walking the path that would lead me to the truth. Betrayal bestowed the bitterest taste causing me to doubt everything and everyone I'd trusted.

Sunaria clutched my shirtsleeve. "Find Paradom and kill him."

My fangs tingled, my rage stirring. "Fabian convinced me finding Dominion was . . . our only hope."

"He knows where Dominion is!"

"How do you know this?"

She lowered her glare. "I too am an ancient. I get to see inside the minds of others."

"Fabian told me to find Dominion."

She looked defiant. "Were those his exact words?"

I broke her stare and thought back to Fabian's last words to me at

London Bridge. *"Keep Dominion safe,"* he'd said.

I resisted frowning, showing my reaction but Sunaria was right. Fabian had hinted that I might know where Dominion was. Fabian's modus was extraordinarily eccentric. Rubbing my eyes, I tried to ease the tension out.

"If Fabian trusted you," she said, "why abandon you on the day you were transformed?"

I tried to shake off the nagging doubt threatening to blind me from everything I believed, the dawning realization that the world I'd left behind when I'd stepped inside this claustrophobic pod was not the world I was returning to.

And I'd forgotten all about my fear of heights.

"Did you really believe they were ever going to trust Orpheus?" Her words faded into the background. "The only worthy leader of our kind. Dominion threatens Orpheus's rule."

As I allowed myself to see beyond the glass, I did for a moment sense the face of the man staring back; that invisible reflection if seen would show the true colors of the vampire standing before it.

Tormented. Betrayed. Damned.

"Find a way to reverse this," her voice sounded distant. "I want him back."

What if I don't make it?

"Then Ingrid will pay the price for your failure."

XXXI

BLINDED WITH CONFUSION, riddled with fury, I flew toward Piccadilly.

Lingering in the foyer of the Ritz Carlton, I tried to still my frenzied thoughts, hoping I could stay calm long enough to have a reasonable conversation with Lucas. Threatened with his possible betrayal, I tried to unravel actuality from conjecture, the truth out of deceit.

If Paradom was Dominion, the plan had been brilliantly executed. No one would have suspected this mad vampire to be the one to lead the rest of us through the twenty-first century. He could just about lead himself to open a can of cat food.

But if separated . . .

Who was Dominion?

Head down, hands in pockets, I used the stairs to get to the hotel room.

Lucas and I had once shared a fondness for the use of code amongst other things, including our love of The Ritz.

I'd traditionally stayed in one of her more sumptuous suites, The Arlington, with its luxurious if not modest décor and a good view overlooking the courtyard. I'd failed to persuade him that the Prince of Wales suite was preferable, but Lucas's simple tastes had won out.

This was easily Piccadilly's finest London hotel, built in the neoclassical style of Louis XVI, with its exclusive Parisian architecture mirroring Paris's most famous street the Rue de Rivoli.

I took in the room.

Though Lucas had delivered on his promise to bring Ingrid here and safely ensconce her in this, the Arlington suite, he himself conveniently wasn't here.

There was an open box of tissues on the coffee table. An uneaten sandwich resting on the oak Chinese cabinet, and next to that a plate of untouched strawberries. An uncorked bottle of Champagne rested on ice.

Ingrid's cheeks flushed when she saw me. "Lucas told me not to open the door to anyone."

Classical music filled the room, the notes tumbling out from discreetly hidden speakers.

"Was Lucas planning on coming back?" I asked.

"Yes."

"You okay?"

Ingrid, the only person I trusted right now, standing there as beautiful as ever, her hair tussled, her eyeliner smudged, vulnerable yet ever resilient.

The small gash on her neck where Sunaria's knife had rested was not the only evidence of her assault.

"Lucas . . . he's fine now," I said, stating the obvious.

"I can't get the image out of my mind of what Sunaria did to him. I couldn't help him." A lone tear fell, threatening others. "I suppose this is where you tell me I'm safe and she won't hurt me again?"

I strolled over to the Chinese cabinet and lifted the bottle of Krug Grand Cuvee out of the ice bucket, pouring the Champagne into the crystal flute beside it.

"Lucas told me all about Sunaria," she said.

"Let's not talk about her."

Ingrid sucked in her breath. "You didn't have her knife against your throat."

"Trust me it felt like I did." I shook my head. "I'm sorry."

Ingrid looked away.

"You need to leave," I said. "It's time to go home."

"What? Why?"

"I'm grateful for all that you've done."

"William, please . . ."

"Being with me is too dangerous for you."

She hesitated. "You and I, we're working together, we're making progress—"

"I have to face this next part alone."

"I'm not going."

"There's something else I've been keeping from you." I offered her the glass.

She gestured she didn't want it. "I'm not going to like it, am I?"

I put the glass down. "It's about James."

"Oh."

"There were so many reasons I couldn't tell you."

"Is it about Lola?"

I waited for her to say it.

"I know," she admitted.

"What gave it away, her name?"

She smiled but it quickly faded. "James was in the shower and his Blackberry went off. I glanced at the screen. I wasn't spying or anything, just kind of did it on autopilot. The text was from Lola, and it was pretty obvious." Ingrid gestured she wanted that drink now.

I handed her the glass. "He's an idiot."

She took a sip. "I can help you find the scrolls."

Moisture on the Champagne bottle had formed into drips, and was trailing over the label and down into the ice.

"You don't think I'll fight for you, is that it?" she asked. "I should have been stronger with Sunaria, but she . . ."

I approached her and brushed a few stray auburn stands out of her eyes. "This is not about me not loving you enough." I took her hand and kissed it. "I love you more than life itself."

"But—"

My fingers pressed against her lips to hush her.

Her sigh was filled with hope for this moment, and for everything that it promised to be as though those words of me leaving could be undone.

Although it wouldn't be easy to leave her, the door was merely a few steps away and all I had to do was walk through it.

Simple and effective.

"William, I want to remember everything. I want my memory back," she said it insistently, locking her gaze with mine.

"Ingrid, we've been over this."

"I need a moment." She sauntered off toward the bedroom, shutting the door behind her.

Sunaria's words ate away at me.

I wanted to forget them.

My attention was drawn to the fireplace and the reproduction hanging above it, an 1842 oil on canvas, *Odaliske and Sklavin*, painted by the French artist Jean Auguste Dominique Ingres. He'd mastered the art of hidden brush strokes, conveying perfectly the young female Turkish slave languishing upon a soft bed while soothed by a nearby musician's lute. The Odaliske's expression was so relaxed, revealing she'd accepted her fate, perhaps aspiring to one day rise to the dizzying heights of the Sultan's Imperial Harem.

A different culture, a different time.

The way Ingres had captured the woman, conveying every curve, her soft blush, her delicate refrain, he could never be blamed for falling in love with her.

The bedroom door opened.

Ingrid was dressed in a daringly revealing low tight black corset emphasizing her waist, complemented perfectly by the thin garter attached to black silk stockings, over a lace trim thong; perfecting this tour de force were her high stilettos, forcing her shoulders back and providing her with a proud, almost defiant gait.

I drank in her beauty.

All this time she'd been wearing this beneath her red dress.

Her expression changed as though realizing that which she desired most may just happen. "I need you to help me reach that part of me I can't get to."

"I'm inside your mind and all I'm hearing is bargaining." I hoped my fierceness might dissuade her.

"I *am* ready," she'd chosen her words carefully and yet it had sounded more like a question. A soft blush arose on her chest. "You once told me you'd know when I was ready?"

"Ingrid—"

"Let me have this," she said. "Have you."

Ingrid's eyes burned with a desire of which I'd never seen in her before, a yearning so intense that questioning she was ready seemed wrong, as though the responsibility fell on my shoulders to guide her along a pathway that would lead her to fulfillment.

In this moment, there came the true lure of forgetting.

With a tilt of my head I said, "You can promise me your complete submission?"

Her lips trembled. "Yes."

Slipping out of my jacket, I threw it across the back of a chair and then rolled up each shirt sleeve, taking my time, exaggerating the quiet, giving her time to think her way out of this.

The stillness of the room reflected Ingrid's thoughts and what she truly wanted won out.

"No going back," I said.

She caressed her fingertips over her parted rouged lips, an unconscious, feminine gesture of readiness. "Free me, William," her voice was a whisper.

And yet, she was the one freeing me.

The way she'd reapplied her make-up provided her with a gothic air, tussled hair, teased curls spiraling downward. She raised her head high, perhaps in that moment realizing the effect her appearance was having on me.

With one look I reminded her that this dark incantation would be led by me alone, forcing my expression to be that of determined master, driving out all empathy so I could take Ingrid as far as she needed to go, and further if necessary.

"Only with complete submission comes freedom," I told her.

She lowered her gaze, letting me know she was ready with that one subtle gesture of obedience.

I bit into my wrist and blood poured into one of the Champagne flutes.

The moment of no return . . .

Ingrid's mouth quivered in anticipation as she sipped from the glass, and then lowering her head, her hair tumbling over her face, the effects to taking hold.

I took the glass from her and pointed to the bedroom.

Once inside, I shut the door behind us . . .

The rush of excitement surged through Ingrid's veins causing her body to tremble, but there was no time for her to savor what the supernatural elixir bestowed and as she turned her head toward me expressing her longing, she revealed she knew all that had transpired so far would pale to what was to come.

Her eyelids closed when I bruised her lips, sharing a smoldering kiss, punishing her with passion.

Soft musical notes came and went, taking her with them and delivering an uncommon enchantment unlike any other. She lost herself in the music, extracting from this moment the rush from giving herself over to me.

I easily controlled her, edging her on with whispers, easing her into that deepest place within her and shining the light it was due, revealing the secrets she'd chased after for so long and bestowing all that she was capable of experiencing.

Notes lifted and fell, dancing around us and sharing joyfully in our illustrious encounter.

Ingrid's face reflected adoration for me and for all that I was bestowing unto her.

More of the scarlet drink was given, a daring amount that a mortal would never be allowed to receive in any other circumstance, and her breaths became shallow; her skin dewy from perspiration.

She was shaking now, seemingly in a controlled frenzy, focusing hard, pouting her concentration. My approval fired her tenacity.

Upon the bed now I wrapped my fingers around her throat to slow down her tempo. "I love you. And now you know that," I told her.

She was motionless, her eyelids closed and her face relaxed, her arms resting by her sides, her mind drifting.

I too let go, experiencing the energy that had intensified around us, and inside of us too.

Eyes closed I went with her . . .

With Ingrid's hand in mine we drifted across time and space, disappearing into the nothingness as we braved to become one with everything . . .

With each other.

"I remember," Ingrid whispered and she intertwined her fingers with mine. "Jadeon?" She let out a moan, seemingly spellbound, the preternatural blood surging within her and prolonging her . . .

Losing myself completely, recalling the image of the way she'd stood in the doorway, her head held proudly, showing off with a delicious self-assurance. Taking full control, I let Ingrid know she was mine, finally crossing that near impossible bridge to her soul.

The music an unfailing classical backdrop to all that had unfolded, where new memories were being forged, and for the first time I believed they might just push out the nightmares of my past.

All that I wanted was her.

Ingrid's auburn locks whipped from side to side as the building ecstasy stole her breath away, sweeping over her and causing her to tremble against me.

Her imminent emotional liberation was fast approaching, her freedom from those last remnants of her resistance.

She arched her back, staring at the wall behind her but not seeing it.

My fangs betrayed me as they grazed her neck, delivering scarlet droplets upon my tongue, carrying her secret desire on a wave of intimacy; Ingrid's silent words found me.

"Turn me," she was saying. *"Make me yours."*

XXXII

THE ARLINGTON SUITE was still now.

The linen Ingrid and I lay upon was now crumpled beneath us.

I pinched the stem of the ripe strawberry, dipped it into Ingrid's Champagne and pressed it gently to her lips.

I had no idea how much time had passed and I didn't care.

She sipped the bubble rich wine in between bites of fruit and I kissed her pink-tinged lips, sharing in the mergence of tastes.

I reached over to the ice bucket resting on the bedside table and lifted out the Krug and topped up her drink, then rested the bottle back into the cooler, crunching it into the ice.

She sat up, resting against the headboard. "I've been thinking a lot about my future." She put her glass down. "It terrifies me I'm even considering it."

"Maybe that's your answer." I climbed out of bed and began to dress. "I have to find Dominion."

"William, we should talk."

I knelt on the side of the bed and kissed her forehead.

"Fabian thinks we make a good team," she said.

I buttoned my shirt. "What you're essentially asking Ingrid, is for me to . . ." I refused to say the words.

"Turn me," she muttered.

"This discussion is over."

Someone was swiping a key card at the front door, trying to gain entry. Though Ingrid was oblivious to the imminent intrusion.

"You're perfect just the way you are." I shot my finger to my lips gesturing for her to be quiet. "Wait here." I headed into the living room.

It was Lucas.

He held up a small bottle and said, "Pain killers. For Ingrid."

"How are you feeling?" I asked him.

"Fine." He looked away, seemingly still rattled. "I thought I'd give you two time to talk. That's why I took a little longer." He peered passed me. "Hey there."

Ingrid stood in the bedroom doorway, dressed now and pulling a comb through her hair.

She approached Lucas and took the medicine from him. "Thank you for getting me that." Ingrid tucked the tablets into her handbag. "I'm going to pop home and get some fresh clothes. Call me, okay?"

"Of course." I tried to hide my frustration of not wanting to waste any time and start interrogating Lucas.

Lucas's eyes glazed over, as though realizing something was wrong.

Ingrid opened the door. "William, I don't suppose you want to come with me?"

"This shouldn't take long," I said.

"Sounds ominous." Lucas strolled over to the bedroom and his expression changed when he saw the disheveled sheets.

The door clicked shut. Ingrid had gone.

Lucas considered the bed. "Was that wise?"

"How's Jacob?" I asked.

He shoved his hands into his pockets.

"Jacob's been rather elusive lately," I said. "We haven't seen him for a while now."

His downcast eyes continued to regard the bedroom.

"Lucas," I said, "what exactly did Jacob promise you?"

"William, please."

"Let's take a wild guess. Jacob promised you'd get Orpheus back."

"What did Sunaria tell you?" he asked.

"Still trying to figure that out."

"You can't trust her."

I leaned back against the doorframe and folded my arms. "Start talking."

He caressed his throat. "Sunaria nearly killed Ingrid."

"Take your eyes off the door."

"Orpheus, I owe you everything. You turned me, after all."

"You were the one secret I thought I'd managed to keep."

He strolled over toward the mantelpiece, pausing briefly to examine his lack of reflection in the mirror hanging above it.

I followed him in.

"Jacob only wants what's best for you," he said.

"How long have you and Jacob been close?"

"A while." He glanced back at the mirror. "Jacob's wisdom became something I couldn't live without."

"So you're for Dominion's rule?"

"Most ardently."

"You believe he can save us?"

"Yes."

"I know about Paradom," I said.

Lucas raised his chin as though his thoughts were racing.

"I know he's joined with Dominion."

Lucas frowned. "Who told you that?" Then he realized. "Sunaria believes that?"

"Is it true?"

He ambled over toward the Champagne and lifted it. "So many luxuries that we can easily afford . . . but not partake in."

"Is Paradom joined with Dominion?" I asked again.

He dropped the bottle back into the cooler. "No."

"Is that another lie?"

Silence filled the room and I let it, hoping that he too would feel the weight of those words.

He slumped down onto the edge of the bed.

I gripped both of his wrists and pushed him back. "I need the truth. And I'm willing to do whatever it takes to get it."

"You're hurting me."

"Have you been spying on me for Jacob?"

"Guarding you. Protecting you."

"You need the scrolls for Paradom, not for me." I said.

He shook his head. "For you. Of course for you."

I tightened my grip. "Is Jacob still a member of the Stone Masters?"

He held back for a moment and then whispered, "Yes."

I was stunned.

"Both Fabian and Jacob believe that mortals and vampires must rule together," he said.

"Are you a Stone Lord?" I let him go.

"My directive comes from Fabian. My orders were to protect you at all cost. You discovered it was mercury that Sovereign was using on us. *You* saved us, William."

I took a step back.

Lucas stood up. "I understand that you don't know who to believe."

"Sunaria warned me that if I didn't kill Dominion, she'd kill Ingrid."

"Dominion's our only hope." Lucas closed the gap between us. "You must see that?"

"Vampire and mortal rule seems an obvious answer. But I need to talk with Dominion—" I shook my head— "Paradom. I need to find out his agenda."

"Paradom isn't Dominion," he said defiantly.

"Why am I being led to believe that?"

"Because Sunaria's connected the dots wrong."

"Then how should they be connected?"

He moved away, head down.

"Something must have happened for Sunaria to assume Paradom is Dominion." I said, pushing Lucas for an answer.

"Jacob's visited Paradom for decades." Lucas's face flushed as though with remorse for not telling me. "Sunaria followed Jacob a week ago. By the time Jacob realized she'd tracked him, it was too late."

"Go on."

"About one hundred years ago, what happened to you also happened to Paradom. His ashes were joined with another vampire." Lucas looked nervous. "Jacob visits him out of guilt."

"Why?"

"Paradom looks the way he does because of a failed attempt by Jacob to separate him."

I wave of nausea hit me.

Lucas looked grave. "Paradom is no longer joined with anyone."

"What?"

"The failure of the attempt left Paradom looking the way he does."

"What happened to the other vampire?" I asked, my voice tense.

Jacob's eyes were downcast.

"He died?" I said it for him, my legs unsteady.

Lucas gestured his reassurance. "That won't happen to you. We'll get the scrolls. Fabian and I will ensure your survival."

I tasted fear.

"Jacob sent you to see Paradom because he didn't want you to disappear." Lucas shrugged. "You seeing Paradom was meant to motivate your desire to revert."

"He's lucky Paradom didn't tell me what happened to him," I said. "I might very well have changed my mind and disappeared." And then it dawned on me. "Paradom still thinks he's joined with another vampire?"

"Yes, I'm afraid so."

I cringed. "So who the hell is Dominion?"

"Jacob refuses to tell me anything," Lucas admitted. "All I know is he's hidden where no one will ever look."

"Lucas, why do I feel I'm caught in the middle of your refusal to trust me."

"Orpheus was unpredictable," Lucas said. "I'm trying to protect you from yourself."

"I'm not Orpheus."

"That's partly true."

"So I'm not going to end up looking like Paradom?" My voice broke. "Unless you fuck up my reversal?"

"We won't."

My shoulders slumped, the tension promising to lift.

"We should have told you the truth about Paradom," Lucas conceded. "I'm sorry."

I lowered my chin acknowledging there was an apology at least. "Have you any idea of the absolute fear you've all put me through?"

"Forgive me," he said. "I'm sorry."

"Anything else you're not telling me?"

"I'm afraid the rumor that Paradom is Dominion has spread." He caressed his temple. "Fear breeds lies."

"Paradom," I said, "can nothing be done for him?"

"I'm not sure." He reached out to me needing to see he'd regained my trust. "William . . ."

I gave his arm a squeeze and then pointed to the Champagne. "Nice touch, by the way."

"I didn't order it. We thought you did."

I studied the bottle and then the china plate where a single strawberry was left uneaten. "I fed them to her."

Lucas bolted over to the window and I quickly joined him.

Across the street, standing on the pavement was Raven, and in his hand he was dangling a set of car keys.

I flung open the window and flew toward him landing a few feet away.

Raven held his hand up. "If anything happens to me you'll never see Ingrid again."

"What is this?" I snapped.

"Bring us Paradom and Ingrid is yours again."

"Why are you doing this?" I asked, already suspecting the answer.

Raven took a step back. "Just bring him. He's been captured by

Sovereign."

"What? When?" I balled my fists, ready to punch him.

"Last night," Raven said warily.

"How do you know that?" Lucas asked.

Raven sneered. "Paradom didn't go quietly."

My anger rose. "And you didn't help him?"

Raven looked surprised. "You'd be hard pressed to find any vampire willing to confront them."

"Where?" I asked.

"They were followed back to Bodiam Castle." Raven's narrow gaze slid over to Lucas.

"They'll kill him," Lucas said.

"We can't assume anything," said Raven. "If Sovereign hand him over to the Stone Masters . . ."

"That place will be locked down," I reasoned. "Impenetrable."

"Not my concern," Raven said.

"If you so much as lay a finger on Ingrid," I warned him, "I will rip your heart out with my bare hands."

"Where shall we meet you?" Lucas asked.

"Stonehenge," Raven said. "I'll give you until tomorrow night."

Lucas grasped the back of my shirt, preventing me from attacking him.

Raven threw me a look of disdain and then disappeared.

Lucas's grip slid to my arm. "William, you can't go. It's too dangerous."

"They have Ingrid," I snapped.

"Fabian would never forgive me if I let you anywhere near that place," he said.

"Lucas, they have the scrolls." My stare stayed on him.

"Still," he reasoned. "You're not going alone."

XXXIII

I CAME UP FOR AIR, having navigated the murky moat of Bodiam Castle.

The stale water tasted fourteenth century. I coughed several times as I pulled myself up the side of the dank underwater cavern. An echo magnified my every move and even my breaths came back exaggerated.

Lucas's head appeared out of the water. I grabbed the back of his shirt to pull him up and onto the ledge beside me.

"Going through the front door doesn't sound so bad now," Lucas whispered, resting back against the brick.

Just up ahead the tunnel turned in a westerly direction; the echo of the water lapping was the only sound.

"Bodiam was built to fend off a French invasion." Lucas tugged at his soaked shirt.

I raised an eyebrow. "The French again."

His expression changed. "I'm going to die down here, I just know it."

"No you're not. Why don't you stay here? You've got me this far."

"I'm not letting you go in there alone."

"Less conspicuous if it's just one." I peered down the tunnel.

"We get Ingrid, and then the scrolls," Lucas said, "and then we get the hell out of here."

"Let's not forget Paradom." I stood up.

"I don't have a good feeling about any of this." Lucas rose and sidled toward me. He jolted back and shoved me up against the wall, trying to hide us from the flashlights sweeping up and along.

There was a loud splash and the water swirled near our feet.

Lucas edged his way further along the ledge again and peered around the corner then held up four fingers indicating the number of men. Suddenly to our right the drawbridge came crashing down, splashing through the water and sealing off our exit.

Lucas grabbed my arm. "They're coming this way!"

"We have to get back in." Though even as I said those words I doubted it was the best idea.

Lucas's eyes widened. "They'll kill us."

Easing myself back down into the water, I gestured frantically for Lucas to follow. He too lowered himself in, his face full of fear. I dragged him under until we were resting on the bottom of the tunnel.

Above us torches swept the surface.

Out of the murkiness a blur drifted behind Lucas's back. Sensing something, Lucas turned to look behind him. A wrinkled bat-like face shot toward his, the eyes black as night, the twisted mouth gasping for air.

Lucas sprung upward, quickly reaching the surface.

Above, there came a scuffle and then yelling, as Lucas was being dragged out of the water.

I sprang out of the water, landing on the ledge—

And flinched.

A silver tipped arrow was just inches from my forehead, pulled taut on a bow. The teenager holding it was dressed in a doublet emblazoned with a knight's coat of arms.

Lucas was gone.

My throat tightened and I swallowed my fear.

A bloodied and ravaged Paradom thrashed at the drawbridge, trying to claw his way out.

"Who are you?" I asked the teenager.

"The one holding the weapon is the one who asks the questions," he replied.

His name rippled as though out of the ether . . . *Aiden Crowther*.

"Paradom," he called out, "I have one of your own here. If you don't return to your cell, I'll kill him."

"How quickly can you reload?" I glanced over at Paradom.

Aiden drew back the arrow heightening its tension. "Once this lodges in your brain you won't much care."

I sent a trance wave directly into Aiden's mind but it had no effect.

Paradom disappeared beneath the surface, leaving behind a trail of bubbles heading back into the castle.

"Who told you about this place?" Aiden asked, now directing the bow toward my heart.

A fortyish bearded monk appeared, donning black rimmed spectacles and carrying his own bow. "Why haven't you shot it yet?" he asked, reaching for an arrow, readying it in his bow and pulling it taut.

Aiden's right eye twitched. "Dad, I can handle this."

I turned my mind gift onto the monk and attempted to trance him out.

"I can feel that," the monk said, and fired.

* * * *

When I came round I couldn't move.

The clang of chains wrapped around my body told me why. I'd been secured to a table. There was a strange tangy scent in the air that I couldn't isolate and despite the age of the castle, this room had been modernized with stark walls and low hung cabinets.

Aiden's face came into focus. "Incredible how they survive that."

"You have to tell your dad *it* woke up," the youthful voice came from behind me.

Aiden glanced up. "Not yet."

"Don't engage it," the voice came again. "Remember?"

"Bring me that knife." Aiden unbuttoned my shirt, though boredom soon struck and he ripped it open, popping off the buttons.

"Aiden?" I said.

"It read my mind," Aiden said. "He's not meant to be able to do that."

"Maybe you need to take more . . . you know," his friend vaguely suggested.

Aiden was now holding a knife. "Even if I cut out its heart it can survive, want to see?"

"I'm not an *it*." My terror turned in on itself as my thoughts turned to Lucas.

"Screaming's permitted, talking isn't." He sliced into my chest and then lifted the blade and blood oozed from the cut.

With my jaw tightly clenched, I barely held back.

"Heals instantly." Aiden snapped his head up again. "Come closer. You can't see from there."

Whoever was behind me stayed put.

I caught a glimpse of the signet ring on Aiden's small finger. The crest was an engraved snake wrapped around a skeleton key.

I tried to breath through my panic. "Who's in charge? I need to speak with them."

Aiden's tongue licked the tip of the knife and he rolled back his eyes, spacing out.

"Let's go now," came the voice.

"My dad doesn't need to know." Aiden offered the knife back to his friend and a hand came out of nowhere and took it.

The room started spinning.

"Not sure if anyone's ever told you this before but you're a perfect specimen." Aiden peered over at his friend. "And like all specimens he must be cut up."

"Lucas?" his name slipped out, but all I could think of was him.

"That's the other one he came with," said the discarnate voice.

"Why did you come here?" Aiden asked.

Nausea welled and I lifted my head an inch and glanced over toward the door.

Aiden bit his lip in feigned concern. "You're friend's probably dead."

His friend gasped. "Shit, don't rile it up."

"It's tied down," Aiden insisted. "Can't do anything with this much silver wrapped around it."

Aiden fiddled with my trousers. "I'm going to castrate you if you don't start talking." He clicked his fingers to get the knife back.

I sent a willful command his way, trying to trance him out.

Aiden's head shot up. "Did you feel that?" His frown deepened. "Shut your mind down," he warned his friend.

I willed a shockwave through the chains and one by one they snapped and fell, clinking when they hit the floor. I clambered off the table and stood before Aiden and swiped his knife, turning it on him. Holding it firmly, I pressed the tip against his neck.

Aiden's eyes widened in terror.

"Where's my friend?" I asked.

"With my dad," he muttered.

I glanced over at Aiden's timid accomplice who was slightly taller than him; pimple faced and teenage thin. "What's your name?" I asked him.

The boy cowered.

"Shawn?" I asked. "Where are they keeping him?"

"Don't tell him," Aiden said.

I narrowed my gaze. "What are you taking to block your thoughts?"

"Nothing," Aiden lied.

"Shawn, say goodbye to Aiden," I threatened.

Shawn mumbled, "Mercury."

"Shut up," Aiden snapped at him.

"Vamps can't metabolize it." Shawn's words spilled with his dread. "It affects their central nervous system."

"Are all members of Sovereign taking it?" I asked.

"Please let him go now," Shawn begged.

"Answer me!" I snapped.

Whirling arrows found their mark and pierced my flesh, sending jolting pain, penetrating deep into my back and trailing behind each one were thin silver chains. I slumped to my knees.

The men who'd shot them were all dressed as monks and they were encircling me, wrapping the chains around my chest and binding my arms to my sides. Aiden wore a look of arrogant pride.

"Did you unchain it?" Crowther seethed with fury.

"No," Aiden replied hastily.

Crowther strolled around me. "You're playing with fire," he said to Aiden.

Aiden's friend was hopping from one foot to the next.

Crowther peered over his lenses at him. "Didn't we discuss the importance of following orders?"

Aiden's voice trembled. "We were trying to get it to talk."

Crowther removed a pistol from his pocket and aimed it directly at Shawn. "Shall I show you what happens when you disobey?"

Aiden flinched. "Dad please."

The shot rang out and the bullet lodged in Shawn's chest; he puffed out his cheeks, his face scarlet, his breath gone from him. He fell forward, his face striking the floor—

Dead.

Crowther glared back at Aiden. "Did I make my point?"

Aiden's stifled moans filled the room.

They dragged me to my feet and we passed Shawn's body out and along the corridor. The shock of each arrow coursed through me, the pain of their tug in my flesh blinding my way. We passed door after door and I sensed other vampires were trapped in those rooms. I was shoved inside a small cell and the monks bullied me to my knees; the chains dangling around me, all strength to fight my way out of them gone.

Crowther appeared in the doorway. "You got inside my son's mind."

"Your son needed no encouragement," I said.

Peering over his spectacles, Crowther said, "You're damned."

"You just shot a boy in cold blood." Struggling to break free I cursed my inability to read his thoughts.

"Imagine what I'm going to do to you." He knelt before me. "During the second world war, Bodiam's dungeons were adapted as a secret bunker. We've updated them since. Reinforced the walls. It's sound tight. Bodiam's secluded location makes it ideal for our purpose."

Words failed me, my gut wrenching with regret for failing Lucas, failing Ingrid, failing everyone.

"No one will hear you." His intensity deepened. "How did you find out about this place?" Crowther yanked on one of the chains.

Sending a jolt of pain into my flesh. "The entire underworld knows about Bodiam," I bluffed.

Crowther twitched. "It's lying."

"My name's William." Concentrating hard, I sent a burst of energy straight into his front lobe.

Unaffected he said, "Your name is *abomination*." Crowther gestured to his men. "We'll use this one instead." He rose and headed out.

The door slammed shut behind him.

XXXIV

AFTER WHAT MUST HAVE been the twenty-fourth hour came and went I struggled to hold onto my aimless thoughts; a stream of internal dialogue that was no longer assuring I'd survive, but had taken on a threatening tone, decimating all hope.

I'd been left alone with nothing but my crazed deliberations and the agony of knowing I'd missed the deadline of meeting Raven at Stonehenge. Although I'd sent mind messages to Lucas, I'd gotten nothing back. The only sounds were the terrified cries of vampires locked up in the other cells.

In between long, chilling silences.

Silver tipped arrows were still embedded, though the shooting pains had lessoned; perhaps my flesh was growing used their intrusion.

Too fraught to sleep, I waited for Crowther's men to return.

And eventually they did, dragging me out down endless corridors. I staggered to keep up with their disregarding strides. We entered a large hall.

Roughly I was secured upon a central table. Taking in the high beamed ceiling, I tried to fathom the mistakes that had brought me here, full of self-hate for delivering myself into their hands.

Squeezing my eyes shut, I told myself this wasn't the ritual of torture once used by the Stone Masters. Though when the long line of monks streamed in, I knew it was. With brutal determination by the men who surrounded me, my arms were stretched out wide to either side of me.

Only now did I understand what Sunaria had endured.

This barbaric torturing of mind, body and soul, stripping away all identity and leaving behind its victim so filled with terror that the fight inevitably turns inward. Regret was all that was left, mourning for all that could have been.

And yet would never now be.

Aiden's face loomed over me. Crowther wouldn't be far away. My throat tightened when that familiar chanting arose, that terrible cadence announcing what was to come. Lord Crowther took his position at the head of the table, the once position of the Stone Master himself, now seized by Sovereign's leader.

The first slice of a knife through my wrist brought excruciating pain; the sound of my blood trickled into a goblet. The fine bejeweled cup was then handed from monk to monk and supped from. Each man's chanting ceased only to imbibe. Unlike the Stone Masters the drink was shared, savored, enjoyed. Gradually, their expressions turning blissful.

All except one, a monk who stood to my left, his hood pulled well over his face, his hands steepled in prayer.

"We gather to celebrate my son's induction," Crowther began. "We welcome Aiden into the fold."

I flinched when yet another slice made its way through my wrist, my teeth chattering.

Lifting my head again, trying to count the number of men, I caught Aiden gulping the entire contents of the bejeweled vessel, his lips smudged red as he violated me with that very act.

Still in denial I wanted to believe I could take them on, all of them, though resistance from the chains insisted my judgment was skewed.

"We offer up this sacrifice to the brothers, our blessed *Watchers of the Night*," Crowther suddenly seemed distracted.

All eyes were on Aiden, who was sitting on the ground wearing a ridiculous grin, his eyelids forced shut, forgetting why he was here as the blood raged through his veins, setting every cell alight with supernatural velocity. His grunts of pleasure were embarrassingly loud.

Crowther watched on horrified, his expression abashed— shamed. One of the monks ambled toward me and from beneath his hood familiar eyes stared back.

Sebastian's.

He reached for the discarded knife and rested it against my wrist though applied no pressure. "Now and again a man glances at the island just off in the distance," he said, his Welsh accent lulling me. "He wonders what goes on there." Sebastian removed the knife. "Then one day he travels to that very island and turns to face the old land and realizes . . ."

My eyes stung with tears.

Crowther snatched the knife from Sebastian. "We finish this tomorrow."

Sebastian stepped back, his hood falling over his face again.

Unsecured now, I was dragged off the table and past the monks who were trying to control a frenzied Aiden. Instead of turning left where they'd initially imprisoned me, I was shoved head first into another cell.

The door locked behind me.

Peering into the darkness, there lying on his side curled up in a ball was Raven, his cheeks sucked in and drawn, his terrified face turned upward at the ceiling.

Paradom was hanging upside down, his clawed feet holding him steady from a low wooden beam, and in his arms lay a barely conscious Angus. Paradom's lips were locked on Angus's throat and he was sucking hard.

"William?" The woman's voice sounded fragile.

There came a wave of emotions, everything from joy at seeing Ingrid to angst that she was here.

She flushed with horror when she saw the arrows protruding from my chest.

"Get . . . them out," I muttered.

Fearing what I asked of her, she carefully ran her fingertips over the nocks testing how deep the arrows went. Despite the wrenching pain, knowing she was alive gave me the strength to stay conscious, and when the final arrow left my flesh it felt like air was filling my lungs properly again.

Ingrid approached Raven and persuaded him to hand over his coat, then carried it back, laying it over me. "What did they do to you?"

I eased myself up and reached for her hand. "Did anyone hurt you?"

She pointed to that circled brand of hers and then glanced up at Paradom. "They saw this and stayed away." She took my hand and squeezed it.

My gaze slid over to Raven. "He kidnapped you?"

"Yes, and him too." She gestured to Angus who was still caught in Paradom's clutches. Ingrid shifted closer. "I never made it out of the Ritz. Within an hour men burst into our room and all three of us were brought here." She frowned. "My captors got kidnapped."

"Raven's plan got derailed," I said, my mouth dry. "This place belongs to Sovereign."

"What is that?" Ingrid whispered, her wide eyes sliding up toward Paradom.

"He's one of us," I explained "But something . . . happened to him."

"What exactly?" Ingrid asked, her fearful stare now locked on the doorway.

Aiden was silhouetted there and he had something in his hands. I staggered to my feet, readying to protect Ingrid despite my unsteady gait.

Aiden took a careful step closer. He was carrying an urn. "You were asking about your friend, Lucas?" Aiden lifted the lid and flung its contents over me.

A cloud of grey dust billowed, covering me entirely in ash.

My chest wrenched and I froze in utter horror.

Aiden was handed a small device and he raised his arm, pointing it toward the ceiling. Paradom screeched and let go of Angus, dropping him to the floor. Paradom landed at Aiden's feet and scampered out the door behind him. The door was locked again.

I slumped to my knees, wiping my face with trembling hands, trying to fill my lungs with breaths that I couldn't catch. I cursed myself for bringing Lucas here, the pain in my heart dimming my vision, blurring my eyes. Ingrid was speaking but I couldn't make out her words.

Raven's voice came out of the dark. "We're all dead."

Angus crawled toward Raven, whimpering.

Ingrid pressed her wrist against my lips. "You have to."

Gently I nudged her hand away. She looked around and I could only assume it was for a sharp object.

"No," I insisted, squeezing my eyelids shut, hating my weakness.

"Otherwise we'll all die in here." She pressed her wrist to my mouth again.

I nuzzled into the crook of her arm and punctured her flesh with a delicate bite, tasting her blood, wanting to turn away but I feared wasting her precious offering.

Sharing in more than just her life source, her essence too, drinking that which might just save me. Save us.

She was trembling . . .

Her love for me pouring out with her blood.

I buried a fang into my thumb and used the scarlet liquid to heal where I'd punctured her flesh. I hugged her into me, holding her tighter than I ever had.

A key turned in the lock and the door slowly opened.

Sebastian's head peeked round and he quickly entered, still dressed in the garb of a monk, throwing an uneasy glance over at Raven.

Sebastian knelt by my side. "Can you walk?" As his eyes adjusted to the darkness he reacted to the grey-tinged ash covering me.

"Have you seen my friend Lucas?" I barely managed to say.

"Lucas told me where you were," Sebastian explained. "They went to find the scrolls."

"Who's they?" I asked.

"Lucas and his friend. A priest? They're getting the scrolls then they're coming back for us."

"Did the priest have a name?" I asked.

"Jacob, I think." Sebastian frowned, studying the ash. "What is that?"

"When did you last see Lucas?" I asked.

Sebastian threw a wary look over at Raven.

Both Raven and Angus were sidling toward the doorway and bolted through it.

"Seb?" I tugged his shirt.

"Five minutes ago," he said.

I threw my head back in relief. "Aiden told me these were Lucas's ashes."

"He's a right little shit, that one," Sebastian said. "You okay?" he asked Ingrid.

"I'm fine," she replied, though clearly she wasn't.

"We have to find Paradom," I said.

Sebastian grimaced. "What exactly is that thing?"

"I'll explain later," I insisted and struggled to my feet.

"Whatever it is, they've inserted a device next his heart," Sebastian said, assisting Ingrid up. "If Paradom so much as makes eye contact they shock him."

I shook my head, disgusted with their cruelty. "Get Ingrid to safety." I grabbed Raven's coat and pulled it on. "That includes you, Seb."

"I'm not leaving without you," Ingrid said.

"You can't stay here a moment longer," I said.

Sebastian pointed toward the door. "There's a fully working laboratory down here."

"They're other prisoners here too," Ingrid said. "We can't leave them."

"First, I have to get inside that lab," I said.

"Perhaps that's where they're testing the mercury?" Sebastian asked.

We headed out into the corridor.

"How did you even know we were here?" I asked Sebastian.

"Didn't. That notebook you gave Alex," Sebastian explained. "Anaïs was able to bring out the writing with lemon juice. Bodium Castle was mentioned in it." He shook his head. "I came here to check out the place. Got caught by the man dressed as the Grim Reaper. Luckily I managed to talk my way out of trespassing because he recognized me. This was the place where I was initiated." Sebastian guided us on. "The lab's this way."

"Sovereign still dress as monks," Ingrid said, "and yet behave like barbarians."

Sebastian peeked round the corner. "White coat heading our way."

The middle-aged laboratory technician, whisked around the corner and virtually bumped into us.

Reading his nametag, I sent a trance wave and said, "Dr. Cass, open the lab."

He stepped back, unaffected.

"Mercury," I said, realizing, and quickly applied a choke hold until he'd lost consciousness. I threw him over my shoulder.

Sebastian unclipped Cass's ID and swiped the card through the mechanism. The small light on the security pad blinked green. The door clicked open and we headed on in.

I laid Cass's unconscious body in the corner. Sebastian, Ingrid and I set to work, searching for anything that might reveal what the scientists were working on.

Ingrid flipped over one of the computer keyboards and peered beneath. "Secret codes are only useful if kept that way." She righted the keypad and typed away.

"Are you in?" Sebastian asked her, peering over her shoulder at the screen.

"Yes." Ingrid began opening files, trying to decipher what she was reading. "Blood results?"

"We have to get you out of here," Jacob called over to us. He was standing in the doorway and he was yet again wearing reverend attire, his clerical collar neatly fitted.

"That's the priest I was telling you about," Sebastian whispered.

"How did you get in?" Ingrid rose from the chair.

Sebastian took a protective step toward her.

"We can trust him," I said.

"I stole one of the guard's ID's," Jacob said.

"How many Hail Mary's will that be?" Sebastian asked.

"I'm not Catholic," Jacob said flatly. "God will understand. I'm assisting my friends, after all." He stepped closer. "Lucas has the scrolls. It's too dangerous for you to stay here."

"Paradom?" I asked. "I'm not leaving without him."

"I'll find him," he said. "Please, get out of here. Before they find you again."

"How did you get into the castle?" I asked.

"Bodium once belonged to the Stone Masters," he said.

"You're still a Stone Lord?" I asked.

He raised his eyebrows gesturing his sincerity. "For all the right reasons."

"Why didn't you tell me?" I asked.

"I needed you to trust me." Jacob relented and gestured to the equipment. "Sovereign are researching the alteration of DNA from continued mercury intake. Their notion is that over many generations of mercury ingestion, human DNA tolerates higher levels."

"Human cell mutation?" Sebastian clarified.

Jacob looked woeful. "Sovereign's long term plan is to alter the DNA of every human on the planet. Provide a form of immunity to vampires."

"Deliberately poison everyone?" Ingrid asked, astonished. "So that we're *all* contaminated with mercury?"

"Yes," Jacob said. "They're adjusting DNA in order to turn off what makes mercury harmful."

"They're planning on contaminating water and food sources," Ingrid realized.

"Ancient Egyptian's were the first to discover the power of mercury," Jacob explained. "They ingested it to aid health and discovered it had other uses."

"Blocked the mind control of vampires," I said.

There came the sound of men shouting just outside the lab.

"This way." Jacob guided us through the laboratory toward a smaller, colder room.

The second laboratory was stark white and at the center was positioned a long examination table.

"You should have told me about this place," I said. "Give me one good reason to trust you."

"William," Jacob said, "I was the one who came here to save Rachel."

"Why not tell me that?" I asked.

"We couldn't risk you destroying this place," he said.

"You feared I'd destroy the scrolls?" I whispered.

Jacob gestured his sincerity. "Now that we have all of them we can separate *you*."

"This is not about me!" I snapped.

"Yes it is." He raised his hand, insisting. "It's always been about you."

Men were now inside the larger lab, their shouts louder, more insistent.

Jacob flew toward the other end of the room and went for the air vent, ripping it from the wall. "Hurry," he motioned frantically. "This leads to a storeroom. There's a stairwell to the left of it. Go!"

I lifted Ingrid up and through the vent and then assisted Sebastian into it.

"I'll meet you back at the Mount," I said.

"William, you too," Jacob said. "I need to know you're safe."

I slid the vent cover back in place.

Crowther and his men burst in, aiming their arrows at the ready.

One of Crowther's men had a silver tipped arrow pointed straight at my heart. I froze where I stood, reassured at least that Ingrid and Sebastian were on their way to escaping.

"*Promise me*," I sent the silent message to Jacob. "*You'll save Paradom.*"

Jacob acknowledged he would. "*William, I failed you.*"

I tried to read from his expression what he meant.

Crowther's glare scanned the room. "Where's the girl?"

"How's your son?" I asked.

Crowther's attention zoomed in on Jacob. "We had an agreement."

"Did we?" Jacob answered calmly.

Studying Crowther, I was left with the distinct impression he had no idea Jacob was a vampire, and though his mind was closed, Crowther's lack of hate for Jacob confirmed it.

Crowther narrowed his gaze. "Father Roch, I let you have Rachel. Our bargain was set. You promised never to return."

"Let William go," Jacob said. "I'll deal with him."

"You gave up any right to bargain when you broke your word and came back," Crowther said. "Now you can help me clean up this mess."

Jacob was stunned into silence.

"We kill the vampire at first light," Crowther said. "Father Roch, you can administer the last rites. Though I doubt it'll do *it* any good."

XXXV

WHEN I CAME ROUND, a hessian sack was covering my head.

The shock of being flung upon a cold hard surface brought me back to consciousness. An excruciating burning went over my entire chest as though the silver from the arrows was leaking into my flesh and spreading out, radiating down my arms.

For at least two days, I'd slipped in and out like this, having been tortured by Crowther's men. Bled . . .

And I'd told them nothing.

The Gregorian chanting sent chills snaking up my spine, and struggling to breathe I sucked in air but hardly filled my lungs. There was a clang of metal chains and the sensation of them being drawn across my body, securing me again. My arms were stretched wide and my feet bound taut and held fast. The chill of dawn and the squawking of ravens were a terrible portend of what was to come.

The hood came off and I caught my breath when I saw the grand rocky gods of Stonehenge surrounding me, inexorably reaching toward the dusky sky and the outer circle of continuous lintels towering over me.

Their sacrifice.

Crowther's face came into focus. "It is with truth and honor that I command your spirit into the afterworld, where you will be judged accordingly."

The slice into my wrist made me flinch.

"It is within my power to grant you forgiveness." Crowther held the goblet over my head.

"Do you repent?"

"Is that question for you or me?" I murmured.

His lips thinned and he tipped the cup, spilling the contents, his mouth twisted in hate. There came another cut and a trickling into the vessel—more of my blood.

Crowther raised the goblet again. "What do you plead?"

"For your death to be slow," I whispered.

He leaned closer. "Death awaits you, vampire." He took a gulp and his eyelids flickered, and he pouted in response to the rush. "Status Regal, this is indeed an honor." He coughed off his reaction. Crowther's eyelids closed as he savored the sensations.

"William?" A man's voice came from behind me.

I took in the upside vision of the monk's face, the deeply etched frown-lines, the middle-aged jowl. I didn't recognize him and I was passed caring.

"My name's Vanderbilt," he whispered. "You understand what is happening? We have waited for this moment for too long."

Crowther opened his eyes and offered Vanderbilt the chalice.

Vanderbilt ignored him and leaned closer to my ear. "You're not alone." He gave a subtle gesture to one of the other hooded monks halfway hidden behind a bluestone. It was Sebastian staring back at me.

"Shall we?" Crowther opened his palm and a silver tipped stake was placed within it. "This is your last chance to admit your sins."

"I confess," I muttered.

Crowther leaned into my ear.

"I confess . . . I never told her just how much I love her." I closed my eyes.

Shutting out the world . . .

We could have been anywhere, but St. Michael's Mount seemed as good a place as any. Allowing my musing to save me from this moment, I went with my imagination, finding myself standing with Ingrid upon the Mount's roof.

Holding each other's hands, we shared these final moments. As I listened to her voice lulling me, telling me not be afraid, I surrendered . . .

But only to her.

And then I realized, Ingrid was here.

My eyes searched for her, fearful she may be in harm's way. There came a scuffle, monks fighting monks . . .

No, it was vampires fighting monks, and even more nightwalkers descended around me, taking up the fight with Sovereign.

Crowther was shoved forward over the central stone, his face looming close to mine, his jaw gaping, his eyes wide in horror; poking out of his chest was the tip of a silver arrow.

He slumped onto his knees, moaning his pain.

Marcus was standing right behind him, having just impaled Crowther with an arrow. Marcus flashed me a crazed defiant smile. The fight ensued, and even more vampires appeared from the shadows, joining the fray.

Still bound to the central stone, I struggled to get free. "Marcus, untie me," I called out.

Though if he did hear me he was too busy fighting.

Mercury, our enemy's only defense, would do nothing to protect Sovereign here. A vampire's warring would leave bodies flung against the stones, others fallen where they'd stood, their necks broken by the swift and unseen attack of the undead.

My kind had not only battled Sovereign's lack of intolerance, but also derailed their plan threatening mortals and vampires alike.

When eventually the stillness returned, vampires peeled off their disguises leaving monk robes scattered. The only victims here were the fallen members of Sovereign.

Ingrid ran to my side and tore at my chains, trying to remove them.

"Here, I'll do it," Marcus said to her and reached for them.

Feeling their loosening I breathed deeply, throwing a glance at Crowther's corpse.

"It's time," came Fabian's familiar voice as he grasped my shoulders and eased me back down onto the stone.

Panic welled within me and I resisted, trying to rise.

Lucas pressed his hands against my chest. "William, I have the scroll we need."

Ingrid reached for my hand. "Is this what you want, William?" she asked, tears welling. "Is this what you want?"

What I want?

Marcus leaned over me and held my shoulder. "Belshazzar's."

I frowned his way.

"Orpheus," Marcus said insistently, "meet me there."

As his words settled into my bones, I knew my time upon this earth was close to ending.

Lucas nudged Marcus out of the way.

"Belshazzar's, remember that." Marcus stepped back, hesitating, holding my gaze. "William . . ." He shook his head, conflicted.

"I'll see you there," I told him, sharing the words he needed to hear.

Seemingly reassured, Marcus was gone.

Fabian brushed a few stray hairs out of my eyes. "Do you have the faith to face the light, William?"

Though I tried to reply, the words were lost forever in a sea of fear.

Sebastian appeared by my side and took my hand. "I'll wait with you."

Ingrid took my other hand. "We won't leave you."

"What will happen?" I asked Fabian.

"We start in reverse," he replied calmly. "And later, we resurrect the ashes."

"Dear God . . ." My throat was dry with trepidation.

"He's here," Fabian said.

Following Fabian's gaze, I took in each stone, focusing on their flawless irregularities, their masterful alignment. Their domineering perfection.

"I want to live . . ." I whispered.

"Death is merely an illusion," Fabian said.

Lucas stood at the end of the central stone looking down upon me. He unraveled the scroll and he took in what was written upon it, his face scanning the Coptic words with a steady eye.

"What does it say?" I asked him.

"It's an incantation," Lucas said.

"We must begin." Jacob's focus did for a minute settle on the horizon as though wary of dawn's imminence.

Sebastian gripped my hand though I suspected it was as much for him as it was for me.

"Sebastian, promise me," I whispered, "you'll dance again."

"I'm counting on you being there when I do," he said bravely.

"Fabian, watch over Catherine." I focused back on Sebastian. "Take care of Alex."

"I promise," Sebastian said.

Above me the clear starlit sky; the first tinges of dawn kissing my flesh.

I held Ingrid's gaze and found comfort there. "I love you," I told her.

She pressed her lips to my hand, her strength feeding mine.

"Sebastian, after we leave make sure William remains on the stone," Fabian said.

My attention fell on Sebastian, checking he'd understood the warning. Fabian, seemingly satisfied, gave a subtle signal to Lucas that he was to begin.

Sebastian squeezed my hand. "It's been an honor."

"You make it sound so final," I said and then swallowed hard.

"William, I'll always love you," Ingrid said. "Always."

Lucas raised the scroll high, interpreting the Egyptian and chanting the incantation with clarity and confidence, his accent thick, his intonation exact. The ancient language carried upon the air, echoing and filling the space around us. Spellbound, I marveled at the way the stones shimmered, their grandness emphasized by the soft blue hue emanating.

"Do you see it?" I blinked several times, fearing the brightness.

Silence found me; the chanting having ceased.

Fabian, Lucas and Jacob had gone.

Reading Ingrid's expression, it pained me to see her so fraught.

I held her gaze. "I *will* find you."

Lips trembling, her hand shaking in mine, Ingrid conveyed her faith that I would.

I sighed my surrender.

These were more than individual pillars brought here centuries ago to be worshiped, and when placed together each was more than a sum of its parts, a profound conduit for power.

Harnessing that which offered itself willingly and trusting in the silent words they spoke to me, I glimpsed the other side . . .

A place of wonder and trueness.

Sunlight struck the stones and the rays caressed the pillars, bouncing off each one and pouring intense crystal shards down and around me. A bright, orange sun bowed low and swept me up into her arms, carrying me into her very center. I willed myself to know her brilliance.

And remember the light . . .

XXXVI

I WRITHED, GASPING FOR LIFE.

Through blurred vision, I made out a standing stone and there, slumped at its base, was Orpheus.

Fragmented memories.

My flesh felt like it was melting but I forced myself to ignore it and rallied my strength, staggering toward him.

Scattered memories . . .

I crashed Orpheus's head against the stone and he struck out, shoving me. He was on his feet again now, flying up into the air toward me, punching my jaw with a crack, knocking me backward.

Stunned, I paused, realizing there was only *one* stone.

Instead of the night sky, there was a high vaulted ceiling painted with intricate frescos, dramatic scenes portrayed from the Book of Genesis and at my feet marble flooring inlaid with emblems.

More striking still, my shirt was off and these trousers weren't my own; I was barefoot. Orpheus too was dressed like me, trousers only, chest bare and shoeless.

He scanned his surroundings, seemingly as baffled.

Orpheus flew at me, grabbed my shoulders and thrust upward, slamming me hard against the ceiling, his fingers squeezing my throat. He let go and we tumbled to the floor.

I rose to my feet and readied for another attack.

Orpheus was standing a few feet away, his face twisted in confusion. "I can't . . . do it." He stared at his hands. Trying to read him, I culled his thoughts for how we'd gotten here.

Orpheus flinched as though struck by an invisible force, his face contorted in horror. "I can't kill you."

"Where are we?" I muttered.

His eyes searched the chamber again, looking for anything familiar.

"Sunaria's alive," I said.

With a suspicious gaze, he considered me. "What the hell happened?"

"I see you've woken up." Fabian was standing casually beside the megalith.

"What is this?" Orpheus yelled.

Fabian stepped nearer. "Orpheus, a part of you is within Jadeon, and he in you."

"What did you do to us?" he snapped.

"Separated you," Fabian said.

Orpheus backed up. "Where . . ."

Fabian threw me a reassuring glance. "St. Michael's Mount."

"Fabian Snowstrom?" His mouth gaped in horror as though remembering. "What the hell did you put me through?"

"I had nothing to do with your joining, Orpheus," Fabian said. "But everything to do with you finding your way back."

Orpheus straightened. "Sovereign?"

Jacob appeared beside Fabian and said, "All dead. Though the son lives."

"Not for much longer." Orpheus faced me again, realizing. "Jadeon doesn't remember, does he?"

Fabian tilted his head. "He will."

"Sunaria?" Orpheus's hands stretched behind him.

Fabian gestured to the doorway. "You won't be stopped."

Orpheus was gone.

Taking the three short steps toward the megalith, I caressed her irregularities, running my fingertips over her coldness. Spreading my hands over her width as though waiting for her to spill her well-kept secrets honored over centuries.

"The incantation?" I asked.

"Went smoothly," Fabian replied. "The scrolls did indeed hold the key to your separation."

"Miraculous," I whispered, "that such a spell even exists."

Fabian lowered his gaze.

I read the trepidation in his expression. "What other incantations do the scrolls possess?"

Fabian raised his hand. "You have visitors."

Catherine appeared in the doorway. "I couldn't wait a moment longer." She ran and threw her arms around me, kissing my cheek.

"You did it!" she said to Fabian. "You actually did it!"

Ingrid was lingering a few feet behind her, watching nervously. Catherine motioned for Ingrid to approach.

"How do you feel?" Catherine asked.

I tried to find the words. "Hung over?" I turned to Fabian. "Is this real?"

"It is." Fabian said.

"How much do you remember?" Ingrid asked.

Caressing my temple I reached for the memories, shocked with the clarity of all that had unfolded. "It feels like a dream. No, make that a nightmare."

"You're safe now," Ingrid said. "It's over.

"And you're both alright?" I asked them.

Ingrid snuggled in, wrapping her hands around my waist and squeezing me tight. "Now that we know you're okay." She looked up at me and a tear fell.

I wiped it away.

Quiet ensued and I felt peace sweep over me, over all of us, a long awaited serenity that had always promised to find us.

Jacob stepped forward and offered Ingrid a rolled up parchment.

Ingrid accepted the scroll, holding it reverently. "Hornub's scroll?"

"Lucas retrieved it from Bodiam Castle," Jacob explained. "Hornub's guide to the other side."

"It belongs with Hornub," Fabian agreed.

"I'll see it's returned to him," Ingrid said. "What will happen to the other scrolls? The book of Toth?"

"They'll be kept safe," Fabian said.

Catherine rubbed Ingrid's arm with affection. "Jadeon, we'll wait for you upstairs." She slid her arm through Ingrid's and they headed out of the chamber.

It felt good to see them both safe.

I found Fabian's gaze again. "I came to you . . . visited you at Leeds castle."

"We talked at length," Fabian coaxed me on.

"It's still a little foggy . . ." I admitted.

"Come." Fabian led me behind the standing stone, through the secret doorway behind it and down the stairwell. Jacob followed close behind us.

All three of us entered Dominion's tomb.

XXXVII

AGAIN I WAS STRUCK with the dramatic standing stone, the way she towered reverently over Dominion's sarcophagus, the other half of her disappearing into the ceiling.

Fabian gestured toward the coffin within. "When something is found," he spoke softly, "what does one do?"

"Cease the search," I said.

Jacob gestured with a sweep of his hand. "The best defenses are the ones you don't know exist."

Fabian stepped toward me. "Jadeon, two hundred years ago, I approached your father Lord Artimas with a proposition. I foresaw that if the Stone Masters continued to wage war on vampires that the suffering of both mortals and immortals would endure. Therefore, I proposed a truce, one that would place a vampire officially within the Stone Masters. The idea being that they would advance with joint rule."

"I had already infiltrated the group," Jacob said.

"Over centuries," Fabian said, "Jacob feigned inheriting the title of Stone Lord from his father, and his father before him. We remained one step ahead. In doing so we prevented much of their persecution of our kind."

"Lord Artimas," Jacob continued, "was informed that we'd chosen one who would govern with an uncompromising hand over vampires. Jointly Lording alongside the Stone Master himself."

Fabian raised his chin. "And his name was—"

"Dominion," I said, my focus finding the tomb again, exploring the ornate carvings.

Fabian broke the silence, saying, "Lord Artimas conceded that a vampire ruler would best reign over his own kind. He agreed with us and took our proposition back to the other Stone Lords." Fabian looked grave. "His men voted against Lord Artimas. They hunted Dominion, intending to kill him. Carnage ensued."

"Lord Artimas and his men refused your offer of peace," I said.

"This tomb was a ruse," Fabian acknowledge.

"A diversion," said Jacob.

"With Jacob securely ensconced within the Stone Lords, he set about building this sarcophagus." Fabian gestured to the standing stone. "She'd been here for one thousand years, carefully hidden. It was the perfect place for a tomb, ensconced within the very heart of the Stone Masters."

"Once this sarcophagus was built," Jacob said, "and secured, we set about choosing the men who would guard it."

"You feigned Dominion had been captured?" I realized. "You asserted he was actually in there." I studied the empty coffin. "Didn't Lord Artimas insist on seeing the body?"

"We waited for a distraction," Jacob said. "We chose the night your mother died in childbirth. Lord Artimas was so riddled with grief that he gave over the power to entomb Dominion," Fabian turned toward Jacob, "to Father Jacob Roch."

"We ordered all vampires to leave Cornwall," Jacob added. "Though they knew not why. And when vampire attacks ceased—"

"The Stone Masters were convinced they really did have Dominion," I said.

Jacob shared a look with Fabian and said, "I chose the men who would guard the tomb. I named them Sovereign. Monks were considered to be unquestioning. They were regularly rewarded with sips of blood offered up in a ceremony."

"For eight years there was peace again," Fabian said. "Harmony."

"Vampires were tempered," Jacob said. "Stayed in the shadows."

Fabian grimaced. "We hadn't accounted for man's greed."

I understood what he was intimating. "Until a member of Sovereign became obsessed with actually drinking from the fountain of bliss, Dominion himself."

Jacob pursed his lips with tension. "One of the monks pried open the tomb. Sovereign believed it was the Stone Masters who'd stolen him. Their allegiance became strained. Sovereign broke away with their own agenda."

My focus fell on the empty sarcophagus again. "Did Dominion ever really exist?"

Fabian raised his chin high. "He does. When we chose him he

was merely a boy. Bright, well educated. His temperament gentle, like his mother's. He was of course mortal. We needed him to grow, flourish and see the world anew. Believe in the possibilities of peace."

"We placed servants around him," Jacob said, "to protect him."

"And great teachers to educate him," Fabian added. "To enlighten him."

"We hoped he would one day join us," Jacob said. "Give his own life over to become a vampire."

"And he did," I murmured.

"But not by our hand," Fabian whispered.

"Orpheus transformed him," Jacob said. "Removing Dominion's free will."

"Orpheus had no idea what he'd done," I whispered, taking in the way the walls threw off a delicate blue hue caressing the marble, the magnificently rising granite stone representing divinity; the way Jacob and Fabian gazed upon me.

"We were waiting for the chosen one to be enlightened," Fabian said. "Illuminated by time."

"Dominion had to be ready," Jacob asserted.

Fabian's irises glinted in the darkness. "To rule wisely."

Jacob gestured to the doorway.

We headed out of the dark chamber and up into the Stone Master's chapel, and onward, ascending the long winding staircase leading out of the once torture chamber. The faint scent of sandalwood lingered.

Though the long lines of cells were illuminated with candles they did nothing to lift the gloom. I followed Fabian and Jacob into the far cell, sensing him before I saw him—

Paradom was crouched low in the corner, and his eyes widened when he saw us.

I knelt close to Paradom. "What are you doing in here?"

"I like it here. Dark and quiet." He held his forefinger to his lips. "Don't tell anyone I'm here."

With a shake of my head I reassured him I wouldn't.

"They took it out." He motioned to his heart.

"We removed the electrode inserted into his chest," Jacob clarified.

Though there was no scar to show what Sovereign had done to him, Paradom seemed calmer.

"No one will ever harm you again." I took his clawed hand in mine. "Come with us out of here."

"I like it here," Paradom said. "Listen."

I could hear nothing.

"See," Paradom continued. "Silence is golden. Like time. Like a poem in my head."

"We'll get you some blankets," I said. "Food. Whatever you need."

"Cat food?" Paradom asked.

Jacob shrugged. "He likes it."

"Then cat food it is," I said.

"You found your way back!" Paradom whispered.

"I did." I squeezed his hand, hoping to comfort him.

His eyes were full of wonder. "And you came back for me. Like you promised."

"Yes," I said. "And you're safe now."

"Can I go back too, now?" he murmured. "Separate."

Jacob shared a wary stare with us. "We won't stop until we find a way . . . back for you."

I rested my hand over my heart. "And that's a promise."

Paradom opened my fingers and pressed a small round object into my palm. I recognized the 1829 shilling crested with King George IV's head. The very coin Paradom had thrown at me when we'd first met.

"Remember me," he said.

"I'll take special care of it." I tucked the coin into my pocket.

I rose and my gaze slid over to the wall upon which was written in blood, "*Find Dominatio.*"

Fabian acknowledged what I was looking at. "Vampires were kept prisoner in here before the Stone Masters took them to Stonehenge."

"That was two hundred years ago," Jacob clarified, "during Lord Artimas's time."

"The vampires found hope in the name Dominatio," Fabian said. "One of the prisoners must have written it as a message to others in case they escaped."

I rose to my feet. "They waited a long time."

"Worth the wait." Paradom looked excited. "All good things come to those who wait."

"We'll take care of him." Jacob peered down at Paradom. "I'll be back in little while."

Paradom clapped his hands. "Premium cat food. Not the cheap stuff."

Jacob smiled my way. "We have expensive taste."

Fabian, Jacob and I headed out of the cell and trekked along the dungeon corridor.

"Is there any hope for him?" I asked them.

Jacob wagged his chin. "We can only hope the Book of Toth offers us guidance."

Fabian patted my back. "You're doing awfully well, considering."

Despite all that had unfolded I too was surprised at my resilience and marveled at my desire to finally face what still lay ahead.

I hesitated when we reached the foyer.

One hundred or so men had gathered there, talking quietly, reverently. They hushed when they saw us. Fabian led me through the crowd toward the central staircase and up it, taking the first ten steps before turning and viewing the many faces staring back.

By the base of the stairs stood Alex, his expression one of hope. Catherine's arm was slid through Alex's and she reflected serenity. To my left Ingrid, her tears staining her flushed cheeks.

I paused, wanting to tell her what she meant to me, reassured to see her still here.

Sebastian's eyes met mine, his expression reflecting his experience of seeing me for the first time, his face crinkled into a smile. Jacob, who stood beside him, gave a gesture of approval.

It was good to see all of them, and I hoped they knew my gratitude for all they'd done for me. Marcus and Anaïs were not here and I could only surmise they were in London, perhaps with Sunaria, celebrating Orpheus's return.

But Lucas was here, having stayed with the others, and he emanated a thoughtful calmness. I owed my return to him. He pressed his hand to his chest in a gesture of affection.

Candlelight reflected off the central chandelier, throwing shards of light down and around us, reminding me . . .

Of Stonehenge.

Her grand rocky goddesses of the night, mystical mistresses of the supernatural, guarding me with their eternal endurance.

Lying upon the central stone I'd faced my fear, and finally the sun's secrets were mine, as all she'd dared to share was now remembered.

Halfway up the staircase, Fabian and I stood shoulder to shoulder, taking in the many faces gazing up at us in awe.

Fabian motioned toward them. "Stone Lords."

Whispers from the past flooded in and settled, saturating my heart and mind like the sweetest promise of divinity.

"Are you ready?" Fabian asked me.

The crowd bowed their heads before us.

I straightened, my eyes meeting with his. "I am."

Fabian's careful face studied mine as though making a decision. He turned and fixed his stare on the others. "Behold . . ." With a sweeping gesture toward me, Fabian announced with a booming voice,"I give you *Dominion.*"

vanessafewings.com
vmkfewings on facebook

23788513R00151

Printed in Great Britain
by Amazon